To Kay

Blood and Roses

Jacqueline E. Waters

Be blessed as you read my story!
Jacqui

J. Waters.

WESTBOW PRESS
A DIVISION OF THOMAS NELSON & ZONDERVAN

WestBow Press books may be ordered through booksellers or by contacting:

WestBow Press
A Division of Thomas Nelson
1663 Liberty Drive
Bloomington, IN 47403
www.westbowpress.com
1 (866) 928-1240

ISBN: 978-1-4908-2065-1 (sc)
ISBN: 978-1-4908-2066-8 (hc)
ISBN: 978-1-4908-2064-4 (e)

Library of Congress Control Number: 2013923037

Printed in the United States of America.

WestBow Press rev. date: 1/9/2014

Acknowledgments

I am indebted to those who faithfully prayed for me and encouraged me during the writing of *Blood and Roses*. Your names are written in heaven! Thanks also to Rhonda Pooley for editing and giving advice when my script needed serious pruning!

Thank you all for your wonderful, selfless support, and I do hope you enjoy the result!

Chapter 1

Early August 1642

The visitor knocked at the door. Eventually an old woman wearing a white cap and pale blue petticoat opened it. A man hovered in the dimly lit interior behind her and then faded from view. At once the woman recognized the visitor as a young man she had known as a boy.

"Why, Master Simon!" she exclaimed.

"Agatha!" he responded. He watched her take in the sight of his plain black hat and cropped hair—the sign of a Puritan—and saw her hesitation as she first extended her arms in welcome and then drew them back. He noticed, too, that the smile, which had so readily spread between the kindly wrinkles, had retracted a little.

Simon studied her blue-gray eyes, understanding completely the distracted look that had disturbed their usual peace, as a randomly kicked stone momentarily disturbs the surface of a pool.

Then suddenly she drew herself up taller.

"Oh, Master Simon, whatever are you doing with all your beautiful curls cut off?" she exclaimed as she welcomed him inside with the gladness lavished on a prodigal. Her boldness surprised him, and it was his turn to hesitate; however, fondness for his old nurse overcame him. He found himself suddenly embracing her in his strong arms and swinging her around on the spot until, laughing, he deposited her once more at the front door step.

"Oh, do come in!" she beckoned.

The smell of freshly baked bread assaulted his nostrils, and he suddenly remembered he had ridden for three days with the message entrusted to him. Simon cast a glance around the dwelling, noticing that the man who had been present in the tiny room when she answered the door was nowhere to be seen.

Suddenly aware of his tiredness, Simon looked around for a seat. Old Agatha pointed to a long bench near the window, steering him away from the seat under whose cushion she had just concealed a rosary. Through the window he noticed the old apple tree and remembered the crisp, ripe fruit he had once climbed for. Now its branches were gnarled, and here and there bare brown branches showed through its leaves. A few hens scratched underneath.

Simon sat down on the bench and placed the austere black hat beside him. Agatha had gone over to the fireplace. He watched her ladle steaming broth into a bowl and set it on the rough wooden table. Quickly she cut thick slices of bread.

"Come, Master Simon, you must eat."

He needed no second bidding. He had eaten little and ridden much since he had left London three days ago.

"Well, Master Simon, what brings you to these parts? You were but a lad when the master and mistress took you to London."

He swallowed and looked earnestly at her kind old face. "I have a message," he said. "Old Oliver was told to bring it, but I persuaded him to let me do it. And anyway, I can ride faster. He would have taken a week."

The blue-gray eyes clouded again, and a frown creased her brow.

Master Simon put down the crust he was eating and lowered his voice. "Where's Matthew?" he asked.

"I don't know," she replied truthfully. "Maybe he's out in the vegetable garden," she said, looking toward the back door but making no attempt to find out.

"I must see Matthew," urged Simon.

"He'll be in later," she promised, but her tone and her frown conveyed to Simon her ambivalence about their meeting. Simon poked at his stew and ate in silence.

"Maybe Matthew is not as happy to see me as you are, Agatha," Simon probed, picking delicately at the edges of the issue in the hope of unraveling it further. He suspected the figure he had dimly seen behind

Agatha as she had answered his knock had been Matthew. His sudden disappearance told Simon he was not at ease with this unexpected visit.

"Matthew never really understood why your father had to leave us," she said with a sigh, "or why this new Puritanism changed their relationship. He was happy as chief gardener at the old manor house. Everything changed when your family moved closer to London. The new master deemed him too old, replacing him with a younger man. I had no wish to stay without Matthew. We had nowhere to go until your father heard of our dilemma, took pity on us, and secured this cottage from the new owners of Hartley Hall." The tiny cottage had been their home for as long as Simon could remember.

"He wanted you to be able to see out your days in peace," he said.

"We are indeed grateful to be able to stay in Harton. Things go on unchanged here in Worcestershire. We hope to see out our days without involving ourselves in religious contention."

Simon kept his eyes on the bottom of the soup bowl, which he was wiping with a piece of bread.

"I must see Matthew," repeated Simon. He searched Agatha's face in the hope of finding clues to the information he believed she was withholding, but there were none.

"What is your message, Master Simon? I will make sure he receives it."

Before he could reply, the back door burst open. Matthew stood before them, holding up a freshly killed chicken.

"How about roast chicken for dinner?"

"Why, Matthew! So that's what you were about," Agatha exclaimed, clearly relieved at his reappearance. She busied herself with preparing the plucked bird for the fire. Simon stood up and turned to Matthew, who nodded a greeting.

"I did not expect to see you in these parts, Master Simon. What business brings you here?"

"I am here to deliver a message from my father, Matthew. No one except Oliver knows I am here. I came in his place because I wanted to bring it myself." From the leather bag strapped to his side he produced a folded piece of parchment on which was penned in ink a letter from his father.

Camberwell
Tuesday, 16 August 1642

Agatha and Matthew:

You have been on my mind of late. There is much unrest in London and elsewhere, and many are stirred to oppose all signs of Roman Catholicism. I'm afraid our queen does us all a disservice by continually haranguing our sovereign Charles such that he takes leave of his senses and attempts to take by force in the Parliament those who oppose him. Many blame her religion and suspect she influences her husband and draws him back to the religion from whose rule this nation has mercifully been delivered. Added to this, the Catholic uprising against the British settlers in Ireland has again fuelled passions in this nation against those who practice the old religion, from which we were happily liberated by our previous sovereigns King Henry VIII and his daughter our good Queen Bess.

I beseech you, therefore, to have a care for yourselves and leave the old practices, if indeed you do still embrace them. You need no reminder, I am sure, of my persuasion about the deception of the idolatrous practices of the Church of Rome and to some extent of the skeleton of Rome preserved in our Anglican churches to this day.

I am mindful of your faithful service to our family and in particular of Agatha's nursing of our son during the fever that nearly robbed us of him.

Please guard yourselves and rid yourselves of anything that might be construed as pertaining to Catholicism and thus endanger your lives and your welfare. I trust this letter finds you well.

Richard Brierley

Matthew listened as Simon read the letter, having never learned to read himself.

"My father is in touch with the mood of Parliament and of the people. He fears there will be much bloodshed and longs to see the nation at peace. He himself is loath to fight, but there are reports from the north that the king is mustering an army. The king's quarrel is with those who oppose his control of the army—on the surface nothing to do with religion, but in fact the king wants Parliament to fund his war against the Scottish Presbyterian bishops on whom he has been trying to force the use of the English prayer book. Parliament is unwilling to fund his cause and indeed to fund any army that might also be used against themselves."

Agatha kept her gaze on the chicken she was cleaning for the pan. Matthew sat down on the chair by the fire and stared at the floor.

"It seems to be a complicated matter, Master Simon, too much for the likes of us simple folk."

"Aye, indeed it is, but it is the likes of you two dear people who are going to get caught up in it, whether you understand it or not."

"Master Simon, I am grateful to your father for his concern for us. I little thought that he would be remembering us after all this time. Tell me— Is he well?"

"Yes, he is well," replied Simon.

"I'm most grateful to your father for considering our safety," said Matthew. "As you can see, we have no relics or statues here, Master Simon. We can say our prayers without those."

Something glinted in Simon's eyes.

"Yes," he agreed, a little too enthusiastically for Matthew's comfort. "The old ways are not necessary for true religion. We must have done with superstitions and dependence on the papal system."

Matthew's silence showed he didn't want to pursue that line of conversation. Ignorant of life outside Harton, he secretly longed for the days when Catholic rule had maintained a rural peace and the rhythm of life from the cradle to the grave was celebrated and controlled by the ordinances of the church.

Like most of the country people, Matthew and Agatha would have been content to live under any system as long as it did not disturb their simple life on the land. Simon, himself passionate about religious and political issues, had heard it said that "the people care not what government they live under as long as they may plough and go to market."

The conversation turned to matters of local interest as the old man acquainted Simon with recent news of those he remembered and his wife busied herself preparing supper. The blacksmith's daughter had married the wheelwright's son, and they were about to produce the next generation of wheelwrights. The wet winter had caused flooding in the lower meadows, and some of the local sheep had been lost. So it went on, and Simon listened, part of him nostalgic at the mention of names he had almost forgotten, part of him listening for clues as to what was happening in the local area in regard to the political developments that took up so much of his attention in London.

The roast supper was good. Agatha raided the herb garden for the stuffing and the vegetable garden for turnips and cabbage. From the cellar Matthew produced a bottle of last year's elderberry wine. In the more relaxed atmosphere that this produced, Simon began to share more of his heart.

"Father's being watched closely for his tolerant attitude to those of the old religion," he confided. "There are those who are all for executing anyone found to be Roman Catholic or even sympathetic toward them. Father does not hold with such persecution. He claims that it's motivated by political ambition. Some suspect Roman Catholics of being not only promoters of papal authority but also of foreign rule. Maybe some of them are. The real problem is that Archbishop Laud is intent on enforcing traditions of the past in the Anglican church—ways that are tainted with Catholicism—relics of the past that should have been dead and buried ages ago. Father wants the new religion to spread by inspiration not force. It is just so difficult to separate religion from politics." Matthew and Agatha nodded their agreement.

"Ever since King Henry took control of the church, it has been so," said Matthew.

"Time was when we could all sleep in our beds without concerning ourselves with such matters," agreed Agatha.

"Times have changed," said Simon. "If the king makes a challenge, we will all need to take sides." Matthew looked grave.

"And which side will you be fighting for, Master Simon?" he ventured to ask.

Simon hesitated and then, shrugging his shoulders, answered, "I have no choice. We cannot stand by and see the king taking arms against so many of our Puritan brethren or using the army to enforce his idolatrous religious ideas, but neither of us wishes to be responsible for the blood of our fellow Englishmen."

"And what about Oliver?" was Matthew's next question.

"Oliver is too old to fight. He'll more than likely stay at Camberwell and look after the women."

A knock at the door caused Matthew and Agatha to freeze. Surely Father Patrick could not have returned already from his trip? Matthew rose to answer the door while Agatha thought to distract Simon by offering more wine and cheese, but they need not have feared. On opening the door Matthew discovered the exhausted figure of a man leaning against the doorpost. Suddenly it was Simon's turn to be on his feet.

"Why, Oliver!" he exclaimed. "What brings you here?" Relief flooded Oliver's face at the sight of Master Simon, and he stood to his feet.

"I've ridden to find you, Master Simon. You must come! Come quickly!"

Matthew, stirred by the sight of this elderly man who had obviously ridden farther and faster that his aging frame allowed, insisted that he enter and be refreshed by food and drink. Oliver searched Simon's face, wondering in whose company he might be, but on seeing nothing there to encourage him to think he was among any other than friends, he gratefully accepted the invitation.

All eyes were on Oliver as he sat on the wooden chair placed for him at the table and hungrily devoured the food placed before him.

"I'm much obliged to you, kind sir, and your good wife. I have ridden fast with news of great import!" They waited patiently until Oliver had taken the edge off his hunger and slaked his thirst with Agatha's good ale. Then Oliver turned to Simon and went on, "The master sent me to find you! Parliament is mustering men, and your father was insistent he wasn't leaving without you. At least if both of you have to go to war, he thinks it good if you serve together."

His words filled the room and hung heavily in the air as the hearers struggled to come to terms with their implication. War was about to break out between the king and Parliament, and they would be expected to fight against their fellow countrymen. Simon swallowed hard, feeling at once a sense of responsibility at being summoned to do his part and a sense of unbelief at the imminent reality of war.

"We are expected to leave London no later than next week," Oliver went on.

"We?" questioned Simon, finding his voice. "Surely you're not thinking of riding to war, Oliver?"

"We'll argue about that on the road, young master! Come now— We must away!" Oliver wiped his mouth on his cuff and rose to his feet.

"My gracious thanks to you for the excellent repast," he nodded toward Agatha and Matthew, who stood, seemingly more stooped by the burden of their freshly gained knowledge.

"You are welcome, sir, though I would that you had brought us better tidings." Then as she looked at Simon with her misty blue eyes clouded with sorrow, Agatha said, "Master Simon, it is a sad day for all of us. May the good Lord keep you and your father from harm!"

"Aye!" agreed Matthew. Simon bid farewell to Agatha and Matthew, and both he and Oliver moved toward the door.

"At least father and I are fighting on the same side. I am thankful for that. Some families have found themselves at odds with one another. I trust we shall not be at odds with you either. May God keep you safe, my dear people, and may we meet again in happier times!"

He replaced his black hat and mounted his horse, which was tethered next to Oliver's at the gatepost.

"Farewell, Master Simon," Matthew called after him. "May God speed you back to that father of yours! Tell him we are well and there is nothing to fear, for we live quietly here and attend the village church with the rest of our neighbors." Agatha stood by him, nervously wiping her hands on her apron.

"Thank you kindly for your visit, Master Simon. May God speed you back to London and keep you from harm."

When Simon turned to look back briefly before they rounded the bend, Agatha was still watching them trot down the lane to join the road that led south as the sun descended into the reddening western sky. He wondered how long she stood there trying to recover the stillness that had been hers before his unexpected visit.

A sudden commotion claimed Simon's attention as a group of cavaliers rode by, plumes waving, horses jostling side by side, their flanks rippling. These were the best horses ridden by the best horsemen—the king's men. They rode with purpose, unmoved by either cheers or jeers in the villages they passed through. Mostly they were greeted by the blank stares of those who had no understanding of their mission—except that their livestock was likely to be plundered as they passed through. Simon watched them until all he could see was the cloud of dust kicked up by the horses' hooves. Soon they would meet in mortal combat on the battlefield.

Chapter 2

By the time they had ridden back to London, Oliver was glad to stay behind and watch over the household. It made good sense after all. With his aching bones, he would make a better steward than a soldier. Simon's mother, Margaret, and his two sisters would be glad of the comfort of his presence. He could be depended upon to help manage the household, and the other servants were happy enough to take their orders from him.

Simon had not been bred for soldiering. He had used firearms solely for the purpose of hunting deer and hare in the woods at Hartley Hall, yet he had more expertise than many who had enlisted as soldiers.

Despite their inexperience, Simon and Richard were recruited into the cavalry. They both rode well and had good horses, sturdy but not too heavy for the chase. Their commander was Sir William Balfour, a Presbyterian and an experienced soldier whose religious leanings were like their own. Previously loyal to the king, he had become disillusioned by the Bishops' Wars and the wrongful dismissal from his post as lieutenant of the tower in the previous December, and he had sided with the Parliamentarians.

"Why, father, under the discipline of Balfour, we shall soon become real cavalrymen!" laughed Simon, exhilarated by the uncommon exercise.

"'Tis to be hoped so, my son! We must rise to the challenge and prevent the king from turning the Parliament into a tool for returning us to the old religion."

There were others like them—men who were more intent on seeing the church reformed rather than a nation without a king—but it was the king who was insisting on the old traditions. It was the king who had insisted on fighting the Scottish church. It was the king who had sacked Parliament for not funding his ecclesiastical war against the Scottish bishops. Since the king was head of the church, church matters and politics had become confused, and the nation was about to be involved in a conflict that could never in fact be resolved by war.

Orders came from the Earl of Essex that they were to march north to muster at Northampton with the intention of confronting the king at Nottingham, where the king had raised the battle standard on August 22. Then news came that the king had moved west to recruit more men, so Simon and Richard found themselves riding toward Worcester.

"Sometimes I wonder why we left this heavenly countryside and moved to London," Richard remarked, somewhat nostalgically. Simon awoke from his reflections on his recent visit to Agatha and Matthew.

"The land was ever full of abundant fruit," he agreed, noticing that red berries now decorated the hedgerows and blackberries glistened from the brambles that straggled across roadside ditches.

"It seems we shall be augmenting our diet with apples and pears, son, though we shall pay for what we eat like good Christians."

"'Twill be a welcome addition to our bread and cheese rations."

"Aye, indeed! Doubtless though some of the ruffians will not be asking for what they pillage!"

"It seems not all march as we do with religious conviction."

"I'm afraid if they do, they fail to apply their religion to their own lives first. We are certainly a motley crew that marches together in this cause."

"I have to admit, Father, that it has not been a pleasant experience to see how some of those fellows have treated those who live along the way. I had not expected to witness such rough behavior, pillaging and taking from the local folk—food, livestock, even possessions—as if they were theirs by right!"

"Well, 'tis inevitable that the men will live off the country as best they can when their pay is overdue. They have no wages or even the promised rations of bread and cheese and ale. Though such robbery is no excuse, I admit."

Richard and Simon found themselves soldiering with men from all walks of life. Puritanism had been embraced by the whole spectrum of British society, from peasants to Lords, and consequently all classes rubbed shoulders together; however, it was not just the class difference that bothered Simon. Some were fighting for religious freedom, others with political agendas. Simon was glad to be riding with his father and to have no need of other company. Evening found father and son sharing the Word together around the campfire.

As they drew near to Worcester, news reached them of the first encounter.

"It seems battle has commenced." Richard's face was serious, and his voice was urgent. "Some of our men were trapped in an ambush near the bridge at Powick and mercilessly slaughtered by Prince Rupert's men. Those who rode with Essex the next day to capture the city of Worcester had to bury the dead. 'Tis said their bodies were horribly mutilated."

"So it begins," was all that Simon could say. Then they were both silent.

The reality of what it meant to be fighting this war that no one wanted set in. Richard and Simon, although not personally involved in the action, felt the shock waves of the first violence and the subsequent general malaise that settled over the army. It made a severe dent in their morale.

Chapter 3

It was autumn, and the swallows had long since departed and ceased to swoop around the little church at Kineton. However, a robin, ignorant of the affairs of men, did sing a cheery song in the frosty air as Simon woke to the dawn of October 23, 1642. Soon other sounds filled the air—the snorting of horses, clanging of cooking pots, and the marching of boots on the frost-hardened ground as men returned from their temporary billets in the village.

Simon's father insisted on carrying a tent to avoid forcing themselves on the local people. In any case it was at least a guarantee of a bed even though it was a straw palliasse. The biggest problem of their self-inflicted independence was providing their own breakfast, but Simon had secured some bacon the previous day and was fully occupied cooking some small pieces of it on a stick. He was, however, not too busy to notice a young lad enter the field and hover at the edge of the camp. After several glances his way Simon took it upon himself to find out what he was about. He looked as though he was about to bolt like a frightened rabbit, but Simon's tone reassured him.

"Have you business with the men, lad?"

"Sir, my mother bade me come with a message, but I know not to whom I should deliver it."

"Well, who is it for, lad?"

"For those that are against the king, sir."

"Then you may deliver it to me, and I will deliver it to the Earl of Essex." With a look of relief the boy hastily blurted out the news that the Royalists were positioning themselves on the ridge at Edgehill just southeast of Kineton.

"My mother says they are getting ready to fight." Then he turned and ran off down the lane back toward Edgehill.

Simon made his way toward the largest tent, which served as a headquarters for the Earl of Essex and his officers. Outside the tent a handful of officers stood around a small fire, drinking ale out of pewter tankards as they conferred about the day's business. Simon saluted.

"Simon Brierley, your honors, I have news of enemy activities." There was silence as all the men turned their gaze on him and waited for him to continue. "News that the king's men are mustering on Edgehill's ridge."

"Indeed!" The Earl of Essex threw back his head and laughed derisively. "I suppose they think we're silly enough to engage them in that high and lofty position! Well, if Prince Rupert wants a fight, he can come down here and get it!" Then turning to Simon, he said, "Young man, you're a cavalryman I presume?"

Simon nodded.

"Then ride over and verify the enemy's position and bring me word at once!"

Since two of Parliament's regiments and most of their artillery had still not caught up with the main body of the army, Essex was not in a hurry to engage in battle, but the proximity of the Royalists could not be ignored, so he reluctantly ordered his officers to prepare to muster.

Simon headed back to his mount, and after he informed his father of his mission, he cantered off down the lane toward Edgehill. It was still early, and a layer of mist shrouded the lower slopes; however, on the higher ground he could clearly see men and horses positioning themselves for attack. It was true. The reality of the upcoming battle settled over his soul like a dark cloud. It wasn't fear that gripped him so much as the stark reality that the men on the hill were fellow countrymen. He watched them for a moment from the cover of a thick oak trunk. The pungent smell of damp leaves assailed his senses. At any other time he would have relished this early morning ride and lingered to enjoy it. As it was he wheeled his horse around and sped back to deliver his report. One thing spurred him on—the tales that had filtered down from those wounded by the Royalists in the ambush at Powick Bridge a month earlier. The blood of such butchery was crying out for revenge. This battle would settle the matter. The king would be defeated. They could all go home then, and Parliament would legislate for religious freedom and an army free of royal control. May God grant it would be so!

Back in Kineton men were already gathering. His father had struck their tent and packed their few possessions ready to strap onto their saddles. Everywhere men primed their muskets and packed gunpowder into the cartouches on their bandoliers. Pike men handled their long pike poles and packed their knapsacks. Simon and Richard attached their armor, steel corselets that protected the back and front of their torso, tied their barred helmets to their saddles, and donned their orange sashes. Simon took courage in these simple acts of preparation. It gave him something to do, something over which he had control. For a while they stood around, letting their horses graze on the long grass at the edge of the mustering field.

As Essex had predicted, the king's men had reassembled in the Vale of the Red Horse below the ridge. Here there was plenty of room for their superior cavalry to maneuver. A bugle sounded, and men moved to their regiments. Simon and Richard moved into position in Sir William Balfour's cavalry regiment. Strictly speaking, these men were cuirassiers with more armor and more sophisticated weapons than the normal cavalry. It had been Richard who had insisted that they equip themselves with proper armor—breastplates and back plates, helmets barred to deflect cutting blows, a pair each of the best pistols they could find, and of course their swords. Pistols were much better than the usual muskets, which took so long to reload. Thigh-length riding boots protected their legs. They were indeed a lot less vulnerable than the pike men or the infantry men with their muskets.

Richard was fifty-one years old, the same age as the Earl of Essex, but with his helmet covering his graying hair and his upright position in the saddle, there was little visible difference between him and his son. Richard's mount was a gray mare that stood fifteen hands high and was bred for the hunt. Simon's was a chestnut that he had ridden on many a chase.

"If we must fight, then we shall take care of ourselves as best we can," Richard had promised. And they had.

"No matter what happens, son, fight like a man! We've come too far to give up now!"

"Aye, father, we must give a good account of ourselves this day. We will see that justice is done in this land. Before God we will!"

"Today we fight for the freedom of religion in this land, though 'twould be better if we did not need to fight at all!"

"Today will settle it! God willing, we shall succeed in securing a future free of popery and go home to our beds in peace."

As the sun began to tilt into the western sky, artillery fire erupted from the slopes of Edgehill. The Earl of Essex, on the defensive while he waited for Hampden's two regiments, had positioned his men behind a ploughed field so the cannonballs would not bounce. Horses whinnied, startled by the noise, but they stood their ground, waiting for the signal to attack. Over on their left they watched, horrified, as Prince Rupert's cavalry swept Ramsey's cavalry from the field and a troop of their own horsemen defected to the king. On their right a similar scene was being played out as the Royalists charged in and more men retreated only to be chased toward Kineton. In front of them the infantry stood firm in the face of Royalist attack, but it soon became apparent that Simon and Richard's regiment were the only cavalry left on the field.

Suddenly they were moving forward, forward as one, charging against an exposed flank in the center of the field. To Simon's relief the opposition melted away before their superior firepower, and they pursued them back up the slopes of Edgehill ridge. After they put an end to the Royalist artillery gunners, they wheeled their horses around to rejoin their own lines only to find themselves shot at by their own side, who mistook them for Royalists.

It was only then that Simon looked around for his father and noticed he was missing. His gray mount was nowhere to be seen. Unable to see much beyond the smoke and noise of the battle, Simon hoped he was somewhere on the other side of the action in the middle of the field.

Balfour led his cavalry back onto the field to rejoin the other cuirassier regiment in the field, and together the two regiments wheeled around the edge of the Royalist infantry at the rear, where Simon hoped he would find his father. Men fell all around Simon, some dead, some badly wounded. In the midst of defending himself, he had little time to look for his father. His greatest fear was of being unsaddled by the long pikes of the infantry, for then he would need to defend himself with his sword and might lose his precious steed.

Essex had sent more infantry troops to attack the Royalist infantry, and the combined attack was so successful that they found themselves approaching the king's lifeguard. In the ensuing melee the Royalist standard bearer was killed, and seizing the moment, Simon spurred his horse into the gap and grabbed the Royal banner. Surprised at his own success and spurred on by the cheers of those around him, he raced away from the Royalist lines with the Royal banner streaming out behind him.

In his moment of glory he looked around again for his father, but it was in vain. Thrilled as he was to have captured such booty, he was far more disturbed at his father's disappearance. He knew his father would never have retreated or defected, so where was he? Even had he been killed or wounded, his fifteen hands high gray mare would have been easy enough to spot. Finding one of the senior officers alongside him, he was glad to pass the standard into his hands and melt into insignificance. The party rode on, but Simon hesitated and then pulled his mount over to the left of the field nearer the hedge. It was there that he spotted his father's horse just beyond the hedge over on this Royalist side of the field. That could only mean one thing, and his stomach lurched. He spurred his horse toward the hedge that marked off a small wooded coppice. Once there he could see his father's unconscious body dangling by the ankle from the stirrup.

A sudden uproar caused him to turn his attention momentarily on the battle, and he saw the Royal banner back in the hands of Royalist troops. Relief and grief became mixed with guilt in a heady emotional cocktail—relief that he had not been killed in the banner's recapture, guilt that he had deserted the field to search for his father, and grief for his father. He dismounted and tethered his horse to a sapling and then grabbed the reins of his father's horse and tethered that too. Then releasing his father's foot from the stirrup, he laid him gently on the leaf-strewn grass of the coppice. Soon he had his helmet off and discovered that his father, although unconscious, was in fact still breathing. He could find no external wounds on him, and it seemed he had fallen from his horse, probably pushed by an enemy pike. With his foot trapped in the stirrup, he had been dragged along by his fleeing horse. Simon reached for the water bottle hanging from his belt and splashed his father's face.

Behind him the battle raged, and his king, surrounded by his lifeguard, looked on as his subjects slaughtered one another; however, Simon's focus was on his father. The water brought a small response, so he repeated the action, and this time Richard opened his eyes and appeared to recognize Simon. Then he was lost again, unconscious but breathing.

Simon's most pressing concern was to remove his father from the battlefield and enlist medical help in Kineton. If he delayed, they were both in danger from enemy bullets. His only option was to lay his father across his horse and lead both horses away, but the gray was rearing and snorting, threatening to break away from its tether. Obviously the battle had totally unsettled it, and Simon was thankful it had taken refuge in the coppice and quieted enough for him to be able to rescue his father; however, he did not trust it to let him lead it quietly back to Kineton, his father's body lying vulnerably across it. Instead he decided to put his father on his own horse, which was less disturbed.

Moving his father brought forth groans of pain, at once distressing and comforting to his ears. Moving him so would likely cause more damage to whatever internal or head injuries he had sustained, but it was his only hope. He managed to muster enough strength to lift him and position him across the saddle, and with the reins of the horse in one hand, he warily untied the gray and led both away from the noise of battle. It would be a slow and painful journey, but he deemed it better to take a circuitous route, coming back to the Kineton road by way of the coppice rather than cutting across the edge of the battlefield again. Once on the road he decided to mount the gray and trust the chestnut to walk alongside.

Kineton was a sickening sight. Hundreds of dead had been brought back for burial, and the wounded lay everywhere, moaning and bloody. Local residents watched with unbelieving eyes the carnage that had turned up on their doorstep. To hear of foreign wars was one thing, but nothing had prepared them to see the fruit of this war, where Englishman fought Englishman on English soil. Not even those on the battlefield had expected to witness such horror.

Simon was at a loss to know what to do for his father, but when he found a barn, he laid him on the straw and made him as comfortable as he could. After he searched for external wounds and found none, he decided to leave him to rest while he went in search of nourishment for both of them. He returned empty-handed to find a young woman, one hand propping up his father's head while she administered mead with the other.

"This'll ease his pain mister," she said, looking up at Simon's questioning face. "Nectar of the gods, sir." Simon was unsure but grateful for her solicitousness, especially when his father momentarily opened his eyes and appeared coherent.

"I have bread and cheese, sir, just a little, if you'd care for a bite." She disappeared indoors and came back with a flagon and a wooden trencher on which she had set bread and cheese.

"I'm most indebted to you, ma'am." Simon was indeed grateful for the food and discovered the flagon contained not more mead as he has supposed but a liberal supply of sweet water from their deep well.

"My husband is attending to others in the house, sir, and we have no room for more, but you may shelter here until your father regains strength."

Simon, remembering a more celebrated family who had been forced to shelter in a stable, gratefully accepted. The horses, tethered to a sturdy post in the barn, were helping themselves to the hay brought by their kind hostess and had quieted considerably. He briefly considered rejoining the battle, but concern for his father restrained him. In any case the daylight was fading now and with it the noise of gunfire. Weary and shaken, he hungrily devoured bread and cheese and had a mind to get his father to eat too; however, either he had lapsed into unconsciousness again, or he was in a deep sleep, no doubt aided by the mead. His attempts to rouse him failed miserably, and he decided to leave him to rest and then fell into an exhausted and troubled sleep himself.

He dreamed of boyhood times with his father in the gardens of Harton Hall, of swinging in the apple tree and sending a cloud of blossoms swirling like snowflakes on a gusty day. In his dream his father came toward him, lifted him from the swing, and deposited him on the footpath where he was free to run along to the ornamental pool and watch the fish. He dreamed he saw his own face reflected in the water and his father's face above it. Then fish tails stirred the water, and when it was still again, his father's face was gone. He swung around only to find himself alone.

"Father! Father!" he cried out, waking himself. It was now dark, and the barn was cold.

His first thoughts were of his father's condition, and he bent over his father's still body and felt his cheek. It was quite cold. Alarmed, he checked for breath only to find none. There were no signs of life at all, and his father's body now lay cold and stiff beside him.

"No, God! No! Not my father! Why my father? Father was a good man!" It was a bitter cup to drink. Self-reproach consumed him for sleeping while his father's life slipped away, and for a while he buried his head in his hands and gave way to grief and disappointment in sobs, glad for the privacy of the barn. Loneliness and grief consumed him until more practical considerations took over and forced him into action. Where could he bury his father, and how? With so many dead, coffins would be in short supply, and even if he could find one, he had not the means to transport it home. In any case he had to consider his mother and sisters. He could not go home and tell them he had buried his father in an unnamed mass grave. He lay back on the straw, overwhelmed and emotionally spent, vacillating between anger at himself and anger at the king for this useless waste of good men but trying to keep his mind clear enough to make decisions.

The darkness was pierced by a lantern, and the young woman returned.

"Oh sir, 'tis a sad day with so many wounded and dying!"

"Aye," agreed Simon flatly. "My father is dead too."

"I'm sorry to hear of it, sir. He will be in better pastures now," she added by way of condolence.

"Aye," said Simon. For all that he was fighting a war fraught with religious issues, his father's eternal abode was a consideration that had been lost to him in his self-recrimination and anger. The young woman's comment gave him fresh perspective.

"He'll not be needing his horse, sir," she continued.

"No, he needs a coffin and a dray to transport him home to rest."

"A hunter like that will not pull a dray, sir, but you could trade him for our horse and cart." Simon knew she was being an opportunist. She could get a good price for the gray mare with so many horses killed and maimed in the battle. He knew, however, it was an offer he needed to accept if he was going to take his father's body home.

At first light he was ready to begin the sad journey home with the farm horse harnessed to the cart, his father's body, his saddle, and few possessions in the cart, his own horse tied to the back of the wagon as well. As he passed through the Vale of the Red Horse, he could see the exhausted soldiers of both sides still on the battlefield, but no one was fighting anymore. It would end that night inconclusively—nothing decided by the sacrifice of those who had suffered through it. King Charles' men would withdraw to Edgecote and then march to London, and the Earl of Essex would return to Kineton to bury the dead and then march south to fight yet more battles. And so it would continue up and down the country for another nine years.

Chapter 4

The rhythm of hooves on the frosty ground, the excitement of the chase, and the sweet taste of success as the arrow found its mark—these were the things that had been for Eleanor such an antidote to the routine of managing Haresby Hall. Since her father's death she had missed those times in the saddle together, missed his shout of encouragement when her body was aching, but the quarry was not yet down. She missed him still and not just in the hunt. There were times when she felt extremely vulnerable as the sole heiress despite her wealth and position.

Lately there had been little time for hunting anyway. The maintenance of Haresby Hall occupied most of her time. It had taken the staff a while to realize that with her father gone, she was assuming full responsibility for the estate and house. She was very conscious of the fact that not only her own welfare but also those in her employ depended on her ability to manage it well. Now she was without a partner in the chase, and she was concerned that the forests would attract poachers. One thing that made her nervous was the thought of strangers roaming at will on her land.

Edmund Whyte had been manager of the estate for some time, and she depended on him heavily to act as gamekeeper and to make it his business to know what was going on in its forests. Sometimes she took her mount and rode alone through the dappled sunlight of the oak and beech woods until she came out into the clearing at the top of the ridge. While Jasper pulled at the grass, she would look down on Haresby and imagine how it might have been had her father been there at her side.

The sheer size of Haresby Hall was at once comforting and

intimidating. As long as people were fed and housed, her position was secure. It was the sheer responsibility of housing and feeding so many that she found daunting. It was all right in a good year when trout were plentiful in the ponds and the sheep bore twins and crops yielded a good return; however, poor summers meant scanty winter feed for stock, and a poor harvest meant basic rations in the kitchen. There had been seasons when she had had to buy instead of sell.

As she stood there, Eleanor thought of those housed in the extensive building below her. Some of them had called Haresby Hall home longer than she herself had. Jacob had been there since he was a boy and had worked his way up until he had finally been promoted as butler by her father. She smiled as she thought of how many miles his bandy legs had walked along its ancient corridors. Then her smile faded as she dwelt on the fact that his once manly stride had become more of a painful shuffle. Soon she would need to replace him. She doubted Hugh, the hostler, would make a suitable replacement, though doubtless he himself might welcome less physical employment than managing the stables. More than likely she would employ someone from the village, though she regretted that she had not already begun to train up a replacement. There had been so much to think about since her father's sudden death and the outbreak of the war. She thought about the assortment of chambermaids and kitchen staff all under the watchful eye of Mary Tilbury, who had even acted as midwife on occasions.

Eleanor's thoughts were also much occupied with the question of the succession. If she married a man of equal social standing, she would be expected to leave Haresby and provide heirs for the estate of another. She was far too independent to be restricted to bearing children and pursuing a life of gentility in a home she had no heart for. If she did not marry, there would be no heir, and it would be left to distant cousins to make their claims on it. No, she would never leave Haresby. It was unthinkable that she should spend the rest of her days away from its familiar stone walls and pleasant acres. Besides that, it was in her blood. Her ancestors had built it, and her family had lived in it. It belonged to her, and she would not let it go to another. No, she would prefer to wait for a man who would make Haresby his home, who would give her heirs and share with her the burden of caring for it.

Eleanor was handsome rather than pretty. She stood tall and refined, her wide-set brown eyes sending out a message that she was not a woman to be trifled with. She couldn't afford to be. She was a woman with responsibilities but a woman nevertheless. Mostly she wore her hair under a crisp linen coif with a lace trim, but whenever she went outdoors, she would don a black hat trimmed with feathers—unless of course she was hunting because then she wore her hooded cape. It was only on formal occasions that her beautiful long brown curls would be set free to play around her fine features, softening their slight sharpness as a rose in full bloom detracts from its thorns.

Chapter 5

From his saddle on the gray mare Hugh watched the woman in the blue petticoat abandon her stockings and shoes on the riverbank and climb warily into the cool shallow water. She stood there for a while, savoring the relief the cool water brought to her feet, and then she climbed out onto the bank and sat down in the dappled light of a hawthorn. He watched as she replaced the stockings and shoes and leaned back against the tree. She moved with a natural grace, though she was not well-bred.

Occasionally the pale October sun glinted on wisps of blond-red hair escaping from her coif as she turned this way and that, searching for something in the trees around her. Presently she found what she was looking for—a hazel tree—and stood to retrieve the ripe nuts. As she stood, she caught her petticoat on a nearby thorn, depositing a remnant of blue cloth. Hugh watched as she unhooked her petticoat from the offending thorn. She picked the nuts and cracked them between two stones, and when she had eaten her fill, she put the remainder in the bag slung across her shoulder. He watched her progress along the narrow forest path from his hiding place among the trees up the hill. When she had disappeared from sight, he descended to retrieve the small scrap of blue cloth.

Ignorant of the damning evidence she had left behind, Nell ran on in the afternoon sun. She was eager to reach Lincoln before nightfall. Another night in a strange barn was a prospect she dared not think about. Robert would know what to do. He would know someone who could provide employment and a bed. Her brother had taken good care of her until the war had forced them apart and he'd ridden away to fight for the king. Surely he wouldn't turn her away now when she came to him in such need. If only she could persuade him to give up fighting for the king!

Let the king fight for himself! she thought. *Let him leave the poor country folk to live out their lives in peace. All they want to do is to plant crops and harvest them, and so long as the sun shines enough to ripen the grain and the rain waters the earth, what do they care if King Charles is on the throne or on the run! Maybe this Parliamentary alliance can make things different for the common people!*

Nell had no wish to see harm come to the king—in fact she could not imagine England without a king—but rumor had it that in his luxurious lifestyle he cared little about the simple folk who gave him their allegiance.

So she pushed on, her anger fuelling her pace. Maybe Robert would listen to her now, and together they could find a place of safety. In any case she would never return to Haresby Hall, never go back to the kitchen, where Matilda's sharp tongue ruled and old Jacob's lurid stares and sly passes as he shuffled past made her recoil into the shadows of its ancient walls. Now she had plucked up the courage to leave, she could not, would not return no matter what happened. So she pressed on with Robert's face before her.

Hugh's hand clasped the blue material, and he smiled smugly, thinking what favor it might bring him with Mistress Eleanor to bring proof of the direction of Nell's escape. Nell was employed as a servant and free to leave as she willed—at least in theory—however, Mistress Eleanor did not take kindly to what she considered her staff's betrayal, and the last girl who had taken it into her head to leave had been found in the village stocks two days later. The blue remnant would lead to the discovery of young Nell, no doubt, and he would ingratiate himself a bit more with Mistress Eleanor.

When he found her, his mistress was on the battlements of Haresby Hall, searching the countryside with her own keen eyes. If she had expected to see the young woman in blue come running out of the forest, she would be disappointed. Good servants were hard to find, and for all her truculence, Nell was indeed trustworthy and hardworking. She knew that replacing her would not be easy, as not many young women could tolerate Matilda's tongue, and secretly she didn't blame them. Hugh saw her from below silhouetted against the late afternoon sky. He took the liberty of joining his mistress on the roof.

"Yes, Hugh, what is it?" she inquired, seeing that he had something to report.

"I have found something of interest, ma'am," he bragged, offering the scrap of blue cloth in the palm of his hand.

"Where, Hugh, tell me— Where did you find it?" she demanded.

"In the woods, ma'am. In fact, I saw her with my own eyes … in the stream a little more than a day's journey on foot toward Lincoln."

"Well, why didn't you bring her back with you, man?" demanded Eleanor. "Now who knows where she is! You've let her slip through your fingers like a trout off a hook! Get away from me, you useless fellow!"

Shocked and disappointed, Hugh backed away. He had not only lost favor, but he had lost face too. Indignant at Eleanor's outburst, he found refuge in the kitchen, glad that Matilda's absence left room to warm himself by the fire. He stared dejectedly into the flames, annoyed with himself for not recapturing Nell, annoyed with Eleanor for being so ungracious. Privately he doubted he could have taken Nell single-handedly. She was a spirited young woman and lithe. He briefly considered re-saddling his horse to pursue her but realized the truth of Eleanor's words. He would have to wait until daylight to find the forest path again, and by that time she could have turned off in one of several directions. If only he knew where she was headed!

Eleanor remained on the roof for a while, nursing her anger. Now she would have to manage the household with less staff until a replacement was found for Nell. She wondered briefly where Nell was. In spite of the inconvenience of her disappearance, she had to admire her courage. Obviously she was spurred on by some secret passion. Wherever she was now, it was far from Haresby Hall.

Eleanor's brown eyes took in the sweep of the land below her—forests where wild deer were hunted, meadows where sheep and cattle grazed, and the broad avenue of poplars leading up to the house. She saw again the funeral procession of her father, the horse-drawn hearse with its guard of honor on either side. For the last year, ever since her father had been killed fighting for the king at Edgehill, Haresby Hall had been her responsibility. Father had always known what to do. She could rely on his wisdom. Since the death of her mother when Eleanor was fifteen, they had been close. Lacking a son, he had poured his affection into her and allowed her to hunt with him, and as she had matured, he had trusted her more and more with the running of the household. By the time he had gone off to fight for the Royalist cause, she was well able to organize the staff and administrate the household finances. At twenty-eight she had more to occupy her thoughts than the lack of a suitor. Not that there hadn't been any, but the ones who were not passionate enough about the Royalist cause to have ridden off to war did not interest her. If she were to wed, it would be to someone who was decent enough to support the king.

The gentle breeze freshened and turned northerly, disturbing her sad reverie. She turned to go in, but as she did so, she caught sight of a man on horseback galloping up the avenue. She stayed to watch as he reined in his horse near the steps. Even from her lofty height, she could see by the state of the horse and rider that he had ridden fast and with purpose. He remained in the saddle for a moment, looked around the courtyard, dismounted, tethered the horse to a post, and ascended the curved steps to the front door. Curiosity got the better of Eleanor, and she descended quickly to the drawing room in order to be ready when Jacob would seek her out to inquire as to whether she would receive the visitor.

The visitor apologized for his disheveled state, but when Jacob discovered his mission, he called for Hugh to stable his horse and showed him to the drawing room.

"A Mr. Duncan Talbot of Tadcaster to see you, ma'am. He says he was known to your father and has important news of Royalist endeavors."

Eleanor thanked Jacob and dismissed him. She beheld a man whose fair complexion, ruddy from exposure to the elements, was framed by a mop of wiry hair that fell about his shoulders like a lion's mane. He regarded her with gray-blue eyes that lent an air of wisdom and gentleness to a face that might otherwise have communicated too much passion. On this occasion they were clouded with anxiety and concern.

"Good day to you, sir. Jacob tells me you have ridden from the battle."

"From Winceby, ma'am. Lord Wheeler bade me come to inform you of the outcome of the battle. He said you ought to know, ma'am. He said your father would have wanted you to know, so you can be on your guard, ma'am." Duncan's brows knit together, and he shifted his gaze to the fire. It would be easier to deliver his message if he did not have to look into the depths of Eleanor's brown eyes.

"I take it the news is not good then, Mr. Talbot. We have seen and heard the commotion—men trampling all over our land as they fight over who rules it!"

"No, ma'am. Parliament has defeated the king's men at Winceby. Sir John Henderson and some horsemen went to break the siege at Bolingbroke castle but were attacked by some of Fairfax's cavalry and routed. Then Manchester and Cromwell attacked at Winceby, and Henderson's men were driven off. Many were killed, some trapped and brutally slaughtered. And the siege at Bolingbroke is still not broken."

"So the Parliamentarians have had another victory in the east?" She looked away, ostensibly through the window, but she did not see the wind-blown sycamore keys twisting to the ground.

"It is more for the sake of propaganda than usefulness," continued Duncan, "just for the sake of destroying a castle that has been the birthplace of a king."

"And so it is! Even falling into ruin as it is, it is still a strategic stronghold!"

"I'm afraid we must accept the fact that those days are coming to an end."

Eleanor sighed and shrugged her shoulders and then turned back to face Duncan.

"Well, bad news or not, thank you for bringing it. If my father were here, he would not have wanted you to ride away unfed, and the hour is late. I'll have a bed made up for you in the green room. This is no time to be riding to Tadcaster."

Eleanor inwardly bemoaned the fact that she would have to ask Susannah to prepare the guest room. She wasn't called "Simple Sue" without reason, but since Nell's disappearance, she had no choice. She was determined to make a priority of finding a replacement for Nell. Till then she would have to get Mary to check on Sue's efforts.

"I don't like to trouble you, ma'am," he said, noticing her frown.

"It's no trouble, sir, just that one of my chambermaids has taken it into her head to run away, and who knows why or where to. I'll have Mary organize another girl."

"I'm most obliged, ma'am, for myself and my horse. He's had a tough time in the battle. They all do. Cromwell had his horse shot from under him and had to wait for another. Pity the musketeer didn't aim a bit higher, I say."

"Would it have changed the outcome of the battle? Can one man make such a difference?"

"He's a good strategist, ma'am, and fired up by religion. He won't stop until he gets his way—mark my words. I know a man with a vision when I see one."

"Surely there's no goodness in fighting the monarch? What other vision could a man have other than an England governed by a God-appointed monarch?"

"There are those, ma'am, who question the divinity of his appointment and his divine right to rule. They want to bring him under control, contain his excesses."

"And to do that, they're willing to kill their own countrymen? Where's God in that?" Anger launched her words like missiles.

"Well, Mistress Eleanor, it was the king himself who raised the standard and challenged Parliament. It seems to me to be a political issue. Now we're all obliged to take sides, like it or not."

"Well, at Haresby we don't like it!" she retorted.

"We can only fight to end it now and believe that the king will rule again soon."

"I hope so, Mr. Talbot. My father gave his life for a noble cause."

"He did, ma'am." Duncan looked away again, moved by her spirit, suspecting that tears lay not too far behind the bold brown eyes. He reminded himself that for all her outward composure and wealth, she was a young woman who had lost much. Behind the fiery spirit was a vulnerability that evoked a compassion in his heart that surprised him. There was silence for a moment, a moment full of emotion where words would have had no more meaning than the crackling of the fire. Eventually Duncan felt bold enough to ask, "How did your father die, ma'am?"

Eleanor gazed at her father's portrait hanging on the chimney breast. "They say he was pushed from his horse by a pike man and trampled by his own cavalrymen." There was a deadness in her voice as she recounted the report brought home by Alexander. She could still see him in her mind's eye, covered in mud from the battle and the ride, standing there and turning his hat in his hands, his lip trembling with the news he had to deliver.

"A terrible waste, ma'am. I'm sorry to be the bearer of more bad news."

"This latest Royalist defeat is indeed bad news, but I do at least know the latest news firsthand. However, there is little I can do. I dare say there is an increased danger that Haresby Hall could bear the brunt of Parliamentary taxation or be subject to plunder by Parliamentary forces looking for what they considered to be the spoils of war ... or merely more horses or food for their troops."

"'Tis true, ma'am, and I cannot help but be concerned for your future, ma'am. I pray you might be protected by the Almighty in these desperate times. Tomorrow I must return to Tadcaster, but I shall be most concerned to hear of your welfare, ma'am."

The next day was overcast with a fine drizzle. Hugh had instructions to have Duncan's horse saddled and ready after breakfast, and they stood together in the shelter of the stable while it finished a bag of oats.

"It seems the mistress is a bit shorthanded," remarked Duncan, reflecting on the lack of hot water in his basin.

"Aye, young Nell's deserted us, sir. I caught sight of her in the forest heading north, but who knows where she is now? Mistress Eleanor is none too pleased."

"I wonder why she'd go off like that."

"She didn't say a word, sir. Just up and went. Just donned her best clothes and took off through the forest."

"Well, I dare say Mistress Eleanor will find another chambermaid locally."

"Aye, I dare say, sir."

Duncan removed the bag of oats and mounted.

"Well, I'm obliged to you, man. Good day to you." Duncan guided his mount back out through the courtyard and eased it into a canter down the avenue. It would be a long ride to Tadcaster.

Chapter 6

For Nell, now also in Tadcaster, the warmth of the alehouse was an inviting alternative to the cold night air. She hesitated near the doorway, hoping to glimpse her brother. Since her arrival on the stagecoach from Lincoln, she had walked the narrow streets in search of his face to no avail. The alehouse would be a good place to ask questions. It was not the kind of place she was used to frequenting, but she had to find somewhere to stay or Robert, whichever came first. She was hoping it would be the latter. As she entered, she saw the few patrons standing around the board that served as a bar, and in a far corner there was a small group of women. One of them swished her ample skirts and approached Nell.

"Come to join us, have you, love?" she inquired in a tone which was less than inviting.

"I'm not here to compete for business!" Nell retorted. "I've got more important business." She was by now guarding carefully the small bag slung across her shoulder, which contained all she had brought with her—a leather purse containing her savings, a hairbrush, and a few other personal belongings, including the last address Robert had given her. It listed a street in Tadcaster that she'd yet been unable to find. Maybe tomorrow in broad daylight she'd have more success. She approached a man pouring ale from a large round pottery flagon.

"What's a pretty 'un like you doing in here then, lass?"

"I'm looking for my brother, Robert Thornby. Is he known about these parts?"

"Can't say I've met him, lass. Ask these gents over here. Anyone know

Robert Thornby? The lady wants to know." The question brought forth more suggestive comments but no information, and Nell decided to find herself a bed instead and continue her search on the morrow.

"I'll be needing bed and board tonight. Do you have rooms?"

"Oh aye, lass, it depends who ye want to share it with!"

"No one!" she glared back.

"Then ye'd best go and ask old Annie down t' road if she can take ye in."

Relieved, Nell left the tavern and went in the direction the barman indicated. Annie looked her up and down.

"My, you've come a long way. I can tell by t' way ye talk!"

"Lincolnshire, ma'am. I came on the stage coach this afternoon. I'm looking for my brother Robert Thornby."

"Never heard of him. If it's a bed you're wanting, it'll be two pence a night, and that includes oatmeal and ale for breakfast."

Nell didn't want to argue about the price but fervently hoped the room was clean and unoccupied. She was relieved to find the small room at the back of the house did in fact have a feather mattress and some covers. Exhausted, she lay down, but sleep evaded her. What if after all she couldn't find Robert? Where could he be?

She wasted no time after her breakfast of porridge and ale in resuming her search. After she bid farewell to Annie, she ascended the rise on the other side of the river, asking at every opportunity about Robert. A thin bent figure watched her from the entrance to one of the alleyways. She didn't see him until he surprised her as she passed.

"Oh, sorry, miss. I di'n't see ye there," he lied.

Instinctively she jumped away, but he came closer again.

"Are you looking for summat, miss?" he said with false solicitude.

Still wary, she replied.

"Yes, I'm looking for my brother, Robert Thornby. Do you know him?"

"I might do, miss … for a price."

"What do mean *might*? Either you do or you don't!"

"What would you like to know, miss?"

"I'd like to know where he is."

"Then follow me, miss."

Exasperated as she was, she hesitated and then decided to follow him and find out if in fact he did know anything. He turned, beckoning her to follow him under the archways and into the narrow alley between the buildings. Nell had only taken a few steps out of sight of the main street when two others set on her from behind, snatching her bag and shoving her against a wall. Then all three melted into the maze of narrow streets, leaving her winded and breathless. All too late she realized it had been a setup. Dazed and distraught, she picked herself up from the gutter and ran down the alleyway, seeking help.

"My bag! My bag!" she yelled. She attracted attention but no help until a well-to-do gentleman pointed with his stick to an area a little farther down the street.

"There's a bag down there, miss, in t' edge o' t' road."

She flew to investigate and discovered her bag with the strap torn but otherwise sound. She knew it was hopeless to expect her savings to be there, and she was right. Now her situation really was desperate. The rest of the contents were intact, including Robert's address. The gentleman who'd seen the bag had walked on. She ran after him. He might know where Field Lane was. He did, but he didn't recall a Robert Thornby.

"I'm going that way right now, miss, if you'd like to walk along."

"Oh, yes, please, sir!" Nell bit her lip and fought to keep back the tears at this the first kindness shown to her for quite a while.

"You're a stranger in these parts then?"

"Yes, I'm from Lincolnshire."

"Have you lost all your money?"

"Yes," she said, the tears again welling up. "I don't know what I'll do now if I can't find my brother."

"What did you do before then?"

Nell found herself telling him how she'd grown tired of Matilda's sharp tongue and decided to join her brother. She omitted to mention his political alliance.

"My name's Mr. Thorpe, Edward Thorpe, ma'am. If you're in need of a bit o' work and lodgings, I daresay our Molly can help ye. My house is just passed t' bridge on t' right. It's called Bethany. Now Field Lane is this one here. I hope you find news of your brother, miss. Good day to ye."

She thanked him profusely and turned into Field Lane. It was a narrow road with houses on both sides. She had tried every one without success when she came to the last one. This one was larger than the rest, with recent additions. Its tiny windowpanes reflected the midday sun. The door was opened by a woman with a pleasant round face. Her answer was a little more hopeful.

"Aye, there were a man o' that name here last year—used to help our Sid wi' t' building on to th' house."

"Really! Isn't he here now?"

"I don't know, miss, I've not seen him since th' end o' last year. In fact, not since t' battle on t' bridge last December."

Nell's heart sank again. "Which battle was that?"

"King's men and Parliament, o' course." Nell was too afraid to ask the outcome. She studied the doorstep, waiting, hoping for more information, but none came. She looked up at the pleasant round face again.

"I'm very grateful to you for the information. I hope it's not been a trouble to ye." Nell walked slowly back up the street.

Once again Nell was to be found cooling her sore feet in a river, this time the Wharfe. The clear shallow water flowed over her feet, carrying away some of her tiredness, restoring her soul a little as well as soothing her feet. The water was also good to drink. She had come down to the river because it seemed that Robert might possibly have been there, fighting for the king. Also it was a good place to think, to decide what to do next. The afternoon sun was sinking lower in the autumn sky, and she had no food, no money, and nowhere to sleep.

As she watched her feet treading carefully on the smooth flat stones of the riverbed, she noticed plenty of musket balls, silent witnesses to the battle that had raged there and that was still raging in other parts, tearing apart the heart of the nation, the hearts of its people, her own heart. If only she could be sure which side Robert was fighting for now, if indeed he was fighting at all, if indeed he was still alive. It was a question that could no longer be stifled—a fact that had to be faced since no one had seen him alive since last December.

A sudden gust of wind stirred the trees, and a flurry of dying leaves floated down and away on the current. Her hopes seemed to float away with them, and loneliness and despair engulfed her. At this spot men's lives had ebbed away, and what for? She could understand the need to fight to defend one's country, to fight a foreign foe, but why this senseless killing of men by their own countrymen and often by their own blood relatives?

The water, which a short while ago had been refreshing, now became too cold for comfort, and she hastened back to the bank. The sound of a horse's hooves on the bridge caused her to look up. A horse and rider obviously in need of grooming and rest trotted toward York. She watched them for a moment absentmindedly as they turned off down a lane and disappeared. Then her thoughts were on herself and her own need of a bed.

She determined she would go in search of Molly at the Thorpe residence. Soon she was pulling the bell outside the heavy oak door, and Molly herself answered. The smell of baking wafted past her, and Nell was reminded that all she had eaten that day was Annie's thin porridge. Molly greeted her almost as though she had been expecting her.

"Ah, yes, is it a room you're looking for, ma'am?"

"Why, yes, I am," answered Nell, "though since I was robbed this morning, I've not the means to pay for it."

"Can you scrub floors, lass?"

"Yes, yes, I can. I'm used to that."

"Well then, come on, and we'll see what we can do for you."

Nell was relieved with such a ready invitation. The house was warm and inviting and clean. She stepped inside and suddenly felt ashamed of her poor appearance.

"I've had a long journey, ma'am, and then I was attacked and robbed this morning by thieves who stole all my money."

"Mr. Thorpe mentioned he'd seen you this morning and suggested you might make a good replacement for our last girl, Polly, who's with child. There's a small room in th' attic you can use. There's a bed and a dresser, and you can fetch up water from t' kitchen. Come, I'll show ye up if ye' be interested. There'll be cleaning to do and fires to keep burning. You'll find a more suitable petticoat and apron in t' dresser."

Molly's warmth was comforting, and Nell needed no second invitation. The room was small but pleasant. The bed was under the window to make the most of the space under the high point of the rafters for standing. A dresser with bowl and jug stood against the opposite wall. It was clean and neat, apart from the remains of insects that had fallen from the uncovered thatch.

While Molly returned to her chores in the kitchen, Nell took care of her own person. Her body felt stiff and sore as she removed her dirtied blue petticoat and shift and set her auburn hair free from the white bonnet. She poured out water and was glad when she felt clean again. It felt almost comforting to be donning servant clothes again. At least she would be housed and fed while she decided what to do about Robert. Working for Molly promised to be easier than suffering torrents of abuse from Matilda, and Mr. Thorpe appeared to be a gentleman. She wondered if there was a Mrs. Thorpe.

Molly's cooking, as Nell expected, far outweighed Matilda's. She had just finished a welcome meal in the kitchen when Molly called her to be presented to the lady of the house.

"Nell, isn't it?" inquired Mr. Thorpe.

"Yes, sir, Nell Thornby."

"So you've decided to join us?"

"Yes, please, sir."

"Well, Molly will show you what to do. You'll be responsible for cleaning and stoking t' fires and generally helping Molly. We'll give you board and a shilling a week. This dear lady is my wife, Mrs. Thorpe."

Nell bobbed a small curtsey and nodded. "This dear lady" looked slightly formidable, with her strong features and her hair swept back under her white cap.

"We're pleased to have you, Nell. You'll find us accommodating enough, if you behave yourself and don't bring shame on us like the last girl. Still you look like a good girl. You'll be expected to join us for evening prayers in the drawing room after supper."

Nell had not been expecting to have to spend time with the Almighty, but at least the drawing room was warmed by the fire she had stoked. It would be no hardship to listen to a few prayers. That first evening she joined the Thorpes and Molly in the drawing room at eight o'clock. It was not customary for servants to sit down with their superiors except in church, and she felt awkward. "A few prayers" also included listening to Edward Thorpe reading from his large Bible. By the time the final amen was pronounced, the fire was dying in the grate, and she had to hurry to fetch more wood.

It was a peaceful night apart from the scratching of a few mice inside the timber walls. Nell slept well on the feather mattress but woke painfully stiff from the previous day's attack. She had little time to dwell on her misfortunes, however, and hurriedly dressed and descended to the kitchen, where Molly was bustling about making porridge. She was eager to make a good impression on her first day, and after she had rekindled the log fire from the embers of the previous night, she was cleaning around the fireplace when Edward Thorpe appeared for breakfast.

"Good morning, Nell. I trust you slept well."

"Yes, thank you, sir." She was still grateful for his kindness and judged him to be a decent sort. At least here she felt secure away from the attack of thugs and philanderers. He nodded and smiled his approval as she rose from her knees, straightened her dress, and bobbed a curtsey. Nell ate in the kitchen, while Molly herself waited on the Thorpes. First though Molly waited at the kitchen door until she had heard her master pronounce the amen at the end of morning prayers.

"Otherwise t' porridge gets cold while they're thanking th' Almighty for it!" she explained. "And I can't see why you'd thank him for cold porridge!" she said and then chuckled.

Nell smiled awkwardly. She had never thanked him for anything, cold or hot! In this pious household she felt quite pagan.

As a young child, she had always attended St. Mary's with her parents, but she had hated the hard pews and enforced silence. No one had ever taught her to talk to God, so she never had. She thought it was the priest's duty to do that for her. She had assumed that God's attention was taken up with more important matters than her own insignificant life. It was to Robert that she had looked for protection. He would be her protector still, if she could find him. She knew he would.

Chapter 7

As autumn faded into winter and the cold northeast wind blew the last remaining leaves from the trees along the riverbank, Nell appreciated the warmth and security of Bethany. Life settled into a routine of cleaning and running errands for Molly. She was backing away from one of the market stalls one day late in November when the sound of horses' hooves behind her made her pause. Two riders, a man and a woman, steered their mounts through the market throng and up the main street. They rode past without mishap, and her eye followed their progress. The man's horse paused to wait for several children to scatter, the woman riding on a little but then turning to wait for her companion. As she did so, a sudden gust of wind blew her bonnet back, revealing nut brown hair. Instantly Nell recognized Eleanor. For sure it was her, head held high, her face animated by a broad smile toward her companion.

Nell caught her breath and all but dropped the basket. Then she just stood, her slight form hidden behind the market stall, and watched as they trotted off up the York road, and turned off into a lane on the right. Then she recognized the other rider as the one who had turned at the same place after he had crossed the bridge that day she had been in the river. Well, it looked as though Mistress Eleanor was keeping company with the gentleman, whoever he was. She hastened back to Molly who had lived in Tadcaster all her life. She'd know who the gentleman on the fine chestnut horse was.

Nell listened avidly as Molly told her all about Duncan Talbot.

"He lives at The Grange, just about a mile down that lane. He's not been around much of late—too busy fighting for the king's cause. His father is Lord Talbot, and he's in charge o' t' king's mustering list in these parts. He knows all t' local gentry and has t' list of those who are fighting for t' king. Now he'd happen know where your Robert is."

Nell's focus changed from curiosity about Eleanor to wondering how she, a servant wench, could get to speak with a gentleman of Lord Talbot's caliber. In bygone days before she'd lost her inheritance, there would have been no problem, but since her father had been imprisoned for debt and her mother had had to take employment as a lady's maid, she'd had no wish to disclose her background.

She was considering these difficulties when Molly raised another.

"Mind you, if you do get to speak with him, don't let on that you've been fraternizing with t' opposition. Mr. Thorpe will not be well pleased. They've not exchanged a word since th' outbreak o' t' war. Mr. Thorpe sympathizes wi' t' Puritans. He didn't hold wi' t' king trying to force t' Scottish church to take on th' English prayer book, and he don't hold wi' all t' pomp and ceremony that goes in t' church ... says it's not in t' Bible. So he'll not be too happy if he finds out you've been asking them for favors."

Nell fastened on the idea of finding out about Robert, but she had no desire to risk being discovered by Mistress Eleanor any more than she had of falling into disfavor with the Thorpes. For now it seemed impossible, so she set her mind on waiting.

Her opportunity came a week later. As she bartered for provisions in the market, she was distracted by the noise of horses' hooves and banging doors. Across the road at The Falcon she saw passengers boarding the southbound stage coach, among them Eleanor. Duncan was on his way back to The Grange atop a small carriage. The coachman hauled up Eleanor's bags and slammed the door. The wheels left trails in the light covering of snow that had whitened the road. There lying on the snow was the glove of her former mistress. It was her deerskin one—the one she treasured since she had shot the deer herself. Nell picked it up and, delighted with an excuse to visit the Grange, hurried back to Molly with the day's provisions.

During her brief time off that afternoon she changed into her own clothes, which she had laundered, and hurried up to the Grange. It was a large, square, two-story house built of stone. It had an air of rather austere grandeur but was much smaller than Haresby Hall and older and more substantial than Bethany. Ivy covered much of the walls, and a tall cedar tree graced the area immediately in front of the house. The whole place was surrounded by a high wall that hid it from view until Nell managed to open the high wooden gate and begin her approach down the path to the front door.

She was greeted by the butler, who after some persuasion admitted her into the large entrance hall. Stags' heads adorned the walls, and she could see that Duncan and Eleanor would share a common love of hunting! She was musing on who would be the better shot and whether Duncan would let her ride with him as her father had when Lord Talbot himself appeared in the hall dressed for outdoors. He was tall and towered over her as he stooped to ask her mission.

"Good morning, miss. My butler said you had something to show me." She proffered the glove.

"Sir, I have reason to believe this was dropped by a lady who was staying here. She must have dropped it as she boarded the stage coach, and I found it. I'm sure she will be grateful for its return."

"I'm sure she will. Much obliged to you, miss." As if he thought it was what she'd expected, he produced a halfpenny from the leather purse on his belt.

"Oh, I wasn't expecting a reward, sir." She turned away embarrassed, but he insisted.

"Thank you, sir." She took the halfpenny, hesitated and then plucked up courage to make her request before she was shown the door. "I was wondering, sir, if you could help me with an inquiry into the whereabouts of my brother, Robert Thornby, who is fighting for the king." Lord Talbot rang a bell to summon his steward, who was sent to fetch his mustering list. Robert's name was on it.

"Yes, he was fighting with us here at Tadcaster, and then it seems he left for the east and is with Prince Rupert's men.

"Oh thank you, sir. I'd be most grateful if you could tell me anything else."

"No, ma'am, I'm afraid that is all I know. I'm sure he would have been fighting at Winceby, but he didn't return here." Nell thanked him, though inwardly she was disappointed—disappointed that the information did not tell her where Robert was now and hurt that it seemed Robert had been fighting at Winceby. There he would have been so close to Haresby Hall and she had traveled so far to find him. She hurried back to Bethany.

Snow was falling again in thick flakes. Nell looked at the halfpenny and almost wished she had kept the glove, but she was glad of the money. Her meager earnings had not yet stretched to afford a winter cape, and she could not run for fear of slipping on the wet road. It was bitterly cold, and she wondered if Robert had warm clothes and shelter. She decided that much as she wanted to find him, this time she would not leave everything to do so—not yet anyway, at least not until the warmer weather. The knowledge that she had left Haresby Hall for Tadcaster when Robert had been so close at Winceby pained her. Even worse was the thought that he might have been killed or injured in that battle.

Chapter 8

At Haresby Hall preparations were being made for Christmas. For one thing Eleanor had decided to make a stand against Puritan influences that wanted to do away with church traditions. For another she needed a good reason to host Duncan Talbot at Haresby.

"Catherine, this year we shall celebrate as we have always done," she declared to her lady-in-waiting.

"Oh, ma'am, that will be grand! In the great hall as in your father's day?"

"Yes, indeed, we shall decorate and feast and make merry once again, and we shall give no heed to those Puritan folk who want us all to be somber and dull as the winter weather!"

"And who shall your ladyship be entertaining? Lord and Lady Ashton?"

"Yes, and Sir Robert Morris and his wife, Anne, and daughter, Elizabeth. They will be happy to come to Haresby again. Father and Sir Robert were fond of hunting together. And I think an invitation should be sent also to the Mortlocks. 'Twould be solace to their grief after their son was killed at Edgehill."

Catherine could no longer suppress her curiosity as to whether Duncan would be invited.

"And will the gentleman from Yorkshire be visiting us again, ma'am?"

"Yes, I shall send an invitation to the Talbots since they have extended much hospitality to me of late."

Catherine was sure that gratitude was not the only motive of her mistress, but Eleanor remained silent about any secret feelings she may have had.

"I shall need to hire extra help in the kitchen and another chambermaid to care for the guests. First I shall write invitations to our special guests and send Hugh to deliver them. Since it's already almost Advent, I shall order Matilda to begin making preparations for the feast. We shall invite all the good folk who used to come and make merry with us, be they rich or poor. Christmas is a time for goodwill, don't you think?"

"Aye, ma'am, that I do, and there's plenty of folks who'll be needing a kindness after losing their loved ones in the fighting."

"Mmm," Eleanor agreed. "We shall set the benches around the great hall for the poorer folk, and there they may eat and drink and watch the plays."

"Oh, ma'am, it will be just like old times!"

"Aye. There'll be the usual mess and expense of feeding them, but it does hold our community together in these times of division and give us all something else to think about besides politics and war."

As Eleanor had anticipated, her invitations were enthusiastically received, and she soon had her replies. To her delight, Duncan would come with his father and mother, which would mean that he could travel in their private coach and not have to ride on horseback. It would be the first time she had hosted so many guests, and she was more than a little challenged by the prospect of fulfilling her role as lady of the manor; however, the thought of seeing Duncan again cheered her, and she applied herself happily to the task of organizing the household to accommodate and feed her guests.

The great house was buzzing with anticipation. There was much speculation about the significance of Duncan's arrival all the way from Tadcaster. Eleanor had insisted that this time there be no shortage of hot water for her guests to freshen up after their long journey. Having done it herself, she understood its rigors.

She determined that despite the busyness of overseeing the preparations, she would dress up for the occasion. A local dressmaker was sent for, and she chose fabrics befitting a young heiress for herself and called for Catherine to select some fine linen.

"I'm not having you looking like a pauper. You shall have something new," she promised.

"Yes, ma'am. Thank you, ma'am!" She chose some russet linen with pink for the undershirt, which would show through the decorous slits in the elaborate sleeves. Eleanor chose cream silk to be embellished with small pearls and lace and worn over a brown silk undergarment. For once instead of a coif, she would wear her brown hair up at the back of her head, but falling in curls around her face and neck. This was one occasion when she needed to look like a lady.

"We shall hold up our heads, Catherine, despite present difficulties. We shall take our place and be here for the Yuletide celebrations as my family always have been."

"Yes, ma'am," Catherine agreed, privately thinking that Eleanor's efforts were more focused on catching the eye of the dashing young man from Yorkshire and that that might be a good thing.

As the day approached, Jacob set the great Yule log in the huge hearth of the great hall. It was cold and empty, and his footsteps echoed in the silence that had pervaded since the last Yuletide celebrations hosted by Eleanor's father in 1641; however, it would soon be full of feasting, music, and merrymaking. Matilda grumbled daily at the extra workload in the kitchen; however, Eleanor had planned ahead, and soon extra staff assisted with the preparation of the festive food. The excitement mounted as they plucked ducks and geese, made the customary pudding of bread and potatoes, and baked mince pies. Outside several pigs squealed as they were slaughtered for roasting, and the frosty air resounded to the sound of a woodman's axe chopping wood for the fires.

Hugh was sent to cut holly, ivy, and mistletoe to make the kissing bush and suspend it from the central beam of the ceiling of the great hall. Eleanor busied herself supervising the decoration of the house with holly and mistletoe. She placed the traditional crib in the alcove near the fireplace. Jacob had spread straw there, and on it she arranged the figurines of Joseph and Mary and placed baby Jesus in the manger, the shepherds with their lambs and the three wise men giving homage. The figurines had been carved from oak felled on the estate several generations before. They were well done, though plain and unadorned. To Eleanor they were precious, and she mused how the simplest of things, when handed on from one generation to another, assume a value not accorded to them in their own time, a kind of mystique, because they have been deemed important enough to preserve and pass on. *Just like Christmas itself,* she thought. Little did she know that it would be the last time she would have the freedom to celebrate it. Before the next Christmas a law would be passed by Parliament banning Christmas festivities.

Around the nativity scene she placed small candles, and on the banqueting table she placed the large Christmas candle that would be lit on Christmas Eve and left to burn until the following day. If it burned until breakfast, it would issue in good luck. Determined not to be secretive, she sent one of the maids to place a candle in every windowsill of the house. Haresby Hall would shine like a light in the darkness.

The banqueting table was set with pewter trenchers and goblets and wooden benches were set out around the room for the common folk. Eleanor ordered Hugh to bring cider from the cellar and wine such as was available to be mulled with spices. Times might be hard, but she intended to make the most of what she had. She would make sure of that. The smell of wood smoke filled the air as fires were lit in all the rooms. There would be a warm welcome for the gentry, and Eleanor would prove herself to be a very capable mistress of Haresby.

The day before Christmas Day was a Sunday, and as the courtyard echoed to the wheels of coaches and hooves of horses, the keen wind hurled flurries of snowflakes across the light of the lantern. Edmund Whyte, who normally managed the estate and was usually out on the land, was sent to assist Hugh in the stables. Eleanor greeted her guests in her previous best dress of green silk. There was much exchanging of pleasantries.

"A white Christmas, my dear, we shall have an early spring."

"Oh, but Christmas on Monday does not augur well."

"No, neither is there a new moon to bring us luck."

"May the good Lord bless you for keeping the traditions, Mistress Eleanor." And so on as she showed them to their rooms.

They spent the evening in the drawing room, where a blazing fire provided comfort and mulled wine flowed freely from jug to goblet. Then they dressed again for the short walk to the church for midnight mass.

The church was less festive than in previous years, decorated only with candles whose flames danced in the dark night, throwing moving shadows across the walls. Eleanor and her guests sat in the special box reserved for her family, while many other local people filled the other pews. St. Oswald's had been a place of worship for Eleanor's family ever since her great grandfather had built it shortly after the completion of the house. Tonight it looked sad compared with the way it used to be decked out for Christmas, lacking even the celebration of a nativity scene.

The service, which came from the Book of Common Prayer, was one that all were familiar with, for it had been used since 1549 and had changed little, despite complaints by the Puritans. It gave Eleanor a sense of permanence in an uncertain world. After a sermon Holy Communion was administered. It was no longer called "the Mass" as it was before the Reformation, but it fulfilled the same purpose of commemorating the sacrifice of Christ on the cross. Catholics argued that the bread and wine actually became his body and blood during the sacrament, Protestants that they were merely symbols. Eleanor didn't care. She had grown up a Protestant, and as far as she was concerned, if she attended church, took the sacrament, and led a good life, she had a good chance of a place in heaven. She was quite content with the status quo and saw no need for the religious rantings of those who declared that it was lacking in godliness.

Eleanor was happy enough to hear the familiar scriptures relating to the Christmas story, but they must also endure the sermon. The hour was late. She was tired after all the preparations, and the mulled wine was taking effect. Only the awareness of Duncan at her side kept her eyes from closing. She forced herself to sit bolt upright to keep from drifting off to sleep. His mother, a rather severe lady whom Eleanor secretly called "the duchess," was not so successful. Soon her coiffured head was nodding onto her ample bosom, and her husband had to prop her up to prevent her sliding along the polished wooden seat.

At last they were invited to proceed to the front of the church and kneel for the Communion bread and wine, which they all did in an orderly fashion, Eleanor leading the way. Finally the congregation filed out into the winter night to return to their homes and warm beds.

Gradually the guests retired, and Eleanor was free to retire herself. It had been a pleasant evening, and she congratulated herself on the fact that everyone seemed to be enjoying the company and the hospitality at Haresby. She was gathering her skirts to ascend the broad sweeping staircase when she became aware of a figure watching her from the opposite side of the stairwell. Looking up across the dimly lit space, she recognized Duncan, his blonde curls falling onto his shoulders and the blue of his velvet coat highlighting his blue eyes.

"Why, Duncan, is everything well with you?"

"Yes, Eleanor, I was merely verifying that all is well with you."

"Yes, indeed, thank you. May you sleep well, Duncan. It is good to have you here with us." She paused on the landing, her head slightly on one side so that her curls fell across her shoulder, her lips parted in a smile.

Duncan paused, taking in the sight of her, and then bowed slightly.

"May we all sleep well and have a merry Christmas!" He nodded, smiled and turned away to enter his room.

It was a merry Christmas. The following night saw the great hall full once again with the local people—people from all walks of life, old and young, musicians and mummers, merchants and millers—all feasting on Matilda's cooking, while the servants were kept busy waiting at the tables. First they observed a respectful silence for Eleanor's official greeting.

"Haresby Hall welcomes you to our Yuletide celebrations. You may eat, drink, and be merry tonight in this place, and may the good Lord grant that we may always be able to do so. We drink tonight to the health of our sovereign, King Charles. Long live the king!" Cheers resounded in the hall as she took her place in the center of the great banqueting table, but her keen eye searched the room for any who kept silence. Since most of the county was now under the control of Parliamentarians, she knew she was not the only one who was keeping a watchful eye on the locals, and she wondered how much the influence of Parliament had affected them. In the present situation it was hard to know who could be trusted.

After the feasting it was time to dance. Couples took their places for the well-known country dances. It seemed natural that Duncan should partner with Eleanor. He cut a dashing figure in his brown britches and elegant dark green doublet, with his cream shirt showing through the elaborately slashed sleeves of his jacket and the cream lace at the cuffs and collar. He was slightly built but athletic. Normally he was not given to too much splendor, but this Christmas night he looked like a gentleman. Eleanor's cream skirts swished, her décolletage discreet with lace but sparkling with pearls as well. There was much foot tapping and hand clapping from those who looked on, and it seemed that everyone was engaged in the community celebrations.

There was a pause in the dancing while some local singers performed "The Holly and the Ivy", and it was during this quieter moment that Eleanor suddenly became aware that Edmund Whyte and his wife and children were missing. He usually took his place in the group of musicians with his viol. Fearing for their health or afraid that some emergency on the estate had claimed his attention, she sent Hugh to inquire after them. Hugh returned without them and approached Eleanor, seeming reluctant to report his findings.

"He says he doesn't hold with all this frivolity, ma'am. It seems he has taken up with those of the Puritan persuasion." Eleanor was at once incredulous, angry, and confused. She had had no idea of Whyte's change of heart. She had worked closely with him, appreciating his dedication and support in the running of the estate. Now it seemed he had turned traitor. Eleanor was speechless. However, although distracted by his absence, she was grateful that his protest against the festivities was passive. In fact, it seemed like nothing more than a personal decision to abstain.

"Well, I hope he keeps his ideas to himself!" she said and sighed. "We don't want that thinking spreading like a cancer at Haresby. And I hope he isn't thinking of fighting against the king. We need him here!"

Duncan watched Eleanor struggle with the issue. He understood her fears. They were not unfounded. It evoked in him again the feeling that he wanted to protect her, to be with her, and to help secure Haresby against physical attack from the Parliamentarians. They were strong amongst the merchants of the eastern counties, and he feared it would not be long before they made their presence felt.

Eleanor put her fears to one side and rejoined in the merriment of the night. Dancing recommenced, and Alexander Mortlock found a willing partner in Elizabeth Morris, whose laughter was a good antidote to the grief of losing his brother. As sole heir now to the Mortlock estate, he would be quite an acceptable match. Eleanor watched them engaging with one another as they shared in the twists and turns of the dances.

"Alexander and Elizabeth seem to be making the most of the occasion, Duncan," Eleanor said, smiling over the top of her goblet.

"Christmas was ever a time of matchmaking!" he replied with a grin.

The more senior couples, Lord and Lady Ashton, the Mortlocks, Sir Robert Morris and his wife, put in a token appearance on the slower numbers but soon retired to watch the dances from the comfort of the seats that had been placed for the purpose near the fireplace. More local gentry joined in the dancing, and the musicians kept up the accompaniment, pausing only to refresh themselves with apple cider and sweetmeats. As was the local custom, mummers—neighbors in disguise—performed some jest until their identity was guessed and they were rewarded with some Christmas treats.

The night wore on, and some of the guests indulged in a little too much revelry.

"Time to blow out the candles," said Eleanor to Hugh, remembering how her father had called the evening's entertainment to a close. Any stragglers would be helped through the door by male staff, where the cold night air would help sober them up for the walk home. Most families could be seen propping up one or two members who had imbibed too liberal a share of the cider or ale. As the clock neared midnight and the candles were burning low anyway, Hugh began to extinguish the remaining candles, leaving the large Christmas candle and those around the crib to burn out. Some of those who had drunk too freely were slow to understand and show respect to their hostess. Their drunken laughter and unseemly talk echoed around the hall, loudly conspicuous in the growing quiet. Sensing Eleanor's apprehension, Duncan stood at her side while, silhouetted in front of the nativity, the firelight and the glow of candlelight behind her, she waited for their courtesy.

"Pray silence for the mistress!" he commanded loudly. The revelers were prodded and shaken by their neighbors and a hush fell in the great room. Eleanor bid them all good night.

"May we all be alive and well to meet again next year." Her words brought a hearty response from around the room.

"God bless you, Mistress Eleanor!"

"We shall keep the Yuletide again!"

"It has been a goodly feast!" With many such affirmations resounding and with much stomping of feet and kissing under the mistletoe, the evening came to a close.

Finally the last guest had left the great hall, and Eleanor had Mary dismiss the chambermaids to cater for the needs of those whom she was hosting. She lingered for a while, remembering childhood Christmases when both her parents had been alive and she had played snap apple and blind man's bluff with the other children. There had been more staff then, and her mother had had little to do apart from checking on the welfare of her guests and keeping them company.

Would that the walls of Haresby might echo again to the laughter of children! she thought. *Haresby needs an heir, so I can pass on the house and its traditions.*

She bent to pick up mistletoe that had fallen to the floor. It was extremely unlucky to let it touch the ground. She hastened to the fireplace to dispose of it, and as she turned, she saw Duncan returned from saying a proper good night to his parents.

"Look, Duncan, I fear we shall have bad luck."

"Not so, my lady!" Snatching it from her hand, he held it above her head. "I think it's extremely lucky! I have an excuse to kiss a beautiful and brave girl!" He kissed her quickly, his action surprising himself almost as much as it did her. He laughed, and she joined him in his merriment.

To one side of them, there was a sudden movement and an explosion of light as one of the last remaining candles fell onto the straw around the nativity and set fire to it. Instinctively Eleanor squealed and moved quickly aside, sweeping her billowing skirts away from the blaze. Duncan grabbed a remaining jug of cider and poured its contents on the blaze. The flames were transformed into a cloud of acrid smoke, which drifted toward the fireplace.

"Thank you, Duncan. I'll have it cleaned up in the morning," she said, hastening to blow out the rest of the candles.

"I can see you are a lady who knows how to kindle a flame!" joked Duncan.

"I hope I am, Duncan," she replied, drawing closer to him and fixing his gaze with her own. The room was almost in total darkness now, and it was easy to let Duncan put his hand under her chin and pull her face gently toward his own. No one saw the sweet embrace and the tender kiss they shared. It was a rare moment of privacy. One that Eleanor would treasure.

Boxing Day dawned crisp and cold. The flurries of snow that had been falling spasmodically throughout Christmas Day had coated the ground with fine white powder. Over a late breakfast her guests were expressing an eagerness to begin their journey home before further snow made roads unsuitable for travel—all that is except for Duncan, who preferred to take up Eleanor's offer of a horse from the stables and a deer hunt on the estate. His mother was less than enthusiastic.

"We cannot travel without you, Duncan. You have no mount to ride home on, and in any case it would be foolish to do so in this weather." Lord Talbot raised one eyebrow as he sipped his tea.

"If we delay our departure, we may be forced to presume on Mistress Eleanor's hospitality indefinitely," he said. "Besides, we have Twelfth Night commitments ourselves, as you know."

"Yes, Father, I do remember. I can make it back by then on the public carriage."

"Maybe you would care to join me in a hunt on my estate too," cut in Sir Robert, "you and Eleanor both. I daresay she would enjoy the sport too. I remember how she begged to accompany her father when he used to chase the deer at Doveton." Sir Robert chuckled, remembering the lithe young woman who ten years earlier had surprised—even at first shocked him—with her ability to keep up with her father.

Eleanor threw him a grateful glance. It was an invitation they were both glad to accept, and arrangements were made for them to visit the Mortlocks the next day. Eleanor was particularly grateful that Sir Robert's invitation had taken care of the duchess's fussing and the Talbots were reconciled to Duncan's traveling home independently, though even he did not relish the thought of the stage coach journey. He would far rather have ridden the fifty miles to Tadcaster, but being without a horse, he had no option.

It was late in the day by the time Eleanor had said good-bye to the last guest and was free to accompany Duncan on a ride across the estate, too late to hunt but time enough for a gallop up to the top of the ridge and a canter along the edge of the woods. Hugh saddled a horse for Duncan and then one for himself to ride out to check on his rabbit traps. The afternoon was still. The only sounds apart from the horses' hooves on the frosty ground were the thin tweeting of blue tits and a robin's warble. Duncan's and Eleanor's breath and that of the horses came out in great clouds in the cold air.

"We'll go up to the top of the ridge," suggested Eleanor. "There's a great view of the estate from up there." It wasn't so much that she wanted to brag about her assets, but she wanted to share with him what was most precious to her. First they urged their mounts up through the woods, now bare, apart from the few evergreens at the top. Eleanor never tired of the vista she enjoyed when she came out of the woods, continued on for a hundred yards or so up a steeper part of the ridge, and then looked back. Haresby Hall nestled in its extensive gardens on the plain below. Today it was a monochrome vista where dark patches of trees mottled the white landscape. Eleanor and Duncan were the only color in it—Eleanor in her voluminous hooded green cape and Duncan in a tan leather jacket and black hat.

An onlooker viewing from a distance would have been unable to pick out the colors but could have watched their silhouettes against the skyline as they rode up the incline of the ridge. They would have been able to see them dismount at the top and stand together between the horses, reins in hand. They would, however, have been unable to see Duncan reach inside Eleanor's wide hood and gently caress her cheek … or the tears that such a sudden tenderness evoked in Eleanor. Neither would they have heard Duncan's words of proposal. Hugh, however, was watching from the edge of the woods just as he had spied that day on Nell, and though too far away to eavesdrop, he had enough information to cause Haresby Hall to buzz with whispers of anticipation.

Chapter 9

In Tadcaster Nell missed the Christmas traditions she had enjoyed at Haresby Hall. Edward Thorpe refused to have anything to do with the traditional religious festivals, but they had ruled the calendar and marked the seasons as much as the changes in the weather and the landscape did. The festivals of Christmas, Easter, All Saints' Days, and harvest—all punctuated the calendar with reason for frivolity. Nell especially missed the Wakes festivities held on the anniversary of a particular church's patron saint, when old rushes were swept out of the church and replaced with new ones to the accompaniment of much dancing, drinking, and reveling. As Molly informed her though, in the archdiocese of York, the Wakes had been banned since 1571 and then restored in 1633 by King Charles I, who had insisted that they be observed. Puritans, however, would have nothing to do with such frivolities, and Nell was expected to abstain too.

The Thorpes, however, for all their puritanical ways, indulged their own household with gifts, and at prayers on Christmas Day Nell was given a cape and shoes. The shoes were new, and the cape, although no longer big enough to cover Mrs. Thorpe's ample proportions, was perfect for Nell. Woven from brown sheep's wool, it was of good quality with plenty of wear left in it. She pulled it close around her shoulders, enjoying the luxury of it, the warmth of the color flattering against her pale complexion.

"Oh, thank you, ma'am. 'Tis most kind of you!" They seemed to take pleasure in her delight. Nell was grateful, for it would have been a while before she could have saved enough to buy her own.

Molly gave her a carved wooden crucifix.

"Take care to keep it hidden. T' master don't hold wi' such things. Says they're of the Devil, but it'll bring you luck, Nell."

Nell was glad of the gift. She had so few possessions of her own. She put it in the deep oak windowsill with the candle she had lit for Christmas just as she had in happier days when she and Robert had shared roast goose and mince pies around the family table. The ivy growing thickly around the bottom of the window hid the candle from an outsider's vision, but she was cheered by its glow, though she knew it was unlikely to burn until the twelfth night and bring her luck. She studied the crucifix as she lay in bed, the candlelight illuminating her earnest young face.

"I need your help, Savior." she said. It was the first time she had ever spoken to God herself. She did not expect an answer, and indeed she heard none; however, a warm glow seemed to penetrate her being in the cold attic bedroom. She could not take her eyes off the effigy of Christ impaled on the cross and wondered why such a cruel death had overtaken the Son of God. She so desperately wanted to believe that somewhere there was a God who cared. Ever since she had become an orphan, she had longed to know love. She had derived some comfort from talking to her mother and at times fancied she heard her reply, but Mr. Thorpe said the Bible forbade talking to the dead. She did not want to get on the wrong side of God. She needed to know that he loved her. She had given a great deal of thought to the problem of knowing God ever since. In the Thorpe household they talked a lot about sin and moral purity. If God was so holy, how could she, a sinner, possibly know his love? She remembered the night Mr. Thorpe had read from the gospel of John, "But to as many as received him, to them gave he power to become the sons of God."

"Does that mean we can be his children?" she had been bold enough to ask. He had seemed pleased with her interest and gone on to explain that God was able to be known as Father through faith in his Son. That was why the Lord's Prayer began with the words "Our Father." Nell desperately wanted a father, even an unseen one. Later that night she knelt in the privacy of her room.

"God, I believe in Jesus. Be a father to me." Immediately she was overwhelmed with a sense of her own unworthiness. She was unclean, too sinful to come close to God. She had been taught that God was holy, hadn't she? She could never be that good. What was the use of trying?

At first she thought it was the shadow of the crossbeams, but then she realized she was looking at a vision of the crucified Christ. It was like the crucifix that now stood in her windowsill, but this Christ raised his hands from the cross bar and extended them toward her, blood dripping from the wounds in his hands. It seemed he was inviting her.

"I'll come," she whispered. Even as she spoke, the heavy weight of guilt lifted from her, and she watched as its blackness went from her to him and nailed his hands once more to the cross. In that moment she understood that her sin had been placed on him. He had borne her guilt away and received her as she was. The transaction was complete. Her sin had gone to him, and his purity had come to her. Now she was a child of God. She could talk to her Father. She blew out the candle, but the room seemed less dark than on other nights. A peace she had never known enveloped her like a warm blanket, and she slept that night secure in the knowledge that she was loved.

Chapter 10

One Sunday afternoon in February Molly was suffering from a fever and unable to visit her sister, who lived on the edge of the moor. Nell had often walked up with her. She enjoyed the exercise and the chance to be outdoors now that she had new shoes and a cape.

"I'll go and tell her you'll not be coming over this afternoon, Molly. You rest."

"Mind you be back before nightfall, young lady. You'll not want to be on t' moor in t' dark." Nell was quite sure she would be back before nightfall. If Molly was still abed, there would be supper to get on the table.

Nell spent an hour or so with Molly's sister. Like Molly she was hospitable, and Nell enjoyed her honey and oatmeal biscuits as they shared local gossip. At about four in the afternoon Nell bid her good-bye and started down the track back to town. The sun was already sinking into the shroud of the wintry, western sky. There would have been plenty of time to get home before dark, but for the fact that Nell stumbled into a hole in the road and twisted her ankle. As it was she hobbled along painfully and slowly as the daylight faded. Suddenly one of those mists she had heard about fell like a suffocating blanket, obliterating everything but the few feet immediately in front of her. She was clammy and cold, her foot swollen and unable to bear her weight. Doggedly she kept to the path, knowing that if she wandered off to the side, she could walk round in circles all night or even worse, end up in a bog from which there would be no return.

Her eyes were so fixed on her feet that she didn't see the old man until he was almost upon her. He just loomed up out of the mist, arms wide like a scarecrow's, his unkempt beard wet with mist and his eyes staring. He was poorly clad and shuffled along slowly. She started, not sure if he was in fact real, for the effect of the mist swirling about him rendered him ghostly. He came closer, and she froze in horror. Then she smelled the drink and knew he must be returning from the tavern.

"Oh, it's a young lady," he said, examining her through squinty eyes. "You'll not be going far t'neet like as not." Nell shrank back. She was unsure of his intentions, and even if they were good, she didn't need the discouragement. Then realizing he had just come up the path she needed to go down, she summoned the courage to ask him how far it was to the town. In the mist she had lost all sense of distance, and all the usual landmarks were obliterated by it.

"You'll not be walking that far t'neet by t' look of ye."

"Oh, I must, sir."

"Nay, lass! You'd better stop at t' next house and get shelter 'til t' mist clears, lady."

It was a suggestion Nell didn't want to consider. The old drunk shuffled his way past her and up the hill. With relief she watched him disappear into the mist. He had obviously trodden that path many times before and knew where he was going. She envied his confidence. Maybe Mr. Thorpe would send someone after her. After all, Molly would tell them where she'd gone. They would be concerned when she didn't arrive for supper, especially if Molly were still abed.

Nell continued to pursue her painful way down. A lighted window glowed faintly through the mist, and she realized she was outside a small cottage. The mist was as thick as ever. She was wet and cold, and her ankle was getting worse with every step. She decided to knock and ask for shelter until the mist lifted. The door was opened slightly by a woman in her middle age. She peered out into the night and gasped when she saw Nell.

"Have you charity, ma'am, for a needy woman? I've twisted my ankle and can walk no further on it tonight. I'm afraid I'll lose my way in the mist."

"Ye can come in and bide a while if ye will. It's a naughty night to be out in, that it is."

Nell gratefully hobbled in through the door. If she had been feeling sorry for herself, her self-pity soon disappeared at the scene of deprivation before her eyes. The house was in poor order and stank of vomit and human excrement. A young woman lay on a mattress on a floor covered with rushes with a baby on her breast. It looked weak and sickly and was making a poor effort at suckling. Its mother looked too tired to care. The woman closed the door. At least the interior of the poor hovel was slightly warmer than the raw cold outside. A small fire burned in a grate, and the woman bent to add small logs to it.

"Our Polly's ailing badly. She's not been well since she had him. And little' un's not thriving either. If you ask me, it's a wonder they're both still with us."

Nell looked at the young woman and the baby. They were a sorry sight, and Nell hesitated to ask about them.

"He's not very old, is he?"

"He was born two weeks ago. Polly's done her best, but with no one but me to help care for her, it's been a sorry plight she's in." Nell suddenly remembered where she had heard the name Polly before.

"Are you the Polly who used to work for the Thorpes?" she asked.

"How do you know? Have you come to spy on us?"

"No, no! Why would I be doing that? I didn't mean to be rude. I'm in service at the Thorpe's and they said that the girl I replaced last October had left because of the baby."

"Aye. She couldn't stay there, so she had to come here with me," volunteered her mother.

Nell was stirred to pity for the girl and the young child. Whatever the circumstances in which she'd come to be with child, it seemed that life had been unkind to her. She wondered about the child's father.

"Can't you contact the father and let him know?"

"We've tried miss, but to no avail. He's gone off to fight wi' t' king's troops and doesn't even know he's a father to this child. He was wounded last year in t' battle at Tadcaster. We took him in, and she would come up from Bethany and help me nurse him back to health. After that they would go walking on t' moor together. Polly thought his intention was to marry her, but in May he joined the king's men mustering in the east. That was the last we heard of him. His name was Robert Thornby." Nell's pale face became ashen, and the room spun.

At that moment the cries of those looking for Nell distracted them. Edward Thorpe had sent a party with lanterns and the horse and cart to search the track from Tadcaster town. The older woman swiftly opened the door and bade them come in and get Nell from where she had just fallen on the rushes.

"One minute she were sitting there on t' chair and t' next she were on t' floor! She's happen had a hard time getting this far on that ankle!"

When Nell came round from the faint, she was looking up at two male faces that she recognized as men who came to the house to the religious meetings. Seeing her condition, they picked her up between them, deposited her in the cart, and departed for Bethany. Nell was too weak and confused to argue and merely mumbled an apology for the trouble she had caused them. She was glad to sink gratefully onto her bed. The next day she also had a fever and was too weak to get out of bed, which wasn't altogether a bad thing as it gave her ankle time to heal. It also gave her time to think and digest the news that she was an aunt to this sick child and that she and Polly had the same thing in common—they were both desperate to find Robert!

Whatever plans she might have hatched were soon thwarted by Molly's news that Polly had been carried out of that cottage and deposited in an unmarked grave outside the parish boundary, as was the custom with women who had borne illegitimate children. Robert's child, it seemed, had been left in the care of Elizabeth Arkwright, Polly's mother. Nell took thought for her little nephew. He would no doubt soon follow his mother. Part of her had been repulsed by the sight of the sickly infant, but this child was Robert's son. She must see him. She must ascertain that he was taken care of. The child's grandmother was obviously unable. Nell determined to visit as soon as she was able.

She had to wait a week before her fever and her ankle were healed. When she resumed her duties, there was much to do to since Bethany had had scant cleaning for a week. At the end of the day she wanted nothing more than to retire to her room and the comfort of her bed again. However, at evening prayers the matter of her visit to Polly was raised with much disapproval.

"I was just sheltering from the mist, sir. I was not acquainted with Polly before that time. My purpose on the moor was to visit Molly's sister, not Polly, and when the mist came down, I twisted my ankle in a pothole. When I came upon their home, Polly's mother allowed me to sit for a while to wait until the mist cleared, but your men found me. Thank you, sir, for searching for me. I do very much appreciate it," she added.

"Well, I suggest you avoid Polly's kind, Nell. We don't want you to be influenced by the likes of her!"

"I understand she's dead, sir," responded Nell miserably. "Molly heard the news from her sister."

"And good riddance too!" proclaimed Mrs. Thorpe. Nell was shocked and secretly wondered if God himself would condemn Polly with such vehemence. Didn't the good book say that he came to save sinners? She couldn't understand religion. Was it all Polly's fault? Wherever she was now, Polly was no longer troubled with the shame of bearing an illegitimate child, but her son was marked as a bastard and would always bear that stigma as long as he remained in Tadcaster.

"Well, I hope the father shows up and takes responsibility for the child," commented Mr. Thorpe. It's law that he should provide for it."

On that point Nell was in silent agreement. She had every intention of making sure that father and son became acquainted. During evening prayers she tentatively offered up her own silent requests for the welfare of her nephew, though she wasn't sure at that point if God would hear her requests for a baby born out of wedlock.

The next day on the pretext of visiting Molly's sister, Nell ventured again to the edge of the moor to the tiny hovel where the life of Christopher Thornby hung in the balance. She had taken leftover dumplings from the kitchen, telling herself that they would most likely have been fed to the pigs. The hovel looked worse in broad daylight than it had in the misty night. Polly's mother sat vainly trying to warm herself by the pathetic fire while the baby lay on the mattress. The pall of death lay over the place, and she sat unmoved and unmoving after she admitted Nell, staring miserably into the grate.

"Now who'll take care of me when I'm old?" she asked. "Polly's gone, and soon this one will be gone too."

Nell could see that the situation was hopeless.

"Would you let me hold him for a moment?" she asked. At least she would be able to tell Robert she had held his son.

"Here— You can have him, if ye want. Not much I can do for him now." Nell knew there was nothing she could do either. By now the child had little more life than a doll, its face like porcelain and its tiny fingers quite still. She looked at the tiny features. Yes, surely it was Robert's with the Thornby nose.

"Christopher Thornby, if I can help you I will," she promised silently. There was something in the dogged determination of this child to hold on to life against all odds that matched her own. She held him closer so that the warmth of her own body would warm his. But even as she held him, she knew he would not live. The little creature had not asked to be born, but it seemed that he soon would soon die.

She knew it would be no good calling for the priest to baptize him. No illegitimate child would be considered worthy of baptism, and if baptism were the only way into heaven, this little one would be banned. One thing that she had learned from Edward Thorpe was that the Word of God was proof enough of the truth of a matter. Suddenly she remembered the words she had heard Edward Thorpe read, the words of the Son of God himself, "Suffer the little children to come unto me." Would God really condemn such an innocent one to hell? No, surely, Jesus, who blessed the little children in the Bible story, would look upon this little one with love and compassion. Tears shone in her blue eyes and overflowed to drop like pearls on her cheeks. Pity for the tiny form in her arms mixed with anger against the injustice of his brief sojourn on earth. Silently she committed him to the Almighty. The church might condemn, but she had heard the words of the good book for herself now. She knew what it said about his love of children. She was learning to pray, learning that God would listen to the prayers of ordinary people, that she did not need the priest, that God would hear her prayers, even the prayers of a woman. She knew little about religion, but faith was beginning to grow in her heart. She would pray to God, and he would hear her prayer. She did not need the priest, and she did not need Mr. Thorpe. Now she had her own faith. And she would not let her nephew go to hell.

"Please, oh please, take this little one to be with you, God." Her prayer was answered even as it fell from her lips. Little Christopher Thorpe passed from Nell's arms into the arms of the Almighty, Nell's tears the only tribute to his passing. Silently she passed him back to his grandmother, and as she did so, she wondered if she discerned a slight smile on the little face.

"I knew he'd not be long for this world," said Elizabeth. "I'll have to see to him now." She placed the tiny corpse on the bed.

"I'll just put him in t' garden," she said. "No good expecting a proper burial."

Molly's sister was walking down to the town when she saw two women digging at a little distance from the back of the house. She knew one was Elizabeth Arkwright, and she recognized the other as Nell from Bethany. Nell took the tiny body and laid it in the grave as tenderly as she would have laid him in a cradle, while Polly's mother looked on. With no priest to say the funeral prayers, Nell made a rough cross by tying two sticks together, and standing at the end of the little grave simply, she said, "Christopher Thornby, may you rest in peace." She consoled herself that in the absence of an earthly father, the heavenly Father had seen this little sparrow fall and cared. There was little more she could do. It was high time she returned to Bethany. Now Robert would never see the son he didn't know he'd sired.

Elizabeth Arkwright was fumbling in a dresser. She took out a small object, looked at it, hesitated, and then came over to Nell.

"I want to thank you, Nell, for your kindness. Please take this. It's just a brooch that that young man gave to our Polly. She'll not need it now. Wherever he is, he's not likely to return either. 'Twould be bad luck to keep it, and I don't want to be reminded of him. I know our Polly would have wanted you to have it."

Nell took the offered brooch. It was shaped like a rose with a cluster of tiny pearls at its center. It had been made by her grandfather, a silversmith, and she recognized it at once as belonging to her mother. She knew that there could be no other like it. It was indeed a most special reward.

As Nell headed down the muddy track she knew she would never return to the dismal home where her nephew had struggled to live for a brief three weeks.

"Why, Nell, wherever have you been?" scolded Molly. "The parlor fire's gone out, and there's cleaning to do! Have you no thought of your domestic duties?" In the numbness of fresh grief the words had little impact on Nell. Murmuring an apology, she set to make up for lost time.

When she returned to the kitchen, Molly began afresh, "And where are those dumplings I left for our tea tonight?"

In the more urgent matters of life and death Nell had forgotten about the dumplings. She had left them behind without so much as a mention, and worse still, she had left the basin in which she had carried them.

"I thought they were going out to the pigs, Molly. So I took them."

"Well, where's t' pot then?"

"I've left it at the home of the poor woman I gave them to," she confessed, not mentioning any names.

"Well, you'd better go fetch it back before t' missus finds out!" Nell promised to do so on the morrow. Before she had time to do so, however, there was a knock at the back door, and there stood Molly's sister with it in her hand.

"Elizabeth Arkwright saw me coming down to t' town and asked me to return this to ye," she said. Nell's relief was short-lived as she saw Mrs. Thorpe at the kitchen door, her expression thunderous.

"Good afternoon, miss, and what's our pot doing at Elizabeth Arkwright's?"

Beatrice repeated the explanation for her visit with the added information that Nell had taken it to Mrs. Arkwright's with the contents of food from Bethany.

"Dear Nell here, she's always thinking about others!" Then to Nell, she said, "I saw you helping her bury t' little one, Nell. Poor little thing."

"She'd be more use if she were inclined to think about her own duties here!" snapped Mrs. Thorpe."

"I'll be going now then," said Beatrice, sensing the prickly atmosphere. "Good day to you, ma'am."

"Good day to you, Miss Thompson, and thank you."

Nell knew that she stood condemned. She stood, flushed with embarrassment, looking at the back door and undecided as to whether or not to follow Molly's sister out through it, but Mrs. Thorpe wasted no time.

"Well, it seems that you have some explaining to do, Nell. You've been forbidden to associate with that family." Nell felt indignation rising.

"I was but helping that poor woman to bury her grandson!"

"And what has that got to do with you?" demanded Mrs. Thorpe.

Nell had no wish to share that the baby was indeed her nephew. She had already borne enough reproach for being there.

"I thought to be charitable, ma'am. I'm sorry if that offends you!"

"Don't you talk to me about charity, young lady! What would the likes of you know about it?" Her mistress had drawn herself up to her more than average height and was looking down her ample nose. Nell knew she had said too much already so she held her peace.

"Don't forget we took you in out of the kindness of our hearts and we can just as soon let you go if you can't be trusted."

With that threat she stalked off, and Nell thumped the pot on the kitchen table and took a broom to sweep the hall. She pressed her lips together and said no more, for words of self-defense would only end in more recriminations. It seemed she had managed to offend all the occupants of Bethany. She wondered if it would do any good to try to explain to Molly and to have her on side, but that would have meant disclosing Robert's part in the whole sad affair. Tears became Nell's wordless but eloquent prayer.

The atmosphere at evening prayers was strained. It seemed that she was somehow wearing the shame that should have been Robert's. In her efforts to nurture the hungry and bring comfort to the mourning, she had taken the blame for sins that were not her own. She was angry—angry with them that their desire to see morality enforced led them to ignore the welfare of their neighbor. She was angry with herself for forgetting the pot, and she was angry with Robert, whose careless indulgence had landed so many in such pain.

Chapter 11

Haresby Hall had seen many an occasion where people had gathered with common purpose. There had been the time when Eleanor's father's body had been brought back from Edgehill, when local people had lined the drive and Royalist soldiers had formed a guard of honor as the coffin was taken into the family church at the rear of the house. On that somber occasion people had stood silent and sad, sympathizing with Eleanor in her loss and sensing the seriousness of the moment. There had been happier days, many harvests when they had gathered in the church to give thanks with hearts glad that the work was done and that there would be food for the cold winter months. This spring day in 1644 they were gathered to celebrate the union of Eleanor with Duncan Talbot, and even the lambs frisking in the fields of the Haresby estate reflected the joyful mood of the day.

Duncan, resplendent in dark blue doublet and britches, a feathered, broad-brimmed hat atop his blond mane, waited at the altar. His bride was elegant in peach and cream brocade over a white satin stomacher with white lace ruffles at the cuffs of the long sleeves and the broad collar. She wore her hair up at the back with long ringlets at the sides and decorated with the same pearls that encircled her neck. She walked alone to stand at his side as all heads turned to enjoy the spectacle. Most of the onlookers were invited guests, largely from Yorkshire gentry, since most of Eleanor's acquaintances had been lost to her through political division or death. Outside, though, loyal servants and tenant farmers gathered to enjoy the happy occasion. There had been precious little to be happy about in recent months.

"Dearly beloved friends, we are gathered together here in the sight of God and in the face of this congregation—" began the priest. They were words known so well to Eleanor, who had attended many weddings in the family church. Although it had been built for and by her family, it was used by all those who lived locally, and its ancient bells had caroled their jubilant chimes on many such happy occasion. The 1549 Book of Common Prayer designated the left hand for the ring, and after the customary exchange of vows, Duncan took the ring of gold and laid it on the Bible, together with the gold necklace he was to give her as a token of his worldly goods. The priest handed it back to him.

"With this ring I thee wed. This gold and silver I thee give. With my body I thee worship, and with all my worldly goods I thee endow. In the name of the Father and of the Son and of the Holy Ghost. Amen." Touching her thumb with the ring at "the Father" and then the first and second fingers at "the Son" and "Holy Spirit," he finally placed it on her third finger at the *amen*. The gold necklace he placed tenderly around her neck.

He spoke the words solemnly after the priest, but not without a smile toward his bride, whose features softened as his promises flowed over her like warm honey. She was not in desperate need of his worldly goods, but his love and protection were priceless treasures.

After the administration of Holy Communion the couple processed down the aisle arm in arm to the greetings and good wishes of guests and then out into the spring sunshine to those waiting patiently at the door. The sun shone from a blue sky decorated with fluffy white clouds, and it seemed heaven itself was rejoicing at their union. Well-wishers threw wheat over the bride and groom as the bells rang out their joyful peal, and then the little party processed formally along the path back to the house for the banquet.

The banquet was decidedly smaller than the Christmas celebrations of the previous year but no less grand for all that. Duncan was formally introduced and welcomed by Eleanor into her ancestral home, and the staff was introduced to their new master—all except Edmund Whyte, who had chosen such a time to inspect his rabbit traps.

The next day Edmund appeared in full livery to lead out the horses belonging to the guests and harness them to the carriages for their departure.

"That fellow assisting Hugh, Eleanor, the one in livery," began Duncan as he watched him from an upstairs window.

"Oh, you mean Edmund Whyte?" said Eleanor.

"I'm not familiar with his name. He was absent yesterday when you introduced me to the staff."

"Yes, he was. Said he was out checking that no poachers were taking advantage of the fact that all the inhabitants of Haresby were engaged in the festivities."

"Did you believe him?"

"Sounds plausible enough. He's used to thinking for himself." Eleanor paused. "I'm not sure though. He's the one who was absent at Christmas too."

"You mean that Puritan fellow?" Duncan's tone was concerned.

"Yes. He's kept his opinions to himself as far as I know, but he's beginning to worry me. There are so many like him in the east."

"Yes. It might be time to dismiss him."

"I was hoping it would not come to that. He has a wife and family to support, and Haresby is all he has ever known. His father was here before him, and I don't know what I would have done without him when my father died."

"It seems to me he is not at all happy with having a new Royalist master."

"I will send to him to come immediately after the last guest has departed, and he will meet you whether he likes it or not!" asserted Eleanor. "I will instruct him to tell you everything he knows. The sooner you get acquainted with the land, the better!"

"Mmmm," agreed Duncan. Then he flashed a smile her way and added "I'd far rather be spending the time getting acquainted with my beautiful wife!"

Eleanor's frown disappeared momentarily as she encountered the warmth of his embrace and returned it, but the frown returned again as she looked over Duncan's shoulder into the yard below and caught sight of Edmund Whyte without a trace of goodwill in his tense features.

At the first opportunity she spoke to him herself. "You must let me introduce you to the new master of Haresby, Edmund. I want you to show him your duties yourself since you know what they are better than I."

"Yes, ma'am," replied Edmund Whyte politely; however, his eyes were hard, and his mouth firm, as though it were a duty he would undertake only because it was a duty, not a pleasure. Eleanor noticed.

"I think we would do well to watch him," she cautioned Duncan later.

"I shall soon be familiar with the workings of the estate, Eleanor, and then we can let him go."

As it was, Duncan had three short months at Haresby before he was summoned to the north to defend the Royalist stronghold at York.

Chapter 12

Nell's best clothes were by now somewhat faded and worn, but they were all she had. Despite the sideways glances of her fellow passengers, she was confident enough. She had paid as much as they for her journey. After much deliberation she had sold Robert's brooch for the fare on the stage coach to York. It was the end of March, and fluffy white clouds scudded across a pale blue sky. The coach jolted along the old stone road on which Roman troops had once marched. Soon it would resound to the march of English feet as they mustered to fight their countrymen. Soon the armies of Lord Fairfax and Lord Leven would join forces at Tadcaster and march north to lay siege to the ancient city of York.

She had no idea what she might do on her arrival in the great city. It was uncommon for women to travel anywhere, especially unaccompanied and especially if they had no connections in their destination. Nell, however, had hope—hope that she would connect with her brother, who for all his philandering was still her brother and her only living relative. But she had more than hope. She had a growing faith that her prayers were not landing on deaf ears. Despite the religiosity of the Thorpes, she had learned from the daily scripture readings that God cared for those who had no one to care for them, even if they met with indifference in the world. He had answered her prayers for a buyer for Robert's brooch. Loath as she had been to part with it, it was the only way she could afford the coach fare. Molly had been sympathetic in the end and provided her with food to eat on the journey.

"I hope you find him, miss. And I hope he deserves your concern and your giving up everything to find him."

"I will, Molly. If he's still alive, I'll find him. If he's not, at least I'll know. Someone will know. God will guide me."

Nell's faith was rewarded. By the time the great walls of York came into view, she had become acquainted with her traveling companions. Lady Asquith and her twelve-year-old daughter, Isabella, were returning to their country home outside York. As Nell shared the story of her quest to find Robert and asked them about their city, they opened their hearts to her and were happy to describe it. Nell listened attentively trying to memorize details that might help her to find a place to stay. She had never been to any place bigger than Lincoln. However, when she shared that she was looking for accommodation, the woman asked her if she would be interested in a position as a maidservant in Darrowby House.

Darrowby House had been the home of the Asquiths for four generations. The present Lord Asquith was serving as an officer with the king's men. Nell considered her options and decided that a Royalist household would be preferable to the streets of York. Darrowby House, it seemed, was close enough to the city to be within earshot of news. Lady Anne seemed kind enough and impressed that her brother was fighting for the king. She decided that this was the Almighty's provision for her present need.

The stage coach swung in under the arch of Micklegate Bar and pulled up in the yard of the coaching inn. James was waiting with their private carriage and all three climbed aboard for the short journey to Asquith House.

Nell was assigned domestic duties—cleaning the grand house and polishing its brass and silver. She was familiar with the process of mixing the wood ash with water to make a paste for polishing the brass. As at Bethany she had to keep the fires burning, and she often assisted Mary in the laundry—hot steamy work where she had to stir the washing in the huge tub with a pole and carry it out in a large wicker basket to hang it up. She was by now accustomed to the work, and it gave her something to do while she waited for any scrap of news that might be a lead to Robert's whereabouts.

The staff consisted of a butler, several cooks, scullery maids, chambermaids, stable hands, and gardeners. They ate together, and any talk of Prince Rupert's men would be sure to find its way into this Royalist household. Nell listened more than she spoke, preferring not to share too much about herself, but it was obvious from her dialect that she was not a local, so she had to field questions about how she came to be at Asquith House. She didn't mind sharing her quest to find Robert since it might lead to receiving information about him.

Nell was past the first bloom of youth, but the flattering light of the evening candles softened her features and lit up the few pale auburn curls that escaped from under her white cap. Mary's fish soup tasted good after the day's labors, but it was not to the liking of Georgie Barnes.

"A man shouldn't have to eat this foul broth. 'Tis only fit to give to t' cats!"

Mary shrank back at the insult, but Nell jumped to her defense.

"You have more manners, Georgie boy! Mary does what she can with the provisions she has! These are hard times, and we must be grateful to be fed!"

"And who asked you for your opinion, wench? I might have to teach you a lesson. Can't have you bringing your high and mighty southern ways up here, can we!" Georgie had jumped up and was stretching over the table to grab Nell's sleeve when his senior, the chief gardener, rose to her rescue.

"That'll do, man! Let her be! And watch your tongue, or you'll be eating with the cats ... outside!"

John Bellamy raised himself up to his full height and eyeballed Georgie from Nell's side of the table. Slowly Georgie backed off and sat down.

"If you have any more problems with this lout, you let me know," John said. "I'll not stand by and see you threatening house staff – and a woman at that!" Nell was shaken by the sudden outbreak of violence and grateful for John's intervention.

"Thank you, sir." She nodded to John and glared at Georgie. "I'm sure Georgie won't repeat his rudeness." She hoped and prayed he would not and was reasonably certain that John's threats would keep him from further attacks. He would not want to jeopardize his position at Asquith House. There were not many places where he would find employment and board with such good conditions despite his accusations about Mary's cooking.

It was a long time since Nell had had someone to champion her cause, and she expressed her appreciation with a warm smile and a greeting whenever their paths crossed. John watched her, inquiring about her health and whether or not she had had more trouble from Georgie. Nell was cautious, too self-contained to encourage his attentions, deeming it wise to maintain a safe distance between them in this Royalist household. As best she could, Nell kept a low profile and listened for news of the king's men.

As far as Nell was concerned, marriage was to be avoided at all costs. Since her father's bankruptcy, she knew it would be impossible to marry into a suitable merchant family. As a maidservant her only option was to marry someone of a lower social standing than she liked to consider. So far she had not found anyone whose attentions she had wanted to encourage. At Haresby Hall all the young men had been recruited into the king's army, leaving only old Jacob and Hugh. At Tadcaster Edward Thorpe had cautioned her about "being unequally yoked," as he called it. He needn't have been concerned. Nell had been too old for the boy who labored in the garden and too young for the Puritan gentleman who had looked at her secretly during prayers in the house meeting. She had kept her eyes closed to avoid meeting his, but could feel his stares through her closed eyelids. In any case she had no intention of being tied down in Tadcaster or anywhere else for that matter. Besides, she was not yet sure if she could live with a Puritan any more than a Royalist. The latter would require her to embrace a religion she no longer respected and a king who enforced it, and her experiences at Bethany had convinced her that not all Puritans practiced what they preached. Neither seemed to express the love of the Christ she had seen on the cross. Her quest had become more than a search for Robert. It was a search for truth.

Chapter 13

It was late afternoon toward the end of April, and John Bellamy was trimming the first spring growth from the hedges of the maze. He was sweating slightly with the labor of it, his cap shielding his eyes from the low afternoon sun. Nell watched from the corner of the maze. He was a good man, honest, kind, and down to earth. She had never seen him flirting with the female staff. He lived quietly in the lodge house by the gate. Nell had a mission, and she had decided she could trust him with it. She knew he rode into York to take produce from the gardens and letters from the mistress to her husband, and she had a mind to ask him to find Robert and deliver a message. He looked up and saw her.

"Why, good afternoon, Mistress Nell. How are you on this fine afternoon?" Nell drew closer within the confines of the maze to avoid being seen from the house.

"I'm well. Thank you, sir. I see you are fully engaged on your work."

"Not too busy to talk with you miss," John replied, pausing from his trimming, and wiped the sweat from his brow. His deep blue eyes studied her face, waiting for her to go on.

"I was wondering if you'd be going into York soon."

"No doubt I will. The missus will have me go and find Lord Asquith again before long. There is talk of a siege from the north, and he is with the Marquis of Newcastle preparing to defend the city.

"Does that mean there are Royalist troops involved?"

"All the locals are rallied, ma'am, but Prince Rupert and the king are still in the south."

"Will Prince Rupert bring his troops here then?"

"I know not what his priorities are. He'll take his orders from the king. We're hoping he will help us here, but he's not near enough yet." John shook his head. "We'll all be summoned to the battle no doubt before this is over." John looked at Nell again. "Why do you ask?"

"I have a brother, sir, who I believe is with Prince Rupert's men, but I'm not sure whether he is already at York. I haven't seen him since he went away to join the king. I heard he was at Winceby and Tadcaster, but after that there's no trace. I was wondering if you might find him while you are in the city."

"I'll see what I can do. Maybe I'll hear of him there. You're a good girl. I'd like to help." He paused and moved closer. "Nell, you wouldn't be wanting to go to him, would you? It's not good for a woman to be around those musketeers." His eyes expressed a tenderness that caused her to blush.

"I want to see him, sir, to know whether he's dead or alive and if I can meet with him."

"I'll ask after him and bring you news, miss, but I'm not encouraging you to go after him."

"Please could you at least let him know I'm here?" Nell removed the locket from around her neck. She had worn it ever since their father had given it to her for her eighth birthday. "His name is Robert Thornby. If you find him, please give him this. He'll know it's mine." She placed the locket in John's large, rough hand, and taking it, he clasped hers for a moment. She caught her breath and backed away slightly.

"Thank you, sir. You are very kind."

"I'll see what I can do, Nell." Her heart was thudding so inside her chest she thought he would surely hear it.

"Thank you, sir," she replied with true gratitude. Then she turned to walk away past the lengthening shadows of the rose trellises and into the house to a safe distance where she could compose herself and tell herself that John's touch had been nothing more than a hearty squeeze. Try as she might, she could not pretend to be unaffected by his interest. In other circumstances she might have encouraged him. With his gentle, dependable ways he would surely make a good husband.

Nell was torn. She could not embrace marriage with a man who supported the king. What had begun as political motivation had become more of a religious consideration. The influence of Bethany had been more than she had realized—not their strict religious ways but a deeper and purer conviction of her own. Somewhere deep inside Nell's being, a candle had been lit, and despite its frequent flickering, her trials had not extinguished it. She had no wish to belong to a system where priest and bishop dictated how she should worship. She had discovered the wonderful truth that she herself had access to the Almighty, and she was not about to give up her freedom. Even John's warmth could not convince her that life in a Royalist household would make her truly happy.

Nell had never been one to let her heart rule over her head, except in her love for her brother. For Robert she held to a loyalty born of gratitude for his care of her as a child. Her determination to find him, her only living relative, was born of loneliness. They had been raised to care for one another, and in their abandonment, that was what they had done. She simply could not stop caring now. The fact that Robert was a Royalist did not deter her. She refused to believe he was truly committed to the Royalist cause. Surely he was just a mercenary. Surely he had found employment the best way he could when their father had died in a debtor's prison and their mother had died from the unaccustomed labor of domestic service or a broken heart. Nell was never quite sure which.

She had often relived that awful day when they had come to arrest her father and drag him off to prison. Her mother's wailing filled her ears still. She and Robert had clung to one another wide-eyed and confused as they were forced from the only place they had known as home. Their mother had eventually found domestic work at Haresby Hall, but children were unwelcome, so they had waited daily by the gate until their mother brought them scraps from the kitchen, and they had slept where they could until they were old enough to be useful at the hall. Then they had been given suitable clothes and a bed in the servants' quarters. Robert had always shared whatever he had with her, until he had joined the king's army and left Nell behind at the hall.

After the Sunday evening meal John took the opportunity to suggest to Nell that she accompany him into York. He was going to take the horse and cart loaded with produce from the gardens to the garrison in Clifford's Tower. He would send Oliver to cover her main duties. Oliver always liked the chance to be in the proximity of Mary, where he could sweet-talk her into parting with a few extra delicacies. Nell welcomed the opportunity. She would be at the stables by sunrise.

Monday dawned fine and full of birdsong. She sat alongside John as he guided the horse along the wooded lanes to the city. The first flush of green covered the hedgerows, and pale primroses lifted their delicate faces to the sun.

"I'm glad you came, miss. It's good to have your company on such a fine morning." Nell smiled. It was good to be out in the morning air, and John was a pleasant enough companion as he whistled to Betsy and coaxed her along with his gentle voice.

"I'm glad too. I'm glad to be out in the morning air instead of stoking fires." On such a day it was easy to believe that God was watching over her. Several rabbits scattered from the roadside verges, and she watched them bounce away to their burrows. Everything was pulsating with fresh life. Blossoms adorned the trees with the promise of fruitfulness, and bees buzzed to their fragrance. If only every day could be like this! She got to wondering whether the excitement rising up within her stemmed from the vibrancy of the spring morning, the possibility of locating Robert, or the prospect of spending it with John. It occurred to her that she knew very little about John.

"Have you always lived here at Darrowby?" she inquired.

"Aye, I were born here," he replied. "My father were t' manager before me for t' late Lord Asquith, and I've worked in t' garden since I were a lad. Prettiest in Yorkshire, I'd say. You wait 'til t' roses bloom. They were planted by my father, and I've always tended them, pruning them and feeding them manure from t' stables. Lord Asquith's pride and joy they are—just as they were my father's. I helped my father build t' trellis for t' climbers, and there's naught so sweet on a summer evening as to walk past those blooms and smell th' air heavy with their scent."

Nell smiled. She envied him his simple life, secure within the walls of Darrowby House. He had never been rich, but then he had never been poor either. His life had a stability she longed for. Would she be so content to have her days ordered by the setting and rising of the sun and the passing of the seasons?

"Do you ever get bored here? Ever want to explore further afield?"

John considered her question for a moment. He had never been more than five miles away from Darrowby.

"Can't say I do, miss. There's allus plenty to do and see here. It's as good a place as any, I'm sure." Nell had to admit it compared rather favorably with both Haresby Hall and Bethany.

They had reached the top of a small rise from where they could see the city walls, and John gave Betsy some rein as she trotted down the other side. The sight awakened both of them to the reality that they were about to enter a war zone. In the wooded lanes it was possible to pretend that that was all there was—John with his easy smile, the clip-clop of amiable Betsy and nature's abundance—a moment in time when Nell could imagine what it might be like to be content. The city would be far removed from this idyll. Nell was not even sure of gaining access to the city, but John reassured her that he was known to the Royalist watchman at Bootham Bar.

"Soon be there, Nell. I'll need to go to Clifford's Tower to deliver this lot to Lord Asquith. He'll be anxious for news from my Lady Anne. Then we can maybe find some o' t' musketeers in t' taverns along t' way and inquire about your Robert."

It had been a few weeks now since she'd come through the city to Darrowby and she was looking forward to doing some exploring. She had learned a lot since her first adventures in Tadcaster and her spirit was not discouraged, but fired by a new determination. She had high hopes that here in this place she would at last find Robert and know whether he could be dissuaded from the war.

In the morning sun York's ancient walls looked impregnable enough, but its future as a Royalist stronghold was about to be challenged. Bitter fruit was about to be eaten by those who had sown the seeds of wrath. York in the spring of 1644 would soon be the site of more bloodshed in the name of religion and political enterprise.

In the crowded streets women carried baskets of goods in their hands and screaming babies on their backs. Soldiers with muskets marched on the cobbles and drank in the taverns. The news had spread that Parliamentary troops had reached Wetherby and were moving toward York to besiege it. For the Royalists the Marquis of Newcastle was poised to defend it with five thousand troops. Nell and John left the peace of the idyllic spring morning outside Bootham Bar. At the gate the watchman was easily bribed with a few vegetables, especially when he learned of John's mission.

They entered into the melee and made their way down to the castle bailey at Clifford's Tower, where John would have to continue on foot.

"Nell, stay here and mind Betsy. I'll find Lord Asquith and come back." He climbed down and put the nose bag on Betsy to keep her occupied. He reappeared with several soldiers to unload the cart and then disappeared within the ancient walls of the tower.

Nell sat there searching the face of every soldier that passed. As long as there was a slight hope, she could not help but look. Betsy continued to be restless, so she held the reins to steady her. She had never learned to manage a horse and cart but had watched John.

Everywhere people were scattering like bees from a smoked hive. The army maneuvered artillery into position, ready to defend the walls and musketeers manned the walls ready to take aim at assailants. Only a few days ago the Marquis of Newcastle had returned with his troops to York to reinforce the Royalist defenses. Hot on his heels four days later were their enemies–the Scots army and the Fairfaxes– who now surrounded it on the east and the south with thirty thousand Parliamentarian troops. It was a wonder Nell and John had gained access and probably only because they had entered through the northeast gate.

Nell was looking up toward Clifford's Tower in anticipation of John's return when she saw a group of cavalrymen approaching. The cart was blocking their access to the road to Bootham Bar.

"Out of the way, woman, can't you see the king's men must be on their way!" Nell could well see the need to move the cart but was hesitant to trust her own ability to maneuver Betsy and get her to back up enough for the cavalry to pass.

"Hurry now! Back up!" the lieutenant insisted. Gingerly she took hold of the reins and had managed to disengage the horse's attention from the nose bag when a musket shot rang out nearby. Betsy shied, reared up, and then took off forward in the direction of Bootham Bar.

Nell had little choice but to cling to the reins and to try to bring Betsy under control. The empty cart did little to slow Betsy. There were yells and screams as people scattered out of her path. Nell was relieved when

Betsy charged directly for Bootham Bar and did not turn into the narrow Shambles. As it was, they left a trail of upturned baskets behind them, their wares scattered over the road. As they neared the wall near Lendal Bridge, Nell stood up in order to better handle the reins and to try to turn Betsy in the direction of Bootham Bar. She struggled to keep her balance. Her coif flew off and her long auburn hair streamed out behind her. Her screams attracted more attention than she would have wanted but did finally produce results. One of the cavaliers was quick to ride his mount alongside Betsy until he could reach over and grab the reins from Nell and bring the horse to a halt. Nell sat stunned and shaken, her breasts heaving under her linen shift. The cavalier dismounted to calm Betsy and her shaken driver and Nell looked up to find Robert at her side.

"Nell! Nell! What are you doing here?"

"Why, Robert! Looking for you! I've been searching for you for weeks!"

"Are you all right?"

"I believe I'm unharmed, Robert, though 'twas a fright, I must admit."

"Thank God you were not harmed, lass. Whose horse?"

"It belongs to Lord Asquith. I'm working at Darrowby House. It's out to the west. I came here to find you, Robert. Thank God you're safe!"

"Yes, I'm safe, Nell. And I thought you were safe at Haresby Hall." He left Betsy's side and came closer to Nell, and she grabbed his sleeve to pull him closer.

"I thought you'd have found a husband to care for you by now, Nell."

"I wanted to be with you, brother, to find a place we can stay together and be safe."

"And where do you think that might be, my little sister? There is nowhere safe in all of England while this war goes on! I must fight for the king to end it, and then we can talk of the future!" Robert turned away to remount his own horse. The press of other riders forced him away from her, and he had to remove himself from the throng to come close again.

"Wait, Robert. Wait!"

"Nell, I'm under orders. I can't stay to talk now. We're mustering to repel an attack! And you, dear Nell, had better get out of here while you still can!"

"Promise you'll look for me at Darrowby, Robert!"

"We'll meet again, Nell, I promise!" Robert disappeared amidst a sea of horseflesh and was lost from her sight.

John returned from Clifford's Tower to find the cart gone, but there were no lack of witnesses to relate the story of Nell's adventure. He found her where Robert had left her. Tears stained her face, and she sobbed uncontrollably. He listened as between sobs she told him of Betsy's flight and her encounter with Robert.

"Nell, we can find him later. Right now we need to get out of here ourselves while we still can. We must hurry before the Roundheads surround us."

Nell sat silently by John's side as he maneuvered the cart through the crowded streets and onto the Poppleton road. He drove without stopping or giving Betsy rest until they were well on the way to Darrowby. It was still only early afternoon, but Nell pulled her shawl around her and shrank into it. John noticed.

"Don't fret, Nell. At least you know he is in the north." He held onto the reins with one hand, put the other arm round Nell, and pulled her to him. She did not refuse his comfort. He felt awkward, but the urge to comfort and protect her overcame his shyness.

Nell's courage, for once, failed her. Her excitement at finding Robert was mingled with the disappointment of losing him so soon. When the intensity of her emotions had spilled over through her tears, she sat like a rag doll, her energy spent. For now she found comfort in the strength and love that flowed from John and stayed resting against him for quite a while until the shock of her rough ride and the disappointment of finding and then losing Robert wore off.

As the hedgerows of Darrowby House came into view, she stirred herself to deal with the present, and John withdrew his arm to take up the reins with both hands and bring Betsy to a halt outside the stables. He helped her down from the cart.

"I'm sorry, Nell. We must pray for the safety of your brother and the deliverance of York and those who are fighting to defend it. If we lose York, Parliament will have a stronghold in the north, and we shall all suffer for it." Nell had every intention of praying, but she would do it in private. John caught her shoulder and swung her gently round to face him.

"Meanwhile I have your locket." He fetched in his pocket for it. "Here, let me fix it." He fumbled with his big hands, and Nell stood like a chided child while he fastened it.

"Thank you, John. I'm grateful for your efforts."

He tipped her chin. "That's my girl. Be content to wait. There's no use fretting. The locket suits you well," he said and smiled. "Now since we haven't eaten yet today, let's see if Mary can be persuaded to feed us."

"If Mary is too busy, I'll wait on you myself," said Nell.

Chapter 14

The season wore on, with the Roundheads pounding York with five cannons from Lamel Hill. Sometimes they could see the flash of gunfire in the night sky, but mostly they just heard about it from those who were nearer. News traveled fast and there were many anxious inquiries from those whose relatives were involved in its defense.

Spring melted into summer, and the first roses bloomed on the trellises that John cared for with such affection—white and various shades of pink, their velvet petals discharging fragrance into the evening air. Nell's favorite job was cutting fresh blooms for the house. She enjoyed the air, the beauty of the flowers, and the opportunity to be alone with her thoughts. It was there that Nell used to pray, though she hardly knew how. Mostly her thoughts turned heavenward, and she would sigh and release the longings of her heart. They were more than she could put into words. She longed for peace, for an end to the civil war where brother fought brother and families were split by their allegiances. She longed for a time when Robert might come back from the battle and come to find her, for a time when she would know that he was safe. She longed for family, and lately she had begun to long for a family of her own.

She wondered if the Almighty heard her silent prayers and whose side he was on in this dreadful war. Word had spread about the cruel torture that both sides used to extract information of military significance. Surely it was wrong to raise arms against one's own kindred. Maybe God didn't take sides—

She was so occupied with her thoughts that she did not see John until he was close beside her.

"May I join you, Nell?"

"Certainly," she said and smiled. For such an uneducated man he was very polite.

"You look rather sad, Nell."

"Just thinking."

"I can see that. Might I inquire what causes a frown on such a pretty face?"

"Oh, everything, John. My brother, the war, my life!"

"What about your life, Nell? I'd like to think I could make it better."

"You do, John."

"I'd like to do more, Nell." He turned to pick a white rose from the trellis and handed it to her.

"A fresh flower for a beautiful girl." Nell reached out, took the flower from him, and put it immediately to her nose to sample its fragrance.

"It's beautiful, John. Thank you." She looked at his face, tanned now by the summer sun, and saw tenderness and hope in the blue eyes. He was so patient. His love for her was obvious; however, she had purposely not encouraged him, and he had borne her indifference patiently, waiting for his little kindnesses to bear fruit.

"Nell, I'm glad you came to Darrowby. I'd like to give you more than a rose," he said haltingly. Nell blushed. The late afternoon sun heightened her color and several blondish red curls glinted in its light. She knew very well what he meant but not how to answer.

"I'm so different, John. I'm not like you and your people here. You belong here. I don't."

"You could if you wanted to," he said, his voice pleading. "Let me take care of you, Nell. I'll not let you feel like a stranger here anymore." His arms were on hers, the basket of roses between them.

Nell felt the pressure of the conflict she hardly understood within herself. She did not want to hurt John or alienate him, but she was not sure what she wanted, not sure she wanted to stay, yet unsure where she would go and why. Robert was in York, but he was too busy fighting a war to take care of her. John belonged to this Darrowby House with its traditions. She had no history here. But where did she belong? Surely it would be good to begin again here in this place and let this kind man make her his and give her a family, but how could she belong to a man who had never questioned the status quo as she had, never wanted to know truth in a deeper way than conforming to the rituals of the church?

She looked at John steadily and then behind him, taking in the clouds gathering over the sunset and reflecting its rosy light.

"I'm sorry, John. I'm just not sure yet. Could you give me more time?"

He looked away, hiding his disappointment. "Aye, if ye wish, Nell, of course." He backed off, bid her farewell, and left her to watch the setting sun on her own. It was beautiful, like the rose she had laid on the grass. She picked it up again, holding it a little too tightly. A thorn pierced her hand, and a drop of blood fell on her blue skirt. She sucked her finger quickly. Beautiful roses, but they always had thorns—she had known that. She pulled back the thorn, breaking it from the stem as the blood red sun dropped below the horizon.

Nell wished she could be as the other girls and keep her mind from troubling about things she could not change. If only she could be content to marry John and settle down to life in Darrowby! Most girls were content to marry and breed, but there was something in Nell that demanded more, that searched beyond the immediate and the temporal. There was a restlessness that refused to be satisfied by the superficial. How she wished she could talk to someone who understood! John for all his love could not. He was satisfied by the simplicity of his life at Darrowby, cultivating the earth and harvesting and eating its fruit. It was enough for him that the sun rose in the morning and set again in the evening, that summer followed spring, spring winter, and winter autumn.

Haymaking came to an end, and the weather grew sultrier. At Darrowby country life went on as it always did, punctuated by religious festivals and Sunday worship. The Darrowby staff sat together at the back of the church, and John was wont to sit next to her. It was getting difficult. It pained her to see his discomfort when she repelled him. Church for him was a social occasion. For Nell it left a strange heaviness in her heart, for she was unable to connect with John or with the God, who had revealed himself to her. She was glad to hear the Bible readings, trying to glean from them something to satisfy her questions, but she was always relieved when the long dreary sermon was over and they were released to stream back out into the natural world where she could at least feel closer to her Creator. Life at Darrowby was becoming burdensome.

News had reached them that Prince Rupert had reached York and broken the siege. York must surely be the place where the Royalists would engage the Parliamentarians in bloody conflict. Nell knew that Robert would be riding with the prince. She had seen the flash of gunfire in the sky, and she knew she simply had to go to York. Maybe there she would be better able to find news of Robert. In the end she decided to bundle together her few personal possessions and leave for York. Nell longed to share her thoughts with John, but she knew she could not take the risk. He would want to persuade her to stay in the confines of Darrowby. He would say it was madness to go to York. She knew it was too, but she had to go.

It was a Sunday morning, and Nell was early in the kitchen and helped herself to some cheese and a small crusty loaf. Then she stole out of Darrowby and past the lodge house, where John would be donning his Sunday clothes. Leaving the protection of Darrowby's weathered stone walls, she scattered the petals from the white rose he had given her outside the gate. It had been a spontaneous gift from his heart. She had kept it until now, enjoying the fragrance and the memory of that tender moment. Now they had to be left behind, consigned to the past. Only once did she look back and wonder if she would regret leaving Darrowby and the love that could have been hers with John. Deep down she knew her spirit could never settle there, and deep down she had known all along that one day she would have to leave and follow a fresh path.

Chapter 15

King Charles' nephew, Prince Rupert, was marching north, recruiting those who were loyal to the Royalist cause. He had left Shrewsbury and marched through Lancashire, where thousands joined him to fight for the king. In the days when kings still led their men into battle, Rupert was a brilliant strategist. He was making his way to York, that city which had ever been the prize of those wanting to control the north. North of York, Sir David Leslie was leading a regiment of Scots bluecoats to support the siege of York—mercenaries who hated the English king. Gunpowder was about to be used once more to dispute church policy in the king's realm. Some fought for money, some for power, and some because they were convinced that they were doing the will of God, and men, horses, and the baggage train that carried the machinery of war rolled steadily on to York.

Nell was also on the road to York. It was quiet apart from an occasional cottage where hens scratched along the hedgerows and children played. Mostly it ran between dense woodland where she came upon unsuspecting deer and sent them bounding off into the forest. She had been this way only twice—once on the day she had arrived and once with John—but she felt confident that if she simply followed the road, it would take her to York.

After she had gone a mile or so, she heard a horse and carriage approaching and took a leafy track into the forest to avoid being seen. Here she found herself walking past a simple wooden home, whose roof was entirely covered by dark green moss. In fact, it was so dark and so camouflaged that she could easily have missed it altogether, but for a small clearing to the left of it. It stood hunched back in the deep shadows of the forest. In the clearing was a small pool where a pair of ducks paddled and dipped in the muddy water. A wooden railing bordered a path to the left side of the building that Nell presumed must be for tethering horses, although apart from the ducks, the place seemed deserted of all life-forms.

Nell paused for a moment in the shade of the tall trees and in the stillness heard the sound of a human voice. She realized after a moment that it was not engaged in conversation but in reading aloud. Curiosity got the better of her, and she ventured closer until she could hear the text.

"He that seeketh findeth—" It had been a while since she had heard it, but the text was quite distinctly from the Holy Bible.

More hopeful now of a warm reception, she rounded the corner and was surprised to find that instead of the dark, leafy cover she had anticipated, the reader of the scriptures was enjoying a pool of sunlight. His wooden bench was on a veranda or wooden platform built up to avoid the soft, wet ground. He had the short haircut of a Puritan but was otherwise quite unkempt in appearance, and for a moment Nell was unsure whether to flee or remain. He looked up at her approach and, although surprised, showed no sign of offense.

"Good morning, ma'am. Are you looking for someone?"

Nell was not quite sure how to answer. She was inclined to speak of Robert but decided to withhold that information and simply say,

"Good morning, sir. I was hoping to find the reader of the scriptures."

"Ye have that," he affirmed with a slow smile. He stood and made toward the door of the wooden hut.

"Martha, we have a visitor." Then he beckoned to Nell to climb up and join him on the raised platform adjoining the back of the house.

"Come. You must hear some more. Martha and I are wont to read the scriptures at home since the nearest meeting of our Christian brethren is too far away." He pointed to a wooden seat. Nell was reluctant to be distracted from her mission, but she was curious to know if she might be among like-minded folk. Martha came out to inspect the visitor. Visitors were rare, especially a woman on her own.

Nell was surprised to see a young woman no older than herself. Somehow she'd expected the hut to be indwelt by an older couple. She judged the man to be a little older, but it was hard to tell under the beard. She smiled.

"My name's Nell. I heard your husband reading aloud and paused to listen."

"Welcome. My name is Martha, and my husband's name is Josiah." She was quietly spoken, but her words and her gaze had a directness that demonstrated self-possession rather than timidity. Her soft, round face was lit by two eyes of the clearest blue Nell had ever seen.

"We have few visitors here, Nell, but if you love the Word, you're welcome." The way he spoke reminded her of Mr. Thorpe, and she wondered if he might frown at her escapades in the same way.

"It's a precious thing, is it not, to be able to read the Word of God?" Josiah continued. Nell nodded in silent agreement, envious of his ability to do so. Her own education had been interrupted at her father's imprisonment. Martha seated herself on the wooden bench beside her husband, and Nell sat opposite where a stool had been placed for her. She was drawn by the warmth of their welcome and the opportunity to sit for a while and enjoy their company. The slight breeze rustled the leaves and made dappled shadows fall across her earnest face.

"Where do you live, Nell?"

"I've been a servant at Darrowby." The other two looked at one another uneasily. Nell noticed. "I'm not of the same persuasion as they are," she added quickly. "I lived with a Puritan family and learned different beliefs. Since I left there, I have not found any like yourselves who read the scriptures at home. My Lady Asquith has been good to me, but I didn't fit at Darrowby really."

"Where are you going?"

"I'm on my way to York." Nell found herself telling these strangers all about her quest to find her brother and the journeys she had undertaken to do so.

"My, you're a brave woman to travel so far. I pray God you'll find him alive."

"I'm afraid that Robert may not be the answer to all my problems now. I had thought he would take care of me as he did when we were orphaned together, but it seems he's too busy fighting for the king."

"I'm sorry to hear it."

"What will you do, Nell?" asked Martha.

"I'm not sure."

"We had to run away from home too," volunteered Martha. "Josiah's family drove him out when he refused to fight for the Royalists. We came here and though we are poor, we have peace."

It was obvious to Nell that despite the lack of physical comforts, they did have peace. Josiah had cleared a small patch of land that was bearing a crop of vegetables, and now that she was at the back of the house, Nell noticed a few hens scratching under the trees and a milking goat tethered by the fence.

"Josiah is able to work in silver, but he refused to make the silver chalices for the church and lost his job. We may have to leave here and find work where the Royalists are not so strong."

"Where might that be?" asked Nell. "It seems that nowhere is settled. Everywhere there seems to be support for both sides, and even if the Parliamentarians take control of York, that won't change people's hearts."

"Indeed!" agreed Josiah. "This war may settle the political future of England, but it cannot settle the issues of faith. Mark my words. This nation will forever bleed from the wounds of this war!"

"Do you really think there will be no end to it?"

"Oh, the fighting will come to an end. May God grant that right soon! But the pain of it will be passed on from generation to generation. Long after the noise of battle has faded away, the blood that has been spilt will always cry out from the ground it has fallen upon."

Nell sat for a moment considering Josiah's statement. She was scarcely able to comprehend his words, but he spoke as one who had understanding and authority.

"Then may God have mercy on us, sir!"

"Our only hope is in the Savior's blood that speaks a better word than the blood of Abel that was shed by his brother. One day people may repent for the great sin of this war and call on him to forgive and cleanse our land of its iniquity."

Nell was not sure she really understood, but she appreciated his sincerity and was intrigued to meet others who like her were prepared to move on if the need arose rather than compromise. She sensed in them a spirit that resounded with her own—a spirit that would accept change rather than become bogged down in tradition. She instinctively knew she could trust them.

"Let us read you some comfort from the Bible, Nell, before you move on." Josiah picked up the heavy black book again and turned immediately to a well-worn page in the book of Proverbs.

"'Trust in the Lord with all thine heart; and lean not unto thine own understanding. In all thy ways acknowledge him, and he shall direct thy paths.' Here is hope for us all, Nell. May the Lord guide you to your brother and to safety."

Chapter 16

As Nell resumed her journey, a gentle breeze cooled her brow. It seemed to pick up her anxieties and carry them away. She lifted up her head to the heavens.

"Thank you," she murmured heavenward. She stepped forward with a lighter step toward York. She would soon need the comfort of knowing that an unseen hand was guiding her very footsteps.

As she neared the city, the breeze dropped. Gray clouds formed and darkened as the day wore on. It would not be long before they dropped their rain on the thirsty land, but Nell wanted to avoid a soaking. Cutting across the fields she kept close to the hedgerows, unaware of whose land she might be traversing. Behind her she heard the cry of a falcon in flight and turned to see it swoop and circle back to its trainer. Unwilling to be rebuked for trespassing, she hurried to the gate in the left-hand corner of the field, but hurry as she might, she was soon apprehended by the falconer, bird on his gloved hand.

"Not so quick, miss. You'll not find a way through there." Nell could see the truth of his statement. The gate led merely to another meadow where a stream ran across and blocked her way in the direction of York.

"So I see, sir. Then I would that you might direct me how I might come to the city."

"You'd best not be going to t' city today, miss. Prince Rupert's men raised t' siege yesterday, and t' city's back in Royalist control."

"Then that's a fine thing, and I might at last find my brother, who is with the prince!" exclaimed Nell

"Well, I doubt you will find him in York. It seems they've ridden west now to encounter the Parliamentarian army. You'll need go back t'wards Poppleton."

Nell knew Poppleton since it was close to Darrowby. Maybe her decision to leave had been hasty, and it would have been better to stay closer to Darrowby. In any case her best option now seemed to be to walk in that direction. The sun was well over to the west by the time she came near to Poppleton.

The news was that Prince Rupert had captured Poppleton Bridge, the only crossing over the River Ouse, and had pursued the Parliamentarians and caught up with them on Marston Moor on the far side of Poppleton. Even now Robert would be there, awaiting the order to engage in battle. Rumor had it that the Marquis of Newcastle had dallied in York and was still on the way with his troops. Nell was desperate for details, listening at every opportunity for more information. She longed to go and see for herself, to run out toward the moor where she would at least be closer to Robert; however, where would she find him in that melee, and what good would it do when Robert was under orders and battle was imminent?

In need of rest and refreshment, she spent precious savings on a pint of ale and joined a group of wayfarers like herself seated on a low wall near a tavern.

"The prince will not fight until he can deploy his troops properly, miss," said one.

"Those men will not be fit to fight again so soon after the breaking of the siege," enjoined another.

"They say the Roundheads have deployed already on the rise above the moor. He may have little choice," countered the first. "He will have to muster his troops among the ditches and hedges of the moor."

"That may well be to his advantage."

Nell thought of Robert, one of a body of several thousand men, even now maybe taking up his position, preparing to face the onslaught of an army racing down the slopes above the moor. It was all very well for them to think in terms of strategy, of deploying troops, but armies were made up of individuals, each one someone's son or brother or father or husband.

"There must be many men mustered for the battle," she said.

"Thousands, miss. 'Tis a grand sight no doubt."

"'Tis a wicked waste of precious lives!" she retorted.

As evening drew near, storm clouds hung low in the southwest, and the air grew humid and heavy. Along with the atmospheric pressure, the tension increased, but no one expected that there would be a battle that night. At 7:00 p.m., however, the noise of gunfire was heard, and for the next two hours the battle raged intensely. The noise of the battle carried on the still evening air even as far as Poppleton. Nell could only think that where Robert was it would be deafening. He would be in the middle of the uproar—cannons blasting heavy shot, hundreds of horses neighing and snorting, muskets firing, and the cries of men. Smoke drifted upward into the darkening sky. Then the storm that had been brewing finally broke, and Nell ran to take cover in a nearby barn.

Eventually the din faded into an eerie silence and the next noise to claim her attention was the clatter of carts along the rough road as the dead and wounded were transported to local hostelries in search of medical help. Local farmhouses became hospitals, and barns became morgues where the dead awaited burial. The horror of war and death overwhelmed Nell. There were so many corpses, many of them shrouded in their own sashes. She despaired of knowing whether her brother was among their number, but she searched, hoping not to see his face among the dead but hoping she would not miss it … if it was there.

Spurred on by the thought that she had been led by an unseen hand to the best place to search for Robert, she turned from one bleeding body to another. In the end she found Robert, not dead but being carried on a stretcher into the farmhouse. She followed him into the crowded house, pushing past those who declared it was no place for a woman until she could speak with him.

"Robert, you're wounded!" she cried.

"Musket ball in the chest. My horse was killed too," he managed to share between gasps. Those in charge attended to Robert's wounds as best they could, while Nell stood by the makeshift stretcher. They made him as comfortable as possible; however, his breathing became more and more labored, and they gave her little hope. When they left him, Nell drew closer and wiped the sweat and blood from his face.

"Oh, Robert, why did you have to fight!"

"Nell, even if I hadn't volunteered, I would have been pressed."

"It's such a waste!" she said angrily, looking at those strewn around the room. "No matter who wins this war, we have all lost!" But this was no time for philosophizing. She had things to communicate to Robert. She stood for a while, her hand on his shoulder, mopping his brow and weeping silently. Then getting her emotions under control, she began to share what was on her heart.

"Robert, I have so much to tell you." The urgency of her voice jerked Robert out of his pain-induced stupor, and he opened his eyes to look at her.

"I want to tell you about your son," she went on.

"My son?"

"Polly had a son. She called him Christopher. She didn't know where you were, and neither did I."

"Polly? What do you know of Polly?"

"I met her by a chance encounter."

"Where are they?"

"They both died, Robert. Polly died three weeks after the birth. Little Christopher died in my arms. I buried him in Polly's garden." Robert groaned, sorrow and remorse added to his physical pain. Nell, relieved to have shared her secret burden, watched his struggle and almost wished she had kept it to herself.

"I'm so sorry. I thought you should know."

"I knew not that she was with child! How came you upon them?" he inquired.

"Maybe the good Lord led me there," said Nell. She told him a little about her time in Tadcaster and how she had gone there to search for him only to find he had been at Winceby.

Robert was quiet for a while, considering her long pilgrimage to find him, fighting for breath.

"Nell, you must find a husband to take care of you. I'm not long for this world now."

"You mustn't talk like that Robert," she said, but she knew it was true. As the early morning light filtered through the leaded panes, Robert's breath became fainter. They both knew he was headed for the grave, but Nell refused to believe that Robert's death was all for nothing, that his life had been to no purpose, a mere sad sojourn on the earth, one full of suffering and death.

"Robert, ask the Savior to receive you," she coerced. Robert opened his eyes.

"What do you mean, Nell? I can't go to him without the last rites. I shall go to purgatory. Pray for my soul, Nell!"

"No, Robert, that's not true! Ask him to save you!" And she told him about her vision of the Savior's cross and his personal invitation.

"And how does the likes of you know so much about what's in the Holy Book?"

"I had to listen to the scriptures daily at the Thorpe's. They read them in English, Robert, so I could understand. I learned from them."

"*What* did you learn?"

"That Christ came to save sinners, not to punish us!"

"No, Nell, not the likes of me. I need a priest."

"No, you don't need a priest, Robert. You just need to believe that Christ died for you. Ask him, and he will give you life."

"Nay! How can I pray without a prayer book?"

"Just pray from your heart, Robert." In the end Robert stuttered out a prayer for forgiveness and received the peace he so badly needed. Nell held him in her arms, even as she had cradled his son, and he slipped away into the eternal presence of God to meet the son he had never seen.

And then Nell wept, wept for the loss of her brother, wept for the loss of life all around her, wept for her own loss until the farmer's wife came to her with bread and ale and they took Robert's remains out to the barn to await burial in a common pit. As she had done with his son, Nell fashioned a simple cross from wood and with a piece of charcoal wrote, "Robert Thornby Aged 22 years." She would at least attempt to put the humble memorial somewhere near his final resting place.

Nell watched as his body was lowered into the common pit, and then she turned and ran. She did not know where she ran, she did not care, but she had to remove herself as far as possible from the place where hope of a future with her brother had died.

Then she found herself on a stony road—the road to York. Scarcely aware of what her feet were doing, she stumbled over stones, her blue shift dirty and bloodied with Robert's blood. As dusk fell, she realized she was near the cottage of Josiah and Martha. Never before had she been more in need of true friends.

Chapter 17

When Nell saw the cottage, her hopes rose. Maybe they would have pity on her and give her shelter until she was able to find work. Martha answered her knock.

"Why, Nell, are you wounded?"

"No, it's my brother's blood. He was killed in the battle," she said, sobbing. Martha's sympathy brought forth more tears. It was a relief to tell someone, a relief to spill out the tears. She could say no more. Numbly she sat on the bench where just the previous day she had heard Josiah read encouraging words from the Holy Book. "Trust in the Lord." The words formed again inside her head, echoing in her consciousness even as she grappled with the reality of Robert's death and her own situation. Trust was hard when your heart was broken and all hope gone. By way of answer Martha sat down beside her and put a comforting arm around her shoulders. They sat that way for a while until the baby's cries demanded Martha's attention and she rose to care for it.

"Come inside and take some rest. We have a little bread and cheese if you'd care for some." Night was falling, and Nell shivered in the growing darkness. As she entered the simple hut, she realized that Josiah was absent.

"Josiah was not fighting in the battle, was he?"

"No. Much as he longs to see the nation adopt godly practices, he sees no point in trying to establish the will of God by force. He went to find out what might be the outcome of the battle on the moor." Even as they spoke, they heard a commotion outside, and Josiah appeared supporting a man with a leg wound.

"This is Simon. I found him trying to ride his horse to York. In fact, there are many even now streaming from the battle site with their injuries, bleeding for want of a bed and a doctor. I've tied the horse to the rail. We'll care for it later."

Nell judged Simon to be about the same age as Robert. His short hair was a clue to his religious persuasion, and it occurred to her that he had been fighting on the opposite side to Robert, maybe had even engaged with him in combat. Maybe he had even fired the musket ball that had lodged in Robert's lungs. Then she noticed that Simon had pistols, not a musket.

The tiny cottage, like most in the vicinity of the battle, had become a refuge for the wounded and weary. They were a sorry sight—Nell with her bloodstained skirt and tear-stained face, Simon with his britches and boots covered in mud and blood, his clothes wet and disheveled under his armor. Josiah and Martha felt helpless in the sight of so much need. One thing was sure. The musket ball needed to be taken out of Simon's thigh, so they braced themselves and lifted him onto the wooden table and took a kitchen knife to the hole where the bullet had pierced Simon's leg at the point just above the top of his thigh boots.

The baby, sensing the anxiety in the little room, was claiming Martha's attention, so Nell made herself useful, mopping up the blood oozing from Simon's wound and holding a candle to the wound so Josiah could see. This was no time for propriety. Josiah prodded the hole until he located the bullet and then pulled back the flesh until he could extract it. It was not deep, but it was lodged in the muscle. It was a painful process for Simon and unpleasant enough for Josiah too. Lacking oil to boil and pour into the wound, the normal practice on the battlefield, they used hot water heated on the fire. By the time they had finished, Simon was weak from loss of blood and suffering, Nell and Josiah from the trauma of having to be part of the procedure.

They decided to leave Simon on the table. There was no other bed or place where he could keep the leg elevated, and common sense dictated that he needed to. In any case they could see he was too weak to move much. Nell tore strips from Simon's ruined britches and bandaged his thigh as tightly as she could in an effort to staunch the flow of blood. She fetched his own blanket from his saddle and made him as comfortable as possible, while Josiah unsaddled the horse and tethered it near a patch of grass where it could graze.

The floor was the only place available for Nell to sleep; however, Martha managed to find her a feather pillow, and she soon fell into an exhausted sleep, grateful that she was not sleeping on the roadside. Even Simon's moans, which continued on through the night in his sleep, did not wake her.

It was a while before the trauma of that nightmare began to fade away at the kind hands of Josiah and Martha. They had little to give but shared as they could, and Simon discovered that the money he had been carrying in his saddle had not been looted. He was more than willing to share it with his gracious hosts and Nell. Josiah took it and had new clothes made for Simon and Nell so they could discard their bloodstained garments. It was without regret that Nell discarded the old blue linen petticoat and burned it on the cottage fire.

During the next three months Josiah made several visits to York. Simon's horse was a blessing, and his money provided meat and cheese, to which they added provision from their small garden vegetable plot. Apart from local information about the decisive defeat of the king on Marston Moor, they heard little other news about the war in their crowded but peaceful haven.

Chapter 18

It was a sunny morning toward the end of October 1644, and Nell was in the woods between the house and the road, gathering firewood. Frost still whitened the ground where fingers of sunlight had not yet touched the forest floor, and the snap of every branch carried in the cold, clear air. Nell's ears picked up the sound of a horse's hooves echoing in the frosty air and the rumbling of wooden cart wheels on the frost-hardened ruts of the track from Darrowby to York. She looked up. It was the horse she recognized first—old Betsy who had given her such a hard time that day in York. Seated on the front of the cart was the once familiar figure of John and seated beside him a woman she did not recognize—her replacement at Darrowby perhaps. She kept herself well-hidden behind the trees as the cart rumbled past about fifty paces away. John was no doubt still responsible for the delivery of produce to the market. She noticed though that this time he had his arm around another girl—her replacement in more ways than one it seemed.

She watched as they continued on their journey, unaware of her presence. Searching her heart in the privacy of the trees, she was glad to find no jealousy or regret in it. She was happy for John. He knew where he belonged, and it looked as though he had found someone to share his life with. One thing was clear to Nell—that door had definitely closed. There was no way back. Not that she had wanted one, but it was good to put the past to rest and to go forward in the knowledge that her heart was at peace.

Nell was so intent on watching them and so lost in thought that she hadn't noticed Simon had come alongside her.

"Two happy lovers!" he said and chuckled. "A man needs a woman to keep him warm on such a cold morning!"

"And maybe a woman needs a man!" she jibed. It was good to see Simon walking again. It had taken a long time for the wound to heal and then even longer for the muscle to build enough strength for Simon to walk again, though he still limped a little.

"I thought this might help," he said, holding up an axe.

"It would indeed." She watched him swing the axe at a small dead sapling and then pull the trunk nearer to the house for chopping. It had been good to nurse him back to health. It had given her a purpose after Robert's death. Now he was strong again, he would no doubt return to his family home in London.

"We'll miss you, Simon, when you go back to London."

"Aye." He turned away, unwilling to dwell on the subject. Nell turned her gaze back to the wagon. It had almost disappeared on the far reaches of the road to York, the echo of Betsy's hooves no longer audible. Tears pricked at the edges of her eyes, and she hurriedly blinked them away, surprised to find them there. She swallowed hard against the emotion that threatened to break loose from somewhere deep within. She was scarcely aware that Simon had stopped chopping and paused to watch her. For a while she was lost in the past, watching those she had loved disappear from view—her parents, Robert, even John to a degree—and now Simon would also leave. Suddenly she felt alone—alone and homeless. If only she could have been happy with John! She bit her lip and took hold of a bent-over birch branch. Just holding something helped to ease the sense of insecurity that threatened to engulf her.

Suddenly Simon's hand was there on top of hers.

"I'll miss you too, Nell." Whether it was an act of compassion or an attempt to communicate his fondness of her, Nell was unsure. Embarrassed to be discovered in her grief, she withdrew her hand and turned away. By now tears were coursing down her cheeks, and she brushed them away with her hands.

"You'll soon forget me, Simon. You'll go back to your family and forget about me."

"But I *will* miss you, Nell!"

"Well, the likes of you have no need of a homeless wretch like me! You'll soon forget Nell Thornby."

"No, Nell, I'll never forget you! I'm so grateful for your kindness in nursing this leg of mine!" he insisted. Nell shrugged.

"Oh! What does it matter anyway?" Gratitude was not what she wanted or needed. What she needed now was somewhere to belong. She turned away and resumed collecting the smaller branches for firewood.

Further conversation seemed pointless. Simon had never known a time without family support, without food, without a future. For three months they had shared the same world in Josiah's cottage, had shared many meals, many thoughts, but never before had they been so personal. Now that time was over, and Simon would return to the world he had come from; however, she had nowhere to go.

Nell took her plight privately to the Almighty. A faint glimmer of hope began to arise in her heart, though what that signified she knew not. She was only slowly moving from hope to trust. She kept her thoughts to herself and tried not to think about the future. In her worst moments she had to admit that panic lay just under the surface. Eventually though there was a strange hope in her heart, an optimism that, though at war with her mind, simply would not go away. As surely as baby Moses was carried down the river toward his destiny in Egypt, Nell felt that her future was in the hands of the One who was directing her course. He had brought her so faithfully to a place of refuge in her hour of need. She could not believe that he would now abandon her to a hopeless future. She clung also to the promise she had heard from the book of Jeremiah "'I know the plans I have for you,' says the Lord, 'plans for good, not for disaster, to give you a future and a hope.'" It did indeed give her hope and confirmed the sense in her own heart that something good was about to follow her season in the woods.

As Nell had rightly said, Simon had been intent on being reunited with his family and furthering the cause of Parliament, but he was stung by her words in the woods and confused by the pain they caused him.

Logically she was right, but his heart knew she was wrong. Her silence bothered him. She seemed withdrawn and preoccupied. He did not wonder at it. Her brother was dead. She was alone in the world, without a home or prospects of employment.

Although Simon had been slow to realize Nell's plight, once awakened to her need, he thought of very little else. He would watch her as she sat by the fire in the simple little home, dandling baby Joseph on her lap. It was one activity that always brought a smile to her face. Her voice, soothing as she crooned a lullaby, had been a comfort to him too as she had dressed his wounded leg. He wondered at her softness, considering the hardships she had endured. Yes, he would miss that softness and the way the auburn curls escaping from her coif glinted in the firelight. And what would happen to her when they went their separate ways?

As the days grew shorter, the four of them discussed their plans by the warmth of the fire.

"It was good to have the news from my sister Elizabeth that your Puritan brethren delivered. Her husband is a merchant at Retford, as you know, but I'm told that he is away now with the Parliamentarians in Berkshire. She will be glad of a visit on my way south to London."

"Yes, there are many brethren in the Retford area, although several have already sailed to the New World and now establish a community free from religious persecution. In the spring Martha and I intend to join them."

"So you have decided!" Simon and Nell both exclaimed together. It was an issue they had discussed before, but now that the decision was made, it seemed so final.

"I have heard it is a perilous voyage, but we must trust ourselves to the Almighty."

"Indeed there are reports of the trials, but also of the triumphs, and few it seems desire to return." Stories of their endeavors had reached the ears of Elizabeth's fellowship—stories of deprivations, of poor decisions caused through ignorance, but of the eventual success of the new colonies that were developing in various places along the eastern seaboard of America.

"Yes, we have decided to sell what we can and join our brethren in the New World. If we leave in the spring, we shall have time to plant a crop and reap it before the formidable winter sets in," said Josiah.

"And I must soon return to London, even now before the spring," added Simon. "My mother and my sister are anxious for my return."

Nell looked down at her feet and kept silent, not having any plans to share and not wanting to sound as though she were feeling sorry for herself. At least she could thank God she still had feet to carry her forward into the plan that had been crafted for her, whatever that was. Her feet had taken her from Haresby to Lincoln, and her feet would take her on to her new destination.

Suddenly Simon cut into her thoughts.

"Nell, I've been wondering if you would like to come with me to Elizabeth's. She would no doubt be happy to have some help with the children during the winter months, and you would be company for her during Edward's absence." Nell was taken aback by Simon's sudden invitation. Her heart leapt, but for a moment she was speechless.

"Why, yes ... I would be glad to, Simon!" The words came slowly, almost under her breath. "I've had experience of domestic service at Haresby Hall and with the Thorpes and at Asquith House," she added.

"I know not if she needs another servant, Nell, but you may come as my guest." Overwhelmed, Nell was unsure how to receive this invitation, but she knew it was right. This must be the door of opportunity she knew would open. However, she still needed time to grasp it, to imagine what it would be like to live with Simon's sister. Life with another set of strangers was about to begin.

"Tell me about your sister, Simon," she urged.

"She's a fine-hearted woman, Nell. You'll like her," replied Simon. Then he added, "Though she is quite strong in her opinions—a fiery opponent in argument but a loyal friend."

Chapter 19

Christmas was less than two weeks away when Nell boarded the carriage for the journey south down the Great North Road. It was an emotional farewell with Josiah and Martha.

"I'm much obliged for your hospitality," said Simon as he shook hands with Josiah. "May the good Lord bring you to your Promised Land!"

"May God go with you, wherever you go," returned Josiah.

"And with you!" added Nell. "I am sorry to part. I doubt we will meet again!"

"If not in this world, then the next!" Martha reassured her with a hug.

Simon gave all the money he could spare to Josiah and Martha to help tide them over the winter. He had been going to sell his sword too, but thought it better to have some means of defense against possible highwaymen on the way home. Simon would ride his horse and keep Nell company at the hostelries along the way.

The body of the coach was slung on leather straps and lurched so badly that Nell felt sick, and despite the cold air, she kept her face near the window and pulled up the leather cover as far as she could. This would be the longest trip she had undertaken since her escapade from Haresby Hall to Tadcaster. She felt a twinge of nostalgia as the carriage pulled away from York but only because it was familiar. Her ears were filled with the noise made by the wheels and the hooves of the four great shire horses on the cobbles. She watched as the cobbles gave way to a much rougher track and the many church spires of York faded into the distance. She had grown familiar with York's great walls and well remembered the first time she had seen them that day when Lady Asquith had befriended her. The few happy times she could remember there were eclipsed by sorrow, and whatever the future held, she felt sure it must be better than the dark days she had known in York.

It was a difficult journey, much more dangerous at this time of year than it would have been in the summer. In the summer the whole journey from York to London could be done in four days. In the winter it would take much longer, and she was glad their journey to Retford was just a fraction of the distance to London. There was no guarantee there would not be long delays, particularly if it snowed. Nell was all too aware that the ruts in the road frequently upset carriages and in some places were so bad that the coaches left the track, preferring to drive through the fields alongside. But both Simon and Nell knew that the danger lay not so much in the precariousness of the carriage as in the threat of attack from highway men who were able to take cover in the dense woodland and ambush the coach as it was forced to slow to negotiate the terrain.

For Nell the journey proved to be more than a traversing of the physical distance between York and Retford. It was also a bridge between her past and her future. The road led south through Tadcaster, where Nell had memories to deal with. The coach rattled over the bridge where she had refreshed herself on her first arrival there. This time she stopped for refreshment at The Angel. From there she could see Bethany, where despite the strict and sometimes harsh ways of the Thorpe's, she had first encountered the Savior and been changed forever. Since then she had been through grief and uncertainty; however, hope had not ceased to live in her heart, and she was learning to trust again. They journeyed on to their overnight rest stop at Bawtry. Simon was proving to be a courteous and kind companion. His provision of the coach fare and a room in The Crown was a rare luxury for Nell.

The next day was overcast, and soon a steady rain turned the road into a quagmire and slowed their pace considerably. Simon rode on ahead, with the intention of preparing Elizabeth to receive the unexpected guest. He was able to travel faster than the coach that would have to slow to avoid the deep ruts in the soft mud. There was much commotion when the coach encountered a flock of sheep being driven to more sheltered pasture. The coach swayed violently as the horses slowed, and the driver, unwilling to steer too close to the soft verges, stopped the carriage in the middle of the road, while the flock of sheep parted like the Red Sea before the Israelites and flowed on both sides of the carriage with much bleating and shouting from the shepherd.

The journey south was slow, and by the time they were drawing near to Babworth, the short December day had given way to night. Here the road ran along low-lying ground and was prone to be muddy even on dry days. Simon had traveled that way before and always breathed a sigh of relief as the horse began the upward pull toward more open and drier countryside.

Nell was wondering what her new home would be like. She had run away three times now. How long would she remain in this one? Would she fit in this smaller household? There had been times when the confines of Josiah and Martha's tiny abode had driven her out into the woods, where she had been free to think her own thoughts. Sometimes alone in the woods she had felt a comforting presence, a quiet reassurance that the One who had died for her watched over her still. It was a communion beyond words that healed her grief, restored her sanity, and gave her a fresh perspective on her sorrows. From somewhere deep within her spirit a new hope was born. Alone in this presence she felt less alone than at any other time.

Nell wondered now how she would fare in yet another household dedicated to strict Puritan ideals. Since her encounter with the Savior's love and forgiveness, she loved to hear the stories and the teachings, which she could not read for herself, but she had sometimes questioned their strict, sober ways, particularly their legalistic views on the Sabbath. Wasn't life as a child of God meant to be more joyful? Wasn't his gift of life something to celebrate in loving praise—something more than a sense of duty, work, and commitment?

Sudden shouts and the violent lurching of the coach disturbed her reverie. The passengers were thrown upon one another in great confusion and feared they would turn over altogether. As it was, the coach lurched to a standstill, and she was able to look out of the window to see a man in a great coat standing in the road with a lantern held high to give him visibility. He lowered the lantern to reveal the body of a horse lying in their path. The horse was sprawled across the muddy road and was quite stuck in the mire.

It appeared unable to move anything apart from its forelegs. Obviously it had been ridden too hard and had been left for dead by its rider.

"Some brigand must have abandoned his mount in the chase and fled on foot!" the man with the lantern said in answer to their inquiry. The coach driver and guard dismounted and hastened to investigate for themselves.

"The poor creature's too weak to stand!" was the unfortunate verdict.

"Have a care, sir! The mire is deep!" warned the man in the great coat.

"We must remove it for its own sake and ours. We have ropes on the coach. If we can get ropes under its belly, we can use the horses to haul it free of the mud."

"Pray God it has the strength to stand, or its carcass will cause us more problems! Had you not been standing there with the lantern, I don't doubt but that we would have galloped straight into it and been overturned." The urgency of the situation propelled them into action, and after they fetched two ropes, they worked up to the knees and elbows in the mud to secure the ropes around the horse.

The sound of hooves signaled the approach of another rider coming from the opposite direction, and soon a horse and rider appeared from between the trees that lined both sides of the road at this point. Nervously the men looked up, aware that this was a likely place for highwaymen, but the rider pulled up his horse alongside them.

"I have ropes too, but I see you are ahead of me," the rider said. "I came by earlier and alerted this good fellow to warn you of the danger."

"Much obliged to you, sir. We can use that rope too. You can fasten it to the bridle, and your horse can assist us by pulling on that, while we attach the two ropes round the belly to the carriage and reverse the horses. That way we may have a chance of pulling it clear of the mud, and if it can stand it will. In any case we must remove it from the middle of the road before it causes an accident."

So they followed that plan, and after much exertion on the part of the men and the horses, they managed to drag it clear of the quagmire. Once on dry land it tried several times to stand and failed, falling pitifully on its side again and again.

"Poor thing's exhausted," said the driver.

"Nevertheless, its limbs seem sound enough. I believe it will recover if allowed to rest." This shaft of optimism came from the rider of the second horse.

The women who had watched from a distance were coming over to see for themselves how the horse was faring since now they could do so without danger of trailing their skirts in the mud. The voice of the rider brought forth a shout of recognition from Nell.

"Why, Simon! It's you!"

"Aye! I found the poor fellow here earlier and hastened to Elizabeth's to get a rope. How fortunate that I returned to find you safe and men to assist me!"

"How fortunate indeed! Will the horse recover?" asked Nell.

"He may. But he needs rest, and he may well die of his ordeal out here."

The man with the lantern held it close to the horse's head to inspect its eyes. It shook its head slightly as if to disagree with Simon's comment.

"In any case we must untie the ropes and let the coach resume its journey." The rest of the passengers readily agreed and hastened to get out of the cold, damp night and climb on board. Nell hesitated. She had never owned or ridden a horse and was somewhat timid around them, especially since her experience with Betsy, but she felt pity for this horse, which had seemingly been abandoned by its rider and now seemed about to be abandoned to its fate.

"Isn't there anything we can do for it, Simon?"

"Not unless we stay with it until it can stand, Nell, and even then it may be too weak to walk." It was the man with the lantern who came to the rescue.

"You must continue your journey, ma'am. The coach is ready to leave. I live nearby, and I will return later to see if it is to be roused. If so, I will stable it. It may yet prove to be a good horse, and its owner will be ignorant of its recovery—the wretched fellow!"

"God bless you, sir." Nell returned to the coach, and the driver maneuvered it carefully around the quagmire. Fortunately its wheels were wide enough to straddle the mud, and they were soon safely on their way. Simon rode on ahead, this time keeping a short distance between himself and the coach so as to be able to meet Nell at Babworth, from where he could make sure that she was met by Elizabeth's small private carriage for the short journey to Retford.

Chapter 20

On their arrival at Babworth the steward was waiting with the carriage to carry Nell to Elmsley Cottage. It had been a long journey, but not as long as the one that Nell had undertaken from Lincoln to Tadcaster by herself. She was curious to see the house that would be her next home. Simon had not given her much detail beyond the fact that it was smaller than his family home but cozy in the winter, and he said there would be room enough for her to enjoy a small room of her own.

Even though Simon had told her it was not extensive, she was surprised how small it was, considerably smaller than either Haresby Hall or Asquith House, but it looked a good deal more welcoming. Nell's first view of Elmsley Cottage with its candlelit leaded panes glowing like lanterns in the dark night put her fears to rest. It was a two-story house with a central door at the front underneath overhanging thatched gables.

William drew up at the front of the house, assisted Nell to climb down, and drove off to the coach house. Nell's only baggage was the small shoulder bag she had carried with her from Haresby. Simon had ridden round to the stables to leave his tired horse in the good hands of the hostler, so she waited, alone and nervous on the doorstep, aware of her poor appearance, wondering how she would be received and how she should respond. Was she a guest or a servant? Inviting smells that promised a hot meal wafted through the door and the happy noise of children could be heard. She wondered at the different kind of world that waited on the other side of the door.

Suddenly the door was opened by Elizabeth herself. Nell need not have been concerned, for Elizabeth was overjoyed at their safe arrival in Retford and bid her a warm welcome.

"You must be Nell. Please come in. We are expecting you. Simon said there was a poor horse blocking the road."

"Yes, ma'am, it's a mercy Simon alerted a neighbor to our approach and the man fetched a lantern to warn us. He prevented a nasty accident, I'm sure. Then Simon's timely arrival with the extra rope helped them to drag the horse to a more secure place."

"Well, 'tis good you are safely arrived!"

Nell was shown to a small room in the attic that reminded her of her room at Bethany. It was on the same floor as the servants' rooms. Elizabeth had few servants—Mary, whose domain was the kitchen; Suzanna, who did the cleaning and laundry; William, whose job it was to drive the coach and act as butler and do general maintenance around the house; a gardener named Percival; and a hostler named Walter, who also maintained the coach.

"I'm afraid this is the only room available, Nell, but I trust you'll be comfortable. I'll send Suzanna with some hot water. You are no doubt weary from the journey."

Nell was glad to wash a little, but with no clothes other than the ones she was wearing, she looked very much the same after her efforts as before, except that she had removed her old woolen cape and brushed her auburn curls, replacing the same linen coif over them.

Simon's mud was soon removed in a hot bath, and clean clothes were borrowed from Edward's wardrobe.

"You feed your husband well, sister!" Simon joked, pulling at the ample waist of the britches.

"And I shall feed you too! Look at you! Wasting away ... both of you!"

Nell had been prepared to serve and eat as a house servant and maybe receive a small wage and accommodation for her labors, but Elizabeth was treating them both as guests. On creeping down the stairs, she had hovered in the doorway of the dining room, still unsure of her place in this household. Was Elizabeth's welcome an act of kindness to a tired traveler or the reception of an honored guest of the family? The way Nell walked through this doorway would influence the rest of her life. Was it to be more of the same or a brand-new beginning? Feeling shabby in her worn out clothes, Nell hesitated.

Seeing her hesitation, Simon bade her be seated.

"Come, Nell, you must eat, and you and Elizabeth must get better acquainted."

"Nell's father was a merchant too," said Simon, sharing one of the few things he knew about Nell and trying to bridge the gap between them.

"And where was that, Nell?" replied Elizabeth.

"In Lincolnshire. He was a wool merchant."

"I have heard they are doing very well out of the war, with the demand for woolen clothes for the soldiers."

"Maybe, ma'am. I know not." While Nell was reticent to share embarrassing details of her family's fallen state, she thought it wise to acquaint Elizabeth with enough of the facts of her background to explain her present situation.

"My father and mother died quite a while ago now, leaving my brother and me without provision."

"I'm sorry to hear it, Nell. I'm sure you have suffered many hardships. Simon tells me your brother was killed at Marston Moor."

"Yes, he was," she replied simply.

"I'm sorry." Elizabeth replied, equally simply. "Our father was tragically killed at Edgehill, so we understand your grief." Nell doubted that they did. It was grievous to lose a relative but devastating to be left alone in the world.

They talked of the war and their hopes and fears, of Simon's need to return to his family home and support his mother, and of his place in politics. Nell was mostly a silent listener, and although interested in their conversation, she was more preoccupied with her own future. Grateful as she was for Elizabeth's hospitality, it would not be appropriate to stay for long as a guest. A place as a servant, though less honorable, would give her more security.

Eventually the conversation did turn to Nell and her plans.

"Ever since my parents died, I have worked in domestic service. I was hoping that my brother and I could make a future somewhere … maybe rent a small cottage and grow our food. With his army pay he may have been able to provide for me, and he had no wife. Now he's dead. I've spent the last four months caring for Simon and helping Martha and Josiah with their chores and their baby."

"Yes, we were four fugitives in a storm!" interjected Simon.

"So you have no family and nowhere to go, Nell?"

"No, ma'am," admitted Nell, but unwilling to evoke pity, she continued, "I have been considering a position as a housekeeper but know not where. Josiah used to read us the Word, and it assures me that God has plans for me that are good. But I am yet to discover them."

"Nell is a brave woman," said Simon, "full of hope and courage."

"I cannot doubt his goodness toward me when he hung on that wicked cross for my sin."

"Tell Elizabeth of your vision of the Savior, Nell."

Nell was reticent to share such a precious personal moment. She had only done so with Simon and the others in the hut in the woods to encourage them all on a day when the pain in Simon's thigh had caused him to be low in spirits. She recounted again how the Savior's bleeding hands had reached out from the cross and beckoned her to come to him and how she had been received and felt his wonderful love. When she had finished, Elizabeth wiped the tears from her eyes.

"Even so he has forgiven us all and welcomed us all into his arms."

Her reply assured Nell that true faith dwelt in Elizabeth's heart, something deeper than a religious striving to earn a place in heaven and more than a superficial righteousness to impress others.

"I have nowhere to go, ma'am, and would be glad to stay if I can be of service to you. I can perform all of the work of the house, though I have never been engaged as a cook."

"Nell, I have not the means to employ more servants, and I do not need a cook. Why not stay on here and help me tutor the girls?"

Nell looked embarrassed.

"I'm afraid I have never learned to read since my education was interrupted when my parents died."

"Then I will teach you too, Nell, and you can supervise their play. They are becoming somewhat boisterous indoors, and winter is here yet for a while. It is high time they began to learn needlework. You can help me care for them so that I may be free to continue the business in Edward's absence. If we do not make and sell our saddles and other leather goods, we will none of us have food or clothes."

Nell was unsure how to respond. She could not sew any more than she could read, but she decided to accept Elizabeth's offer and do her best to learn.

Sunshine sparkling through frosty tracery on the leaded window panes greeted Nell as she awoke to her first morning in her new home. It was cold—very cold—but she was warm under the woolen blankets and comfortable on the goose feather mattress. Although the room was small, after she had shared the limited space at Martha and Josiah's home, she considered such personal space a luxury. Footsteps descending the wooden staircase alerted her to the fact that it was already late, and she hastened to dress, doing the best she could to look as if she belonged in this family.

After she opened her bag, she took out the wooden crucifix, and she was about to place it in the windowsill, as she had at Bethany, when she thought better of it. There was no guarantee that it would not be discovered and considered offensive in this household. To her it was a precious keepsake, a vessel through which she had come to understand the significance of Christ's crucifixion. To them it was a symbol of the influence of the Roman church with all its idolatry and worldly pomp. She stroked the polished wood and placed it back in her bag. She had few enough possessions and had no desire to part with this one.

She descended to breakfast to find Elizabeth, Maisie, and Emily already at the table.

"Come and join us, Nell. I deemed it good to let you sleep late after your journey. Simon has departed to check on the welfare of the horse at Babworth, though his leg is giving him some pain after riding so far."

"I rather feared it might," said Nell. "He will need to rest before he rides on to London."

"Yes, he will, especially at this time of the year." Then changing the subject, she went on to say, "Nell, maybe you would like to accompany me into town. We will have William drive us there in the carriage. I must go to inspect the tannery and make sure the men are performing their work and getting paid. Then we will buy linen for new clothes for you and woolen stockings and leather shoes so that this winter will not be your last!" Nell was embarrassed by such charity but thankful. It was the beginning of a new season—a season of nurture and education. Later that week she celebrated her new season by discarding her old clothes and putting on the new ones that Elizabeth had sewn for her. In her new green skirt together with a white shift and a new black shawl draped around her shoulders, woolen stockings and leather shoes on her feet, she felt less like the stray she had been on her arrival.

Simon returned with the good news that the horse they had rescued was recovering in the barn of the man with the lantern.

"And I have arranged, Nell, that when it is strong, he will deliver it here for you."

Nell gasped.

"But Simon, I have never ridden a horse!"

"Then you shall learn ... along with Maisie and Emily. We can surely find a spare saddle in the stables." Nell was overwhelmed. It seemed she was to learn many things.

Gradually she persuaded Elizabeth to allow her to contribute to the household by doing the things she was good at—polishing the furniture and the copper, keeping the fires burning, helping Suzanna with the laundry, and cleaning the tiny diamond-shaped windowpanes. It made her feel better to work, to be useful rather than just receive charity, and in spite of her reticence to employ Nell as a maid, Elizabeth held to the notion that work was sacred and accepted Nell's labor as such.

Chapter 21

Simon had been slow to understand his love for Nell. Preoccupied with his need to see his home and be reunited with his mother and sister, it took time for him to realize there was a vacuum where Nell's tenderness had been. In Nell he had found a rare combination of strength and courage blended with a true servant's heart, and he had to admit that he felt considerably poorer without the daily comfort of her presence and that it was only the difference in their social status that had blinded him to her true worth. It simply had not occurred to him that their relationship might continue after their refuge in the woods had ended.

In April parliament passed the Self-Denying Ordinance, which ruled that a man could not simultaneously hold a position in the army and Parliament. They then created the New Model Army, a specially trained body of men who would fight in the war against the king. Simon, disillusioned with both the army and Parliament, began to agree with Josiah that the nation could better be influenced by winning people to God one soul at a time and educating them through the preaching of the Word. The will of God, he decided, could not be brought to bear on a nation by physical force. Unsure of his future as he was, he was growing more certain of one thing—his intense desire to have Nell by his side.

With this in mind he set off to Retford, anxious to test the plans of his mind against reality. It was toward the end of June, and Edward was home from the war with the news that Parliament had just won a decisive victory at Naseby. He greeted Simon warmly.

"Welcome! We meet again in these dangerous times!"

"Indeed! Thank you, and I trust you are well."

"By the grace of God, I am. And you?"

"I am well. Thank you. And happy to be away from the fighting. It seems the army is surviving quite well without my services! Naseby is taken from the king?"

"Indeed it is!" replied Edward. "If the king would surrender and negotiate with Parliament, we could all be spared more bloodshed and heartache."

"I fail to see how the king can maintain his army further with so many losses."

"We captured his baggage train too and all his personal correspondence, and it seems he has been secretly trying to buy the services of Irish Catholics, though he denies it of course."

"It seems he is determined to prolong this misery at all costs in order to save himself from loss of personal power."

"I doubt he will succeed. Fairfax and Cromwell have a strong army now, and the sword rules, it seems."

"Who would have thought," questioned Simon, "that one quarter of the nation's population would have been engaged in fighting a sordid civil war! And all to prevent the king from ruling Parliament with a rod of iron and appointing Catholic sympathizers to office," he continued.

"It seemed we would continue enjoying unprecedented peace until the king looked to make himself as absolute a ruler as his counterparts in France and Spain."

"Maybe true peace will always be elusive unless we establish God's rule. When the king thinks he is God, there can be no peace. The question is do we attain it by the sword or by education."

"You are becoming quite a philosopher!" teased Edward. Then when he saw Nell riding across the courtyard through the window, he added, "Look! See how well Nell rides now! And that horse you rescued has made a remarkable recovery!"

Simon watched as Nell cantered across the courtyard and disappeared around the side of the house toward the stables. Horse and rider seemed made for one another, and it occurred to him that they had both been rescued from difficult circumstances and delivered into a better future.

Would to God that England would soon follow suit! Yes, he had to admit, he was becoming seriously philosophical.

Nell came in shortly afterward, wearing a dark blue riding cape, her face flushed by the exercise—or was it excitement at seeing Simon again?

"Simon! I saw your horse in the stables! It's good to see you again!"

"It's a pleasure to see you, Nell, and to see how the fine air of Retford is suiting you." Simon was astonished that he never noticed how blue her eyes were. In fact, her whole appearance was transformed from the poor, thin refugee he had known in York to a well-formed and confident young woman who stood before him, examining him with eyes that sparkled with warmth and life.

"Yes, Edward and Elizabeth have been very good to me, and I have been happy here. And how is your leg after the long ride?"

"Well enough, Nell. Thanks to your care."

Edward, who had been watching their interaction, said, "Yes, it's a long ride from London. You must be in need of refreshment, Simon. Nell, be so kind as to tell Mary to bring some victuals."

When she had departed for the kitchen, Edward was curious to test his observations of their relationship.

"A blossoming rose, don't you think, Simon? I think you'll find your sister has been showing Nell a few beauty treatments—how to make a cream by pounding strawberries and water cress to remove her freckles and how to use a combination of apple pulp, swine's grease, and rosewater to soften her skin. You know, the sort of things our girls do!"

"Yes, it's surprising how well things grow with the right cultivation and some good sunshine," he answered, giving nothing of his own feelings away. "But I rather think Nell's transformation is more than skin deep."

"There is a perfect time to pick a rose, you know, Simon," went on Edward quietly with meaning. "Just as the bud begins to open. If you leave it too late, you may lose it." Simon smiled. It seemed he would have no opposition from his brother-in-law.

Apart from having a chance to woo Nell, Simon wanted to meet some of the local Separatists who met for worship with his sister's family. Several from the area had been the first to leave for the New World, and despite opposition the sect prospered among the merchant classes of this rural community. He was hungry for their fellowship and for any information he could find about the fortunes of those that had left for the colonies.

The family carriage would accommodate only its four members, so since the world was saturated in sunshine that summer morning, Simon and Nell rode to church. The sky was filled with the trilling of skylarks and the hedgerows filled with warblers and thrushes, and in this quiet corner of England one could have believed that all was well with the world. They rode their horses at a walk, eager to drink in the beauty of the countryside and the novelty of being alone together.

"Nell, I have something to tell you," started Simon. She turned her gaze on him, wondering if it was to be good news or bad. "I am considering pursuing a career in the church, Nell. Maybe I will be able to bring some influence to bear on the old traditions from the inside."

"Where, Simon, and when?" she asked, unsure what the implications of this piece of news might be. "Since I already studied before the war intervened, I shall soon qualify, and I hope to secure a place in London so I can continue to live in my family home there."

"Will your nonconformist ideas be tolerated, Simon?"

"In London there are many who pursue religious freedom, Nell. I shall try to extend our influence. I want to preach, Nell. It is the best way to change this nation."

Nell was silent, considering his answer.

"It has to be better than slaughtering one another!" she agreed. "I'm glad, Simon. You often said that you had no wish to follow in your father's footsteps in Parliament."

Since Nell seemed to accept the news with equanimity, he felt able to bring up what was really on his mind.

"Nell, you once said I would forget about you. Now you can see that isn't true."

"I'm sorry, Simon. I had no idea you would invite me to Retford."

"Nell, even in London I missed you. I had to come back to see you … to see if you were happy … to see if you—" He pulled up his horse and waited for Nell to do the same and come alongside. Then when her attention was fully on his face, he said, "Nell, I need you alongside me. I want to share my life with you, Nell. Will you marry me?"

"Marry you? You want to marry *me*, Simon? *Me*?" repeated Nell, trying to grasp the reality of Simon's offer.

"Yes, Nell, be my wife! Come and share my life in London."

Two tears welled up in Nell's blue eyes and dropped like jewels on her cheeks. At last she would belong! At last she would be loved and protected and by a man she could respect.

"Oh, Simon, yes! Yes, yes, yes! That would make me very happy," said Nell, feeling in that moment more happiness than in the rest of her life put together. Unable to contain her joy, she took off at a gallop.

"Race you to the church!" she challenged, laughing. Simon took off after her and soon caught up with her just before the spinney that marked the boundary of the church grounds. Here they both had to slow down, and as they steadied their horses, Simon brought his mount alongside Nell's, confining her by the little wooden fence, and then leaned over and grabbed her reins.

"I can see we shall have much sport!" he said and laughed. He quickly dismounted and lifted her from her horse.

"Now, Miss Nell, may I seal my proposal with a kiss?"

She leaned toward him, lifting her chin, her smile radiant.

"Indeed you may, Master Simon!"

Chapter 22

Although it was summer, a fire was still burning in the cottage, smoke curling lazily upward in the still afternoon. Maisie and Emily bounced up the path. Maisie turned to Emily and gave her a posy of fresh flowers picked from the garden. She took it and put it to her nose to smell the fragrance.

"Now hold it like this Emily. In front … like this." They practiced walking side by side along the path where the sun had hardened the mud. Nell caught sight of them from the upstairs window and paused to watch. Emily was trying hard to keep in step with her older sister, her round-cheeked face framed by the bonnet Elizabeth had stitched from linen and tied with a blue ribbon that matched the blue of her long-sleeved dress. Maisie's attention was on her feet. To trip and spoil their beautiful clothes would ruin the day.

"Come on, let's go inside now. I'll show you how to curtsy." She took her sister's hand and led her inside, where they could curtsy without dipping their skirts in the dirt.

"Mamma, Maisie picked some flowers." She thrust her posy toward Simon's sister.

"Beautiful!" she said without looking up from the dress she was stitching. She had only a few hours before she must wear it. Today her brother, Simon, would marry the woman he loved, the woman he believed God had given him not only to nurse him back to health after the battle but to be his lifelong lover and companion. She came without a dowry but with virtue. She came without experience of running a large house, but she was learning. In Nell Simon was sure he had found a woman he could love and trust, whatever his mother might think. Elizabeth and Edward knew that Nell's real worth lay in her indomitable spirit and genuine faith, and they had given their hearty approval to the marriage. Simon's mother and older sister, Mary, had not yet met Nell and continued to be vexed by Simon's odd choice of wife. Despite that, they had agreed to travel to the wedding.

Babworth church—their closest church—was the setting for the happy occasion. Its gray stone walls, solid as the tradition it represented, stood square and imposing in the sunlit glade. The surrounding woods, where Simon had chased his bride-to-be for his first kiss, were pleasantly shady rather than somber, covering the arriving guests with dappled sunlight.

It was from here that those called dissenters had migrated to the New World, but those nonconformists had long since fled and the parson replaced by one who would not threaten the status quo. Obliged to attend services there, Edward and Elizabeth found fellowship and teaching elsewhere in the homes of others like themselves; however, it was in the church that bans were published, and here the wedding was to be performed by the incumbent minister. Since the prayer book of 1549 required the use of rings in the ceremony, there had been much discussion about the wedding, for Puritan beliefs rejected the use of rings, considering them popish. Simon decided not to make an issue of it and to give Nell a simple gold ring, which she was not obliged to wear afterward.

"After all," he said, "we do not have to embrace the popery in our hearts."

"Simon, I care not whether I be wed with or without a ring, so long as we may be man and wife."

Simon smiled. "We shall be wed according to the law of this land, Nell, and no one will be able to dispute it. Nevertheless we shall not decorate the church or have the organ play, Nell. Your beauty will be decoration enough."

Simon had traveled to the church with his mother and sister in the family carriage, while Nell arrived with Elizabeth and Edward in theirs.

Waiting at the front of the church, Simon had never seen his bride without a coif, and he looked around to see her wearing the smallest of little caps, around which a circle of tiny white rosebuds crowned her auburn curls. Her simple dress of blue silk, cinched at the waist after the fashion, fell in soft folds to the ground. The bodice was cut away and laced over a white stomacher to make the shape of a heart, tapering up to a wide white collar that fell over her shoulders. In her hands she carried a posy of white rosebuds.

It was Edward, resplendent in royal blue britches and white shirt, who escorted Nell down the aisle, since she had lived under his protection for the last eight months. All eyes were on Nell, but her gaze was on her groom. It was for her an unbelievable moment, and she scarce felt the stone floor of the ancient building beneath her feet; however, she trod with dignity and grace. Elizabeth, who was wearing a dress of darker blue, walked behind with the two girls. Simon had dressed simply, but he was elegant in a fine mulberry doublet over a white shirt and matching knee-length britches with brown stockings and shoes.

The rest of the family and some friends of Elizabeth and Edward sat in the pews while Simon and Nell made their vows and the minister tied a piece of cloth around their hands to symbolize their union. The minister had been willing to grant their wish to keep it simple in accordance with Puritan tradition, so no music played for the reading of the psalm. They knelt together for the reading of the prescribed scriptures and the administration of Holy Communion. It was all very somber, but Nell's heart was singing as they turned to process back down the aisle and the sun shone through the high windows and kissed them with its golden shafts. Surely this was a marriage made in heaven, and despite the differences of social status between them, it would endure till death parted them.

Later Edward, leading more heartfelt prayers as the family gathered at his home, prayed in the words of a Puritan prayer, "Dear heavenly Father, give both of them a great spiritual purpose in life as they seek your kingdom and your righteousness. Loving you best, they shall love each other the more and faithful unto each other they will be. Now make such assignments to them on the scroll of your will as you bless them and develop their character as they walk together. When life is done and the sun is setting, may they be found then as now, hand in hand, thanking you for each other. May they serve you happily, faithfully together until at last one shall lay the other into the arms of Jesus."

"Amen," chorused the family. It was done. The great assignments that lay ahead would unfold as they shared their lives together.

Chapter 23

Their journey back to Camberwell took three days, as they had to allow time for the horses to be refreshed, and they needed to obtain stabling and accommodation at hostelries on the way. Simon and Oliver took turns to drive the carriage, sitting together on the seat outside at the front, while the women sat inside. This gave them ample time to get better acquainted before they arrived home.

Nell was a little intimidated by the other two women. His mother was somewhat aristocratic with fine features, and her brown hair was pulled back in a way that accentuated her high cheekbones. Mary was very much like her mother, but thinner in the face, with thinner lips that were rarely decorated by a smile. They were righteous women, but they lacked warmth. They both complained about the long journey to London and London itself, and Nell discovered that they both regretted ever leaving the quiet Worcestershire countryside, where they had enjoyed the benefits of a large estate and the comfort of familiar, long-term relationships. She also suspected that they both still grieved for Simon's father, for whose career they had made the move.

On arrival at Camberwell village just south of the city, Nell thought the house charming and the locality more rural than she had expected.

"Welcome to Tall Chimneys," said Margaret sincerely, for she was indeed glad that Simon had chosen to bring his bride home. The house was of three stories, a brick and timber building of generous proportions. It had a fireplace in every room, a recent innovation in the new London homes and a feature that advertised their wealth. Richard had spared no expense in making it as comfortable and pleasing to his wife as he could. There was ample room for Simon and his bride.

Nell regarded the polished oak-paneled walls of the hall and its floors of oak covered with woven rush matting. The ceilings were plastered and lime-washed and the walls brightly decorated. Its many windows were hung with warm woolen curtains, and Margaret and Elizabeth had made a fine new patchwork quilt for the bed in Simon and Nell's room. They would have two rooms on the east side of house. Other than that they would live communally, and Nell would need to get used to being served instead of serving.

Nell was happy enough with her new life; however, life as Mrs. Brierley was very different from life as Nell Thornby, and she faced some challenges at first. Simon's warmth compensated for the coldness she felt from Mary and his mother treated her well, but once again she had to adjust to a new household, and this time she had to adjust to being part of the gentry instead of serving it and to observing their strict religious ways. Ironically her difficulties were exposed by a kindness.

Noticing that Nell, even though she had learned to dress in keeping with her new station, still held on to the small leather bag that had been hers in poorer days, Margaret took the liberty of buying her a new one.

"A new bag for you, my dear, so you can discard that old one," she said, proffering it one afternoon. Nell thanked her, took it up to her room, and laid it on the bed. It was made of beautiful soft leather drawn together at the top by a long cord, unostentatious and smaller than her old one but of excellent quality. After supper she would transfer to it the contents of the old one. Before she had opportunity to do that, Simon noticed it.

"A fine bag for a fine lady!" he said. "You must use it at once!" Picking up the old one from where it sat on the floor by Nell's side of the bed, he turned it upside down and then stood staring in unbelief as the wooden crucifix clattered to the floor. Before Nell's embarrassed gaze, he picked it up, inspected it closely, and demanded to know why she kept such an idolatrous item among her personal treasures.

"Nell! I little thought to find such an idolatrous thing in your possession!"

"Simon, that's the cross that first showed me the way to the Savior," she explained. "It's not an idol! I don't worship it! Don't you understand? It's special to me because he used it to demonstrate his love for me?"

"If my mother or Mary find out, they'll not approve, Nell."

"So am I to live my life according to what your mother and sister approve or according to my own desire?"

"Nell, you must leave the past behind now! You belong here, and you must learn to fit in!"

"I am trying to fit in!" she asserted tearfully. "Ever since I arrived here, I have been trying! I try to behave right and speak right and address the servants properly. I try to dress right! I try to respond cheerfully to Mary's complaining! I try not to offend your mother or embarrass myself by doing anything contrary to their usual way of doing things! Now you tell me I have to ask them for permission to keep my own few possessions! Simon, if you are against me too, it's just too much!" Simon sank down on the end of the bed. Knowing he was the cause of her tears hurt him too.

"Nell, don't you see? If anyone found this in here—the servants for example—there would be much gossip that you are not sincere in your religion. They will say you are a secret Catholic sympathizer, and there will be much talk, talk that will harm us, harm you. I don't want that, Nell."

For a moment Nell was back at Bethany, listening to Molly's warning not to let the Thorpe's know of her gift of the crucifix. Then she remembered the vision of the Christ extending his bleeding hands to her. She swallowed. It had been precious to her because it had led her to question its meaning and had been instrumental in her finding God's love, a love that had kept her sane in the madness she had lived through. One thing was sure though—she did not want any more trouble from religious persecution. She had a faith that went beyond religious effigies. She had only wanted to keep it for sentimental reasons. It had meant so much when she had so little.

"Very well, Simon. I will put it away from me." she said and then sighed. "It seems one must always conform!" She threw it into the fire that blazed in the hearth in their room and stood watching while the flames devoured it, resenting its loss, angry and sad.

"There. Now it's gone."

"I'm sorry, Nell. It's been hard for you."

"It was my first Christmas present," she said sadly.

"Nell, we don't keep Christmas here."

"I know that! I have accepted that too! I was merely thinking of Molly's kindness. She kept Christmas, and she gave me a gift when I had nothing of my own."

"And now you have a new gift, Nell. Isn't that new bag a gift too?"

"Yes, of course," she admitted. "I'll enjoy it of course."

She picked up the remaining personal items and placed them in the new bag. Simon was right. She must leave the past behind, but adjusting to the present was not easy.

"I'm trying, Simon. Please give me time. It's not easy living with Mary's stern tongue. She's not helpful like Elizabeth. Elizabeth was like a sister to me. Mary is jealous of me, Simon. She is not used to sharing your affection with anyone except with your mother. Deep down I feel her disapproval too. I'm sure she feels you should have found a more fitting wife—one more nobly bred."

"I'm sorry, Nell," said Simon softly. "Mary is very set in her ways. Be patient. She will see what an excellent woman you are. She will be glad to be in your company." He looked at her where she sat slumped in the chair, weary with emotion, her face still tear-stained.

"Come, Nell, I'll read to you if you like." That brought a smile to Nell's lips, and she embraced him fully.

"I would like that," she said. "I read so slowly still. It would be lovely to have some time together."

Soon the fruit of their love ripened in Nell's womb, and by the summer of 1646 they had become the proud parents of Adam. As Simon watched Nell with their child at her breast, he was content and thankful. God had given him a good wife.

Chapter 24

It was a sunny Sunday morning with a light easterly breeze, a bit fresh but pleasant enough for the young lad running along the path by the river, whipping a wooden spinning top. Sauntering along in the opposite direction, a middle-aged man, his rather large nose tilted to the sky, hands clasped loosely behind his back, was also enjoying a rare moment of pleasure in the morning sun. This was about as relaxed as Oliver Cromwell ever got. He was not predisposed to leisure, not even on a Sunday, *especially* not on a Sunday!

Billy Cooper, free from worldly burdens, was totally engaged in the innocent pastime of trying to keep the wooden top spinning on the rough path. It was of no great consequence if he failed. He would just pick up the top, bind the whipping cord around it, and pull it sharply away, sending it spinning along the path once more. Oliver Cromwell, on the other hand, was keeping several tops in motion simultaneously and could not afford to fail. Nevertheless, he walked with an air of self-confidence. With King Charles surrendered to the Scots, one of his tops was spinning nicely. Now it was a matter of how to get the Scots to deliver King Charles into the hands of Parliament and to get him to negotiate terms of a settlement between Parliament and the monarchy by which the country might safely be governed.

With such weighty matters on his mind, you would think young Billy would have passed by unnoticed. Not so. Cromwell, ever in the role of one who sought to establish religious law, rebuked him sharply for pursuing recreation on a Sunday.

"For shame on you, lad. Don't you know it's the Sabbath? Stop your playing and get to your prayers, boy!"

Young Billy hastily gathered up his top and fled, as many others would, at the stern railings of Cromwell. King Charles would have done well to follow suit, but convinced that he should be ruling by divine right the nation and the church, he continued to seek ways to pursue his return to supreme power. With the New Model Army growing in power and expertise, he stood little chance of succeeding. The Parliamentarians were now a force to be reckoned with, and they spared no quarter to the Royalists.

As the summer of 1646 wore on, more Royalist garrisons fell like dominoes—Newark, Oxford, which was the king's own operations base, Worcester, Wallingford Castle, and Raglan Castle. All were spoiled and rendered unusable, as the drum-roll and redcoats of the New Model Army was making its presence felt. The army, trained and led by Sir Thomas Fairfax with Cromwell as second-in-command, was proving to be the deciding factor in the war. The country was indeed being ruled by the sword, and that sword was about to make its force felt at Haresby Hall.

Chapter 25

At Haresby Hall Eleanor and Duncan woke one morning to find a minion installed on the rise above the house and a mob of soldiers firing musket balls at the windows. Eleanor sent Catherine scurrying around the house to make sure no one was still sleeping, and Duncan ordered the servants to secure all the doors and take cover from the windows. Then armed with pistols, he and Hugh took up position on the flat part of the roof, where they were afforded some protection by the low battlements. From here they could pick off any who approached the house from the front.

Eleanor knew it would be useless to argue with Duncan about going with him; however, she had a keen eye and a steady hand, and she could not stand idly by while her beloved home was destroyed. A cannonball slammed mercilessly into a wall at the back of the house, and Eleanor sped upstairs to a door that gave out on a small parapet at a corner of the house, not in direct view of the soldiers but overlooking the minion. Crouching where two merlons met to form a corner, she carefully took aim at those loading the minion. She could hear the commands,

"Load your ladle! Empty your ladle! Poke your powder!" Before they heard, "Load your shot!" Eleanor had fired three shots, wounding two of the party and sending them all running for cover. She held to her position. If she could keep them from using the minion, the walls of her family home might survive.

Downstairs they carried in Hugh, who had been mortally wounded by musket fire. The women flocked around, crying and panicking until Matilda gave orders to fetch ale for his thirst. Before the ale came, however, she had to send for a sheet to cover him. Duncan reappeared, hurriedly securing the door behind him. Gone was his usual self-possession. Addressing everyone, he said, "They are too many for us! We are outnumbered. We must get away while we can! If you leave by the kitchen door, you will be shielded by the stables. Then by keeping close to the stables, you can gain access to the woods and find your way secretly to shelter." Most he knew had family in the nearby villages—all except Matilda and Jacob, for whom Haresby Hall had been home for many years.

"Where's Mistress Eleanor?" he demanded to know.

"She's gone to the east wing, sir."

Duncan raced off to get her. They must leave and quickly, while they still had their lives. Eleanor had withdrawn again to the relative safety of their room.

"Eleanor, we must go! We'll take the carriage and go to Tadcaster!"

"No! We'll ride!" protested Eleanor. "I'm not leaving my Silver for those Roundhead rebels to ride! Anyway, we shall make more haste on horseback!"

"Very well! Quickly!" He wanted to protest that Eleanor would have more protection in the carriage, but she was right. It would be slower, and it would also draw more attention to themselves and mean that they would have to travel on the road.

There was no time to fuss. She had hastily dressed as simply as she could and now donned her riding cape. No time to grab her father's portrait from over the fireplace in the drawing room. No time to bury poor Hugh. After they left by the same door as the servants, they quickly saddled their horses and rode off into the woods, and taking the same path as Nell had done when she had begun her escapade, they made for Lincoln and then north to Tadcaster to the relative safety of The Grange.

The Roundheads, when they realized that the occupants had fled, stopped firing and moved in to make Haresby Hall an army base. Matilda and Jacob were instructed to continue with their normal duties, serving their new masters in place of Eleanor and Duncan. Edmund Whyte, while keeping to his former home in the cottage, became more concerned with matters of soldiering than of maintaining the upkeep of the grounds.

Chapter 26

Despite choosing not to follow in his father's footsteps as an MP, Simon kept abreast of political developments in the nation. In his chosen role as a spiritual shepherd, he still hoped to influence the church and therefore the Parliament toward religious toleration. Many of his father's colleagues were still well disposed toward him, and Simon made the most of every encounter.

He was well abreast of the news that the king had escaped from Hampton Court and had sought a refuge on the Isle of Wight at Carisbrooke Castle, where Colonel Robert Hammond was the governor. He was also up to date with the strategic victory of Cromwell's New Model Army over the Scots and the Royalists at the battle of Preston in the preceding August.

It was a blustery October afternoon when Simon encountered one of his nonconformist acquaintances in one of the new London coffee shops. They greeted one another formally with a handshake and polite inquiries after the welfare of each other's families, but what was on the heart and mind of both was the stalemate situation of the king's captivity.

"I believe Colonel Hammond is the nephew of the king's chaplain?" queried Simon.

"Indeed so, but he was appointed by Cromwell. The king has little influence now in the affairs of this nation, though I am led to believe he is treated reasonably well enough by the colonel."

"Where do you suppose it might end?" asked Simon. "Cromwell cannot detain the king indefinitely."

"Parliament tries even now to negotiate a settlement with his majesty, but the king manipulates at every turn, attempting to set the army and Parliament at odds with one another. Parliament seeks only to see Presbyterianism installed instead of the power of the bishops and the monarch. The New Model Army, on the other hand, wants total religious toleration. The king would do well to agree to Parliament's terms while he can."

"Indeed, he would. It's a wonder the Scots believed him when he promised to establish Presbyterianism in return for their support in invading England," commented Simon.

"The Scots would indeed have done well to remember that that was the very reason Charles had taken up arms against them in the first place. In any case, Cromwell so brilliantly routed them at Preston. There seems little hope now for the monarchy. The king continues to be imprisoned in a very small part of his kingdom. He is running out of options, and his attempts at escape have all failed miserably."

"Even should he escape, it seems he has no hope of resisting Cromwell now. His only option is to settle by negotiation. Would that he would see sense and allow us all the religious freedom we desire!" Simon along with many others were hopeful that the king's lack of options would drive him to a compromise.

"The problem is," continued his friend, "he sees himself as appointed by God to rule over all the church, not just a part of it. He and Cromwell are both religiously motivated, but it seems Cromwell is now the one with power, albeit temporal. He sees himself as God's deliverer."

"Does the king think likewise?"

"Yes, I believe he holds to the notion that he is God's chosen too—or else he will be a martyr to monarchical rule."

Simon left the coffee shop in a pensive mood. With neither Cromwell nor the king willing to compromise, it seemed that time was running out for a peaceful settlement.

Chapter 27

Simon was eventually assigned a living in Dulwich, and the moment of his first sermon arrived. He had spent much time in meditation and preparation of his message. Most but not all of his congregation would likely be supporters of Parliament and inclined toward a Puritan way of thinking, so he hoped that together they could affect some changes to traditional conformity. It would be worth his studies in an institution that hadn't been entirely to his liking if he could now be used as an agent of change for the betterment of the English church.

Sunday came, and a hundred or so people were seated in the wooden pews, their serious faces lit by strong rays of sunlight that pierced through the high arched window like unsheathed swords. Clad in their best Sunday apparel, they waited to know if this new vicar would be to their liking. Would he be on the side of tradition or nonconformity?

The service proceeded as normal from the Book of Common Prayer. When it came time for the sermon, Simon ascended the little steps up to the wooden pulpit and turned to the book of Matthew to read out the text on which he would base his message.

"'Master, which is the greatest commandment in the law?' Jesus said unto him, 'Thou shalt love the Lord thy God with all thy heart, and with all thy soul, and with all thy mind. This is the first and greatest commandment. And the second is like unto it, Thou shalt love thy neighbor as thyself.'" He looked down at their faces, wondering what thoughts were forming behind the solemn expressions, all conformed to a proper aspect of devotion.

"Brothers and sisters," he began, "today we meet in the name of our Lord and seek to do his will. His Word tells us his will is for us to love one another. We were made for love—his love—and when Adam and Eve rejected that love, he pursued us through Abraham and the patriarchs, David and the prophets, until finally his own Son, Christ, paid the penalty for our rebellion and by his own blood brought us into his kingdom—the kingdom of love. Then the epistle of the beloved apostle John tells us that 'we love because he first loved us' and that we are to love one another."

He had the attention of his listeners, and they were nodding in agreement. It seemed that the flock was feeding out of his shepherd's hand like lambs. But his father's blood still ran in his veins, and he could not help but apply his message to the political state of the nation.

"In England two giants vie for supremacy, both claiming to serve the purposes of God and the people. In reality both seek for absolute power by which they might rule *as* God instead of *for* him. One is a religious megalomaniac, striving to bring about the kingdom of God by suppression and ungodly control—a leviathan with whom it is dangerous to struggle! A Pharisee who 'cleans the outside of the cup' but neglects the state of the heart! The other manipulates and uses anyone who will join him as long as they are willing to serve the purpose of establishing him in absolute power. Then afterward he discards them like a worn out garment. He has proved his inability to shepherd his people by appointing ungodly and unprincipled men to run God's church for their own ends. The bishops allow all kinds of licentiousness, as long as the people give their tithes and keep them well-shod and overfed! Both of these giants seek to establish control by the sword. Neither has any idea about the God of love they claim to serve. Meanwhile a whole nation is like a herd of sheep without a shepherd, savaged by wolves of depravity, sickness and ignorance.

In his passion Simon had left the confines of the makeshift pulpit and had begun to pace in front of the people. His audience sat in silence, stunned at his passionate invective, shocked that he had left the pulpit and continued to preach outside it. Simon continued, unable to stem the flow of what was bursting out of his soul like a river released from a broken dam wall.

"We must cry out to God to deliver us from the blood guilt of fighting our brothers! We must ask for mercy and for his face to be turned toward us once again so that peace might be restored and that the land might once again yield to us a harvest!"

Pearls of wisdom poured forth from his mouth and landed like gunshot on the floor. In his naivety Simon had hoped they would be received as an offering from God, but in his fervor he discovered he had unwittingly "cast his pearls before swine." While he had intended to turn their focus from politics to explore more spiritual realities, he had done the opposite and offended those on both sides of the political spectrum. Suddenly the church was in an uproar.

"For shame on you to call Cromwell a leviathan!"

"Quite right, my boy, for so he is!"

"You speak of things you do not know!"

"How dare you defame the king and his bishops!" Everyone it seemed had an opinion, and no one was keeping it to themselves. There was much disagreement, and Simon, taken by surprise at the reaction to his message, retreated quickly into the pulpit, while Nell and Margaret and Mary shrank back into their pew and prayed silently for his deliverance from the fire that been sparked within the cold ancient walls.

"Gentlemen and women, I beseech you," he began. "Let us not display such uncharitable sentiments!" The congregation settled a little, but the mood was ugly, far removed from the brotherly love that had been the subject of his sermon.

"Young man, get on with the service! We shall be late for our dinners!" demanded a portly elderly man at the front of the church.

Simon swallowed hard and composed himself. Then quietly but with great determination he said, "I hardly think we may come to the Holy Communion in such a state of disagreement. I shall not be administering the rite until we are at peace with one another."

At this the man, obviously used to being a leading figure in the group, waved his stick and shouted, "Then we shall see what the bishop has to say about the incumbent who is refusing to administer the sacred rites to his congregation!" So saying, he walked out, followed by two rather sheepish women and a trickle of others whose angry footsteps echoed on the stone floor, until the sturdy oak doors slammed behind them.

"I hardly think," said Simon sadly, "that we are bringing much joy to the Savior today. I am sorry. It seems we are divided in our opinions, but let us not forget that there is a court far above our earthly realm that makes decrees that are both just and merciful. Let us sing a hymn and allow ourselves to be more composed thereby." For once Simon was glad to include a hymn, and it did produce a more congenial atmosphere, after which he felt able to suggest they show their peace with one another by a handshake. Peace and order thus being reestablished, he proceeded to celebrate the Communion according to the normal practice.

Later he reflected on the experience and discussed the issue with Nell.

"Tell me— Who is going to save this people? Who is going to put salve on their eyes so they can see? Who is going to bind up their wounds? Who is going to shine a light into the darkness of their souls that they might see their way to God?"

"You are, my dear Simon! You must preach about the Savior's redeeming love and avoid controversy. Only he can rescue this nation and deliver us from the mess we have made of the church. Only his love can turn around a nation torn apart by power struggles over who controls the church. It was birthed out of humility and self-sacrifice, and it ought to be led the same way now!"

"Yes. Even if I have to resort to preaching the Word in the fields and byways, outside the confines of the church! There the common people might respond to the invitation of the Great Shepherd! In the church I suspect I will be just a voice crying in the wilderness!"

Chapter 28

In Tadcaster the autumn of 1648 was dragging into winter. Eleanor was slumped in her chair in the parlor on the south side of the Grange. The chair had been a gift from her husband, beautifully upholstered in green brocade, a rare jewel in the furniture world, something to comfort her in her exile from Haresby Hall. She sat immobile, gazing out onto the leafless trees of the Yorkshire landscape, where recent gales had torn the last remaining leaves from the trees. However, there was a new life within her own body, and she could feel the new heir to Haresby making his or her presence felt. Soon it would be delivered into the world.

"Oh, would that it was a different kind of a world I was bringing you into!" she said aloud to the babe in her womb. She looked forward to cradling it in her arms. At least caring for the child would give her something to do. At least there was that to look forward to, but the strong irony of the fact that now there was an heir to Haresby there was no inheritance dented the joy in her heart.

"One day," she promised it, "one day we will return. One day law and order will return, and the king will rule again." For now she must endure the bleakness of Yorkshire, the bleakness of this comfortless home in the cold north and the coldness of Duncan's mother, who having welcomed Eleanor into the family as a wealthy heiress was less than impressed with having a daughter-in-law who seemed to have lost everything. The one thing that was constant in her changed circumstances was Duncan's love. She knew he would do anything to make her happy and at least he was still alive and had not been lost like so many others in the Royalist ranks. Eleanor's misfortune had merely made him more compassionate and more determined to care for her in his own home. The problem was that Duncan's passion for the Royalist cause had drawn him away from home to engage in battles far from her.

Eleanor closed her eyes and thought back to the days when she had responsibility for the whole estate. She had found it difficult at first but had grown into the challenge until she could walk with confidence in the responsibility of being the mistress of that household. Even now she often wondered what had become of Matilda and Jacob and the others on that fateful day. Here at Tadcaster she certainly was not mistress, and Catherine Talbot definitely was. Duncan's father had an obvious affection for his new daughter-in-law. As far as he was concerned, she replaced the Talbot's own daughter, who had been stillborn, and he enjoyed having another woman around to soften the austerity of his life. To his wife though, Eleanor still felt like an intruder, tolerated rather than welcomed, and unaccustomed to leisure, it was hard for her to get used to the inactivity her present situation necessitated.

Like Nell, Eleanor was struggling to adjust to her new household, but there was nothing she could do. She simply had to accept her changed circumstances and get on with life, but she would not give up the fight. She would return to Haresby and return it to its former glory. She would return now if she could, but in her present state she could not.

There was a knock at the door, and a maid came bustling in.

"There is a gentleman at the door who says he needs to speak to Mrs. Talbot."

"Which Mrs. Talbot does he wish to speak to?"

"I know not, ma'am."

"Then ask him and find out what his business is."

"Yes, ma'am." She exited. Eleanor, alone in the house apart from the servants, waited for her return, hoping it was something that could wait. The maid returned a moment later with the news that his name was Edmund Whyte and he had come to see her.

"Send him in at once please, Emily!" said Eleanor as she braced herself for whatever news he had come to deliver. She was sure that whatever the reason for his visit, it was not about to improve her day. A moment later Emily returned, behind her an austere-looking man dressed all in black apart from the broad white collar under his pale face. Edmund Whyte had never been a big man, but now he looked decidedly thin and haggard, his dark brows knotting over his thin, tired face.

Eleanor stayed where she was in the chair and opened her hand toward another to indicate for him to sit. He hesitated and then said, "No, thank you, ma'am. I'd prefer to stand. My message is but brief."

"I little thought to have a visit from you, Mr. Whyte." He was silent for a moment, hesitating and studying the floor as if searching for words, while Eleanor waited impatiently.

"It is good to see you looking … er … so well, ma'am," he said rather formally, raising his eyes and taking in more fully the sight of her pregnant form. At last he continued, "I have ridden myself to deliver news and an invitation."

"And what might that be?"

"I have ridden to inform you that your husband has been taken prisoner by the army and is being held in the garrison that is now at Haresby."

Eleanor felt sick at the thought of Duncan being held prisoner anywhere, but the thought of him being held at her former home was more than she could bear. She struggled to contain the swirl of emotions that threatened to undo her composure. She wanted to rebuke Whyte for being the bearer of bad tidings but thought better of it since he had ridden so far to deliver the message personally, and it was obviously an unpleasant task for him to deliver it.

"I thank you for your trouble, sir," she said as graciously as she could. "I can hardly thank you for the news you bring. How exactly did my husband come to be imprisoned in my home?"

"I can tell you, ma'am, had he not come to meddle in the affairs at Haresby, he would not be held hostage now. I knew, ma'am, he would be investigating the place on your behalf. Not so, my comrades. Thinking him to be spying for information to pass on to the Royalists, they apprehended him and would have shot him had I not intervened. I persuaded them to spare his life. I have restrained my comrades from doing further damage to the house so that both your husband and your home are preserved."

"I am indeed indebted to you for that," she said, sincerely grateful. She had always appreciated his loyalty. "I am at loss to know why you serve on the side of those who oppose our king, Edmund," she said, using his Christian name deliberately

"I would that you and your husband would turn to Parliament since it is the way of the future. Join us and return as mistress of Haresby."

"Return? Return? And betray all that my father died for! Throw in my lot with a handful of rebels?"

"Maybe you have not heard, ma'am, that the army has taken the king from his captivity on the Isle of Wight up to London. Soon the army will rule this nation, and the Parliament will negotiate new laws. And we shall have a different order." This last crushing blow was more than Eleanor could bear. She was at a loss to know how to contain her emotions and how to keep the anger she was feeling from spilling out over Edmund Whyte. She had no wish to alienate him or he would return to Haresby feeling that his journey had been in vain and any loyalty that he had felt toward her would be totally destroyed, her husband and home both endangered. She swallowed hard, trying to think clearly and give him an answer that would not betray the panic rising within her.

"As you can see, I am in no condition to undertake a journey to Haresby. Nor do I expect to in the foreseeable future. You may tell my husband that I am well."

"Your husband is a brave man. But I doubt if he will be released in the foreseeable future, and I beg of you to think of your husband and your child and to join forces with those that are set to rule this nation."

"I do not understand why you declare yourself to be a godly man and turn your hand against our sovereign."

"A man cannot serve a sovereign who imposes on us forms of worship we no longer want to embrace and penalizes those who choose to follow other ways than that of the bishops. May I remind you, ma'am, it was the king himself who drew first blood in this battle and forced us all into this abominable situation. Since I cannot change your mind, I shall take my leave of you. I wish you well."

"I thank you for your concern, and I trust you might continue to preserve both my home and my husband. I leave them in your hands," she said, thrusting these words almost as a charge, for it had occurred to her that he might continue to undertake that responsibility even as he had undertaken his responsibilities in the past.

"I make no promises, ma'am, but I surely hope to see you well delivered of your child and your husband returned to you, and I pray that you might yet see sense and return to his side."

"You well know, Mr. Whyte, even should I return to Haresby, I am no longer its mistress so long as it is full of Roundhead soldiers. One day I shall return to Haresby, and I shall return as its mistress. One day my child will be the rightful owner of Haresby, and proper law and order shall return to this land."

"As you will, ma'am. I take my leave of you. Good day."

Chapter 29

It was around midnight in a London home, and a man sat at a simple wooden table. Despite the fire blazing in the hearth behind him, the room was still cold. Putting the final words to the letter he was earnestly penning, he sighed, signed it, reread it, nodded in satisfaction, and attached his seal. Then he rolled it and placed it into a cylindrical leather pouch.

"Thomas!" he called. The footman appeared. "You may tell our visitor his wait is over."

A few moments later a man wearing a blue cloak ready for travel entered the room.

"The letter is ready as you wished. It is most providential you are able to deliver to it. Godspeed! There is no time to waste. Without Cromwell's leadership, Parliament will fail to carry through what we all know is necessary for the freedom of this nation. The people have had enough of war—we all have—and if we make another agreement with the king, he will again try to deceive us and drag us into yet more confrontation."

"I will see that Cromwell receives it early on the morrow, sir."

So saying, he took his leave, mounted the white horse tethered outside, and began his night ride to Ely. It was a moonless night, and that suited his purposes perfectly.

A few hours later a milestone indicated Ely was another twelve miles, and the rider pulled his cloak more tightly round his chest, tucked it into his leather belt, and put his head down once more into the northeast wind. The purse beneath his tunic was full of gold, but the real treasure lay hidden under the saddle. Curled inside its protective leather case was the parchment containing the edict concerning the king. The rider cantered on through the night. He was sure now to reach his destination under cover of darkness.

The cobbled streets echoed to the horse's iron shoes, and a servant awaiting his arrival ran across the cathedral courtyard to meet him and stable the horse. The rider fumbled in his saddlebag for the giant key that would open the heavy wooden door to his private chambers at the cathedral—his by way of favor for his support of the school. His footsteps rang out on the cobbles in the chill morning air as he strode to the door and admitted himself. He locked the door behind him. After he placed the scroll and its leather case inside a secret compartment in his escritoire, he locked that too. Only then did he permit himself to relax a little, and a slight smile spread across his thin lips.

His movement toward the bedroom was halted by a loud knock at the door. After hesitating momentarily, he decided to answer and was both relieved and pleased to see a servant boy on the doorstep with something steaming in a pot and ale.

"The master had me prepare this for your arrival, sir."

"Then convey my thanks, Oswald."

The servant departed, and he sat to enjoy his meal, reflecting on the fact that soon the bishop might be redundant and that he himself might be the master and that it was such a wonderful coincidence that Ely Cathedral lay next to Oliver Cromwell's home. In the morning he would deliver the letter, and Cromwell would make all haste to return to London to support the Parliament in the trial of King Charles—a trial that would hopefully lead to the release of the church from the control of king and bishops. More importantly in the eyes of some, it would open the way for Parliament to rule the nation. Cromwell would do it—he knew he would. He must.

Cromwell himself was tired of negotiating with the devious king, who seemed as determined as ever to have his own way and return as absolute monarch. More fully understanding the king's duplicity, his attitude hardened. As he rode to London, he reflected on the three-day prayer meeting at Windsor Castle, where his army leaders—many of them in tears—had concluded that Charles was "a man of blood who must be punished for his crimes." Oliver Cromwell was a man of conscience, and the blood of many devout men was crying out from the ground for vengeance. If the king lived, it would lead to the bloodshed of more Christian Englishmen. And by Christian he meant nonconformist.

He thought about the letter as he rode. It seemed they were waiting for him, waiting for him to give credence to what would otherwise be unthinkable. And in the absence of a monarch, might he be just the man to rule the nation? If he had any doubts, it did not show as he cantered his black steed toward the capital, his rather ugly face fixed with resolve under the round black hat. He was a man of resolve, not emotion, with a profound sense of timing.

The timing of Oliver Cromwell's arrival in London was crucial. Parliament was locked in bitter debate over the removal of the king. After they had sat all night to discuss the issue of the king's future, they had decided that the removal of the king was illegal. The army was not going to succeed in removing the king unless all those who would not vote in favor of the king's removal were blocked, but it would be better if he himself was not seen to be responsible. He would arrive after the deed was done and appear to be the savior of the situation.

The deed fell to Colonel Pride, who, using soldiers from the New Model Army, prevented Presbyterian MPs, who were in favor of negotiating with the king, from taking their places in Parliament. The remaining fifty members authorized themselves to act without consent of either the House of Lords or the king. When the deed was done, Oliver Cromwell appeared in London and expressed his approval of what had taken place, although he denied he had any part in the planning of it. Now the way was clear for their solution to go ahead. He declared to his peers that they would "cut off the king's head with the crown on it." It seemed the only way to solve the impasse. Their only option was to remove the authority of the king, and the only way to remove his crown would be to remove his head. The stage was set for the trial of the king.

It was January 1649, and London was buzzing with the news that the king had been brought up to the city. The High Court of Justice had been convened for the purpose of putting him on trial. Simon could barely believe what he was reading. Kings had been murdered before, but never before had the king been tried by his own subjects. That he had caused the death of many good men was hardly to be doubted, but who were the men who considered themselves able to try the monarch?

"It seems that the army have taken things into their own hands." Simon shared the news with the other members of his family seated around the dinner table. "The king is on trial in Westminster Hall for high treason."

"We must pray that he will repent of his misdeeds, come to his senses, and agree to rule more moderately," said Simon's mother. "Maybe the Lord will use the army to bring about his purposes and free us from the domination of bishops as well as king."

"He must surely see that he has had long since lost the power to rule absolutely. This nation has paid too high a price to submit to his high-handed ways," said Simon, "but surely Parliament cannot itself act in so high-handed a manner as to find the king guilty of treason."

"Treason is punishable by execution," added Nell, "and it cannot be that they will carry their actions so far. It would be so utterly unreasonable to execute the monarch!"

"Whatever they do, it seems they are determined to take control. Parliament is now reduced to those in favor of removing the king, and the High Court has appointed those who are likewise determined to carry it through."

Simon was silent for the rest of the meal. What would his father have thought of the present proceedings? In that first battle at Edgehill, they could scarcely have imagined the way events would unfold. Scenes of the king seated on his horse behind his bodyguard, watching the slaughter of his own subjects, came back to Simon, followed by the memory of his father's body hanging limply alongside his horse. On searching his heart, he could not deny that a trace of desire for the revenge for his father's death lay there. There might even be a sense of justice in the execution of the king—that is, if he were not in fact the king.

The trial continued all week in Westminster Hall—a very public affair. Many were the stories that circulated among the people. Mostly they told how the king was being humiliated. He had been shown no respect by his judges. They had all kept their hats on, and when the head fell off his silver cane, he had been obliged to pick it up himself. This pathetic illustration of his loss of power and dignity touched Simon's heart, but it seemed that even now the king was failing to appreciate that he could no longer expect unwilling subjects to obey. He had lost their respect, and Simon was fervently hoping that he would win it back by agreeing to Parliament's terms.

By the end of the week the crisis had worsened. The king refused to accept the court's legitimacy and enter a plea. Therefore, the court proceeded as if the king had pleaded guilty. Finally through political lobbying, fifty-nine members were persuaded to sign the death warrant, and the execution set for January 30. Soon the city was in an uproar at the news of the king's imminent execution.

Chapter 30

Many of those thronging the streets of London could remember the grandeur of King Charles' coronation. It had been a five-hour ceremony loaded with symbolism and tradition dating back to the first sainted king of England, Edward the Confessor. No one had been left in any doubt that he believed himself to have been consecrated by God as king. Nor could they possibly have imagined that the day would come when not only his crown but his very head would be cleaved from his body.

Unable to believe that Parliament would actually follow through with their plans to execute the monarch, Simon felt propelled to Whitehall along with a great crowd of men and women who had lived with political and religious upheaval for six long years and who were becoming desensitized to it and anxious to know where it might end! Simon's feet moved relentlessly along the road toward the River Thames from where he could be ferried to Whitehall. He was forced to wait for a barge as a sea of people surged forward, intense and full, like the river at full tide as it pressed toward the sea.

Simon had not eaten, and hunger pains gnawed at his stomach. Waves of nausea rose up at the thought of what he was about to see.

"Surely the king will agree to toleration." It was a desperate hope. "Oh, God, let us not bring the blood guilt of killing the king on ourselves!" He was unaware that he had prayed out loud until a man pressed up against him in the crush added his amen.

"Yes! Amen! Maybe the Lord will stretch out his mighty arm and stay this madness!" But with every step he knew that this day the heavens were as brass and that the spirits of violence and death that had rampaged over the nation would soon turn against the man who had opened the door to them. His feet felt like lead, and it was only the press around him that kept him moving forward. As he turned a corner into Whitehall, there suddenly before him was the scaffold on an elevated platform draped in black outside the Banqueting House, which ironically had been designed by Inigo Jones to celebrate the glories of the Stuart dynasty. Simon knew it was too late for either justice or mercy, for both had failed.

Soldiers from the New Model Army stood at the front of the crowd and on the scaffold. Recognizing one of them as a comrade from his army days, Simon pushed his way through the crowd until he was close enough to call out to him.

"James! James! Why this tyranny? I scarce thought to see you involved in such a vulgar crime! Tell them to halt! This cannot be!"

"Stand back, man! Today we liberate England from a tyrant!"

Simon looked up as the king climbed through one of the windows of the banqueting hall and out onto the elevated scaffold. A hush fell on the crowd. The January day was bitterly cold, but it was not the temperature that sent a shiver down Simon's spine. There before the vast crowd stood the monarch of the nation clad in a simple shirt. He removed the splendid onyx and diamond Order of St. George insignia from around his neck and gave it to his attending bishop. Simon was close enough now to hear the king's last words, "I go from a corruptible to an incorruptible crown." He appeared calm, and after he prayed briefly, he placed his head on the scaffold, more as a martyr to the absolute rule of kings than as a victim of politics. In one swift blow it was removed from his body. If the soldiers had expected the crowd to join them in their cheers, they were disappointed, for all that issued forth from the king's subjects was a loud groan followed by an eerie silence.

Simon along with many others stood stunned by the enormity of what had just taken place. Suddenly the silence was broken by the screams of a young woman behind him.

"They've killed the king! They've killed the king!" she screamed at no one in particular. Simon turned and recognized his servant girl, Abigail. As the soldiers celebrated the success of their mission by holding up the bleeding head of the king, she began to run hysterically away from the sight, but the press of the crowd behind her made it impossible to put much distance between herself and the horror she had just witnessed.

"Abigail! Abigail! Stop!" He ran after her, apprehending her and forcing her to a standstill.

"They've killed the king," she sobbed, covering her face as if to blot out the horror.

"Hush, Abigail. Hush!" He tried to quiet her, but in shock himself, he was hardly able to offer comfort, only to stop the hysterics.

"Come, Abigail, we will walk home together over the bridge since it will be a precarious business securing a barge today."

Abigail fell into step beside him, and they walked in silence along the Strand until Abigail burst forth again.

"Oh, Mister Brierley, sir, who will reign over us now?"

"It seems we are ruled by the sword, Abigail, so no doubt the army will attempt to rule." Ever since Colonel Pride had forcibly removed from the Parliament all Presbyterians and those in favor of negotiating with the king, there had been little doubt in Simon's mind that that was the case.

They turned south over London Bridge, where the river was full and its cold, dark waters flowed swiftly down to the sea, as if even they were running away from the horror that had just overtaken the nation. Farther downriver Simon could see sailing vessels, their skeleton masts and spars stretching out against a dull gray sky. It was no weather for sailing, but Simon longed to sail away from this land of death and disorder to a new world, where hope might again rise up and inspire him to believe once more in Christian brotherhood. He pondered on the fact that it had almost been thirty years since the Pilgrims from Retford had sailed to the New World with its tiny band. By now there must have been a sizeable colony, and he wondered if Josiah and Martha had settled there successfully.

Chapter 31

While most of England mourned the king, soldiers of the New Model Army were celebrating their success. At Haresby Hall the Roundheads were in high spirits. Although the hour was late, Matilda was in the kitchen baking pies, for the soldiers planned to feast.

"It breaks my heart to see that poor Mr. Duncan confined in that tiny room, while the rebels have the run of the place. They haven't even the decency to care for it!" she said to old Jacob. She glanced around the kitchen, checking for eavesdroppers. "And that Edmund Whyte ought to know better and not be so busy with his soldiering that he's forgetting there's work to be done on this land." She brushed flour from her hands and placed them on her ample hips.

"If you ask me there is nothing good coming from that religion! They are just getting all fired up for nothing! Just look at this place! If Mistress Eleanor were to see it, 'twould break her heart! Don't tell me that the Almighty is in favor of locking up gentlemen in their own homes!"

"The man was at his prayers when I took up his breakfast," answered old Jacob.

"You mean, Mr. Duncan? Well may the good Lord answer him and get him out of there and back to his poor wife!"

It was as Matilda continued vehemently kneading the pastry that she fastened on a plan to be the answer to Duncan's prayer. When Duncan received his soup tureen, he was surprised to find a thin coiled rope inside it with a scribbled and misspelled note to say that a horse would be saddled and ready in the stables when indicated by a flash from Jacob's lantern.

It had been a long time since old Jacob had saddled a horse; however, he was sick of the rudeness of the Roundheads, and it would be good to know that Mistress Eleanor would have her husband by her side, even if she was unable to inhabit her home. For that he would make the effort. They would never suspect he had had a hand in aiding Duncan's escape. Duncan quickly burned the note. If he could climb through the window onto the flat roof below, he could secure the rope around one of the merlons and climb down from there. He would then be at the back of the house, and from there it would be easy to gain access to the stables under the cover of darkness.

Matilda and the maids were once again setting the banqueting table, but this time for the revelry of the soldiers.

"Put out plenty of the strong ale and wine," she instructed. "And make sure the guard outside Mr. Duncan's room has a bottle to himself. And I shall make sure the food is plentiful enough to keep them feasting until late into the night."

Matilda kept her word, and the table was spread with venison, pies filled with rabbit, pigeon and mutton, fresh bread and pastries. The ten men posted at Haresby drank to the health of the army and to Cromwell, its commander, with much bravado.

When Jacob saw Edmund Whyte take his seat at the table, he hurried out to the stables to saddle up a horse. Edmund was shocked to find most of them had already enjoyed more ale and wine than was proper.

"Men, you have drunk more than is fitting for a soldier of the realm."

"Nay, sir, the realm is gone, and we are now living in a free country!"

"Then let us behave with a little dignity, lest we gain a reputation for indecency!"

"And who are you to tell us what to do?"

"Aye! You are the gardener, not the lord of the manor!"

"Lord Edmund, sire!" mocked another, doffing his hat and bowing outrageously.

"Enough! Enough!" yelled the captain, jumping to his feet. "Eat your victuals and be at peace, men! This is no time for disputing!" The men settled down, and Edmund helped himself to food and wine; however, finding the atmosphere full of contention, he left with his trencher and goblet to eat in his own home.

Outside Duncan slid down the rope at the signal from Jacob and made for the stables, where he found a mare saddled and bridled in the stall. Jacob faded away into the night, and Duncan took the reins and led it toward the door, his hand over its muzzle. As he reached the doorway, he heard the snap of a pistol being cocked and looked up to find Edmund Whyte's silhouette blocking the doorway.

"So you think to leave us, sir?"

"Edmund, let me pass! Parliament has control. What good will it do to kill me, save make a widow of my wife?"

"It will do me no good to let you go."

"You have less to lose than your former mistress, who kept you on at Haresby, even though she knew you were a supporter of the Roundheads, so that your wife and family would not be homeless!" Edmund slowly lowered his pistol. There was silence. Duncan heard nothing but the beating of his own heart as he waited with bated breath.

"Make haste! I will give you time to clear the property before I raise the alarm."

"You have no need to raise the alarm. I am no criminal. The guard will discover my escape soon enough."

"Go then! For the sake of my lady, go!"

Duncan leapt into the saddle and urged the horse to a gallop as soon as he was out of earshot of the hall. Edmund returned to where he had found the rope dangling from the open window, and leaving it there, he returned to replenish his trencher. He found the men considerably the worse for the wine. It would be easy enough to blame them for lack of watchfulness.

Duncan rode through the night, pressing on under the cover of darkness to arrive at a hostelry he knew to be owned by a Royalist sympathizer. It was bitterly cold, and his fingers were so numb he could scarcely hold the reins. He missed his riding cloak that had been stolen by the Roundheads, and the freezing fog permeated to his very bones. The mare was tiring, and the saddle was badly fitted. At dawn he was glad to see the warm brick walls of The Swan appear through the mist. He approached cautiously, looking for any signs of Roundhead presence, but the place was quiet. He turned into the inn yard and let the mare drink at the water trough. Then he found a stall for her in the stables. He unsaddled her himself and found oats in a sack. No one stirred, so he decided to stay in the relative warmth and security of the stables until he could be sure of finding the innkeeper awake. He decided to climb up into the hay loft, and he promptly fell asleep.

Presently he was awakened by the loud quacking of ducks on the pond near the stables, and he rolled onto one side to spy from behind a bale of hay. As he had hoped, it was the hostler come to ready the horses for other guests. The latter was startled to see another horse in the stall and even more alarmed when Duncan jumped down in front of him from the hay loft.

"Good day to you, sir!" Duncan greeted him.

"You surely haven't spent all night in here!" exclaimed the other when he recovered his equilibrium.

"No, indeed, I have ridden all night to escape from being a prisoner of the Roundheads, and I thought it wise to make sure if you were friend or foe."

"I see you have stabled your own horse."

"Yes, though she is much the worse for being ridden so hard."

"As it seems are you, sir."

"Yes. I am badly in need of hot oatmeal porridge and bread and cheese."

"Then you will find the cook in kitchen and the master serving the guests, sir."

Duncan lost no time in hurrying inside.

"Duncan Talbot. Good morning," he introduced himself.

"I scarce recognized you, Mr. Talbot. You look as though you have fallen on hard times."

"Indeed, I did, sir. I have just escaped from being a prisoner of the Roundheads and find myself without money or goods with which I might pay for my breakfast."

"Then you shall eat for free and pay me on your next visit. And you must wash and tidy yourself, lest you frighten your lady wife on your return."

"I'm most grateful, sir.

"You have heard, of course, of the king's execution?"

"Oh, aye, the army was making much of their success. But by killing one king, they have made another. His son, Charles, is now the rightful heir, even though he is in exile in France."

"News is that the 'Rump' Parliament—as they call themselves—will abolish the monarchy altogether."

"Trying to rule this nation without a king will be like trying to control a chicken with its head cut off. Most of its citizens are law-abiding. But the present anarchy has made them insecure, and who knows what they will do now!"

"Quite so, sir. Now when you have eaten, you may use one of the guest rooms to wash and shave, and I shall send the maid with hot water and towels. You will be anxious to be getting back to Tadcaster no doubt."

"I am indeed, sir. I am much obliged for your hospitality."

"I understand you have fought well for the king, sir, and I would not have you hungry."

Duncan considered the possibility of resting a little before he traveled on, but he decided against delaying further. He could travel faster by daylight, and he was well out of the clutches of the men at Haresby. It seemed that Edmund had kept his promise.

Whereas Duncan had news of the nation's fortunes, he'd had none at all of his own family—of Eleanor's health, of the birth of his child. His thoughts went back to the wedding in the church at Haresby and how elegant Eleanor had looked in her wedding gown. Now dispossessed of her home and family fortunes, she still retained her dignity, even in pregnancy; however, her spirit was crushed, and she thought of little else except how she could regain Haresby. And he had only bad news to share. Maybe the birth of their child had given her another reason to live—something to treasure more than she treasured the stone walls of her family home.

At last the ivy-covered walls of The Grange came into view. The mare was all but spent, and so was he. He almost fell out of the saddle and walked the mare into the stables to leave her in the capable hands of the hostler. It was worth the long ride home to see Eleanor's look of surprise and delight when he strode into the parlor in his riding boots.

"Duncan! My love!" Eleanor's head reeled with the suddenness of the reality of Duncan's presence. For so long she had longed for this moment, and to have Duncan suddenly standing before her had an air of unreality. It had begun to seem like an impossible dream, and she had all but given up hope of seeing him alive again.

"Eleanor, my love!" Words were superfluous as they embraced. Then they were joined by his father and mother, who were equally ecstatic at the reappearance of their son.

"So you escaped from the rebels?"

"Yes, with some help from old Jacob and Matilda, I did, though I thought to be shot when Edmund Whyte encountered me as I led out the horse. Thankfully the fellow relented when I appealed to his sense of loyalty to you, Eleanor."

"Then he did not disappoint me in the end."

"It would have been unforgiveable to kill the father of your child, Eleanor, after your patience with him, and thank God he had enough conscience left to admit it."

"And you do have a son, Duncan."

"Yes, a perfect little fellow," added his mother.

"Proper little Talbot too," joined in his father.

"Then I must see him, Eleanor!"

"Yes, indeed! He was born on the eve of the new year, and I hoped it was a sign that this year would bring us better fortune than last!"

"Then he is five weeks old. Did you give him the name we chose?"

"Edgar Duncan Talbot. Had you not returned, I would have called him by his second name. As it has happily turned out, we shall call him Edgar. I was waiting in hope of your return for his christening."

They had reached the nursery, and Duncan peered into the crib to see the tiny features of his son in peaceful sleep.

"So innocent," mused Duncan. "How is it that men become vile enough to stoop to kill their brothers?"

"I know not, Duncan. Let us hope the land returns to peace and order before our little Edgar is old enough to care about it!"

Chapter 32

On the eve of Duncan's escape Edmund had decided it would be prudent to be seen in the hall with the men. In any case Matilda's apple pies were very good and the last he would taste for a while since Matilda must surely have used all the apples in the store. On his return though, he had found the men brawling again and the captain unable to restrain them. What had sparked off this hostility he never discovered, but his respect for the men with whose cause he had united slid further down the scale from disappointment to disillusion.

"Ye shall know them by their fruits" were words that echoed around his mind as he retreated to the cottage that had been his home for as long as he could remember. His wife was in bed but woke when she heard his footsteps on the wooden stairs.

"It's late, Edmund."

"Yes, my love, the men celebrate the demise of the king and the advent of the new reign of true godliness." Emily did not answer, unsure how to interpret his answer. He lay for a while, thinking about what he had just said, for his words refused to line up with the scene he had just witnessed. He tossed and turned, trying to ignore his thoughts and find sleep, but despite his tiredness, sleep evaded him. He thought back to the days when, as an esteemed member of the household, Eleanor had entrusted him to oversee the maintenance of the entire estate—gardens, pastures, and woods. Now no one valued him or his work. The woods were full of poachers, the pastures ill-managed, and the gardens overgrown and ruined by the careless boots of soldiers and their horses.

He had believed it right to fight for religious freedom, but now it seemed that his Christian brethren were more bent on violence than showing any kind of reverence for man, property, or God. Sensing his inner turmoil his wife put a solicitous hand on his shoulder.

"Edmund, whatever disturbs you so?"

For answer he poured out the sad reflections of his troubled heart. Finally he concluded, "Mistress Eleanor took good care of us, Emily. I just pray her husband arrives safely home."

"You mean you have released him?"

"Aye ... well, he escaped—no doubt the servants gave him aid. I discovered him leading a horse from the stables, but how could I prevent him when all the while we enjoy the home Eleanor provided? But hush now! Not a word! The captain will blame the men for their drunkenness and lack of care for their duties, and I shall say nothing."

"It's not the way I envisioned it might be now we have no king to fight. Where is the peace we have fought for all this time?"

"We must be patient, my love. I shall keep myself occupied as I used to, caring for this estate before it fails to support us. We took it from Mistress Eleanor, and we must maintain it in proper order. If we do not, it will cease to provide for us."

"Then where would we go?" Her question echoed the one in his mind. It was a question that remained unanswered for a while, but it remained nonetheless.

Chapter 33

When Edgar was almost three years old, what Eleanor and Duncan had been hoping for happened. Prince Charles returned to fight for his crown.

Sunshine filled the walled garden of The Grange, and Eleanor was enjoying watching her son collecting daisies from the lawn. He formed a tiny posy, and clutching it proudly in his tiny hand, he ran to present it to his mother. Eleanor smiled.

"You're going to be as gallant as your father," she said and chuckled.

"Daddy … see Daddy?"

"He's gone to fight for the king."

"Why?"

"Because he needs to get the crown back."

"Why?" Edgar was demonstrating the usual curiosity of a young child whose mind is not yet controlled by worldviews he has learned from his superiors. *Why* was a word he used often.

"Because bad men took it away."

"Why?"

"Because they were wicked."

"Why?"

"Because they were fighting."

"Daddy wicked?"

"No!" Eleanor laughed and decided that the subject was far too complicated for the mind of a child to comprehend.

"Daddy coming home?" This was a question Eleanor would have liked to answer, but could not.

"I don't know, Edgar." She sighed, lifted him up, sat down on the wooden bench at the edge of the lawn, and set him on her lap. She hugged him, enjoying the comfort of his little face next to her own. His childish love was reassuring.

No, she thought, *Duncan was not wrong to fight. He was nobly endeavoring to see justice done, the rebels put down once and for all, and what was rightfully hers returned to her.* As she watched Edgar, his attention on the flowers in his tiny fingers, she fervently hoped his father's efforts were bearing fruit.

Duncan's father had been at pains to muster troops for Prince Charles' cause; however, many of the men on his list had been killed or wounded in the battles led by King Charles I, and many others were disillusioned. At last Duncan had ridden off with a group of cavaliers, their red sashes bright in the dull morning. Eleanor had watched them go, watched the jostle of horse flesh and heard the sound of hooves mixed with the shouts of the men. They rode with purpose to recapture the crown, the lost power of the crown over England. Theirs was the duty to do justice to those who had dethroned the king. They were ready to take vengeance on all who stood opposed to royalty. Children stood wide-eyed and waved at the spectacle, ignorant of the blood about to fall again on English soil.

They rode west to join the Earl of Derby in Royalist Lancashire. Duncan had high hopes that with the Scottish troops that were marching down from the north with Prince Charles and Sir David Leslie, they would stand a fair chance of defeating Cromwell's troops. Charles expected the Royalist west to support him, but he was disappointed. Then an unexpected battle at Wigan cost them the lives of many officers and men. By the time Charles reached the Royalist stronghold of Worcester, he had less than sixteen thousand troops. Meanwhile Cromwell was sweeping down through eastern England in anticipation of a Royalist attack on London with thirty thousand troops.

Chapter 34

In rural Worcestershire a young man was returning from the mill empty-handed, for the land, desolate with the bloodshed upon it, had failed to produce enough of a harvest to feed its people. Concerned for his wife and newborn child, he was considering walking to the next village to try to obtain flour—or even wheat if he could get it—but as he approached his cottage, he saw three cavalier soldiers enter it. Fear for his wife sprang up into his throat and stifled his breath as he pushed homeward as fast as he could.

The young woman leaned forward to put the baby in the cradle, carefully so as not to waken him. His tiny features were peaceful. Then she stood composed to face her intruders—three men clad in leather tunics, woolen britches, and riding boots.

"We have no bread or ale," she said truthfully, for they had finished the ale that morning. She had not baked bread for three days, as she had had no flour with which to bake.

"Then we'll take what you have! The king's men have need of it." Without waiting for an invitation, they raided the larder of cheese, pickled pork, and eggs.

"And what are we to eat then? For pity's sake leave us food!"

"Stop your whining, wench! The men are hungry and must eat. How are starving men to win this country from the rebels?"

"Sire, I have a babe to feed, and I must eat too!" For an answer he pushed her roughly, and she tottered backward against the table.

They were distracted by a musket shot in the street, and the three men departed. Mary peered from the window to discover a man lying in a pool of blood. Others stood by in shock, as the gun smoke dissipated and the man's lifeblood drained away.

"This is what happens to those who refuse to join with the king!" the musketeer announced to the gathered crowd.

The young woman watched, her hands clasped over her mouth in horror, sobs choking in her throat. The man whose life had been so brutally and suddenly taken was hers.

Other men were gathered and were marched away like sheep at shearing time, leaving her alone with her dead. He was buried with due respect, the single bell intoning its monotonous, mournful tones over the countryside, which mourned more than the death of one man. The very land itself was mourning the violence that had been wrought upon it.

On the other side of the hedge a fox crept away into its lair. Today was not a good day for hunting. Today people were watching, and the stalker might too easily become the prey. Today was a day to lie low and wait for a more opportune time. Prince Charles might have learned a lesson from the fox and stayed in France rather than attempting too soon to turn the tide of events in his favor.

At Worcester the rivers Teme and Severn created tactical difficulties that the prince hoped to exploit, but Cromwell had spent three days building bridges of boats and was able to cross and attack the Royalist armies grouped south of the city on the northern bank of the River Teme. The foot soldiers on the eastern side were also defeated, and the prince, positioned at the top of the cathedral tower, watched as his men were routed. A courageous charge by two of his officers gave him a chance to escape on a fresh horse and avoid capture. The last battle of the civil war had ended where it had begun nine years previously, and Cromwell stood before God and gave thanks for the crowning mercy of this wonderful victory.

In and around Worcester lay the dead and the dying and those too wounded to flee. Many of those who fled were captured and brought in to Cromwell—officers to be executed or imprisoned in the tower and others to be shipped to Barbados to work on the sugar plantation. The nation was beginning to populate the colonies with those it desired to punish.

Chapter 35

Darkness was falling, and Duncan, wounded in the charge, barely made it out of the city gate. He was bleeding profusely, but his horse was unhurt. With the red sash discarded, he thought to make haste along the road that led north, but with all the roads being watched for the prince, he realized that there was little chance of escaping capture by the army or their sympathizers. In any case he was rapidly becoming weaker through loss of blood, and just when he felt he no longer had strength to stay in the saddle, he found a small barn in the village of Hartley.

In the moonless night the darkness in the barn was total. Finding his hand on a post, he tethered his horse to it and was relieved when it found hay and quieted since there was only a small piece of land between it and a cottage. He listened for clues that might tell him whether he was among friends or not, but before he could find out, he lost consciousness.

Presently the back door of the cottage opened, and an old man walked down the little path toward the barn, carrying a lantern. The old man was too deaf to hear the movements of the horse, but sensing the presence of intruders, he lifted the lantern high. He discovered the body of a man lying in a pool of blood.

Shocked, he hurried back inside to summon his wife, who returned with him.

"It seems he is dead. Royalist I should think by the look of his clothes." The woman bent down to examine Duncan's face, and detecting breath, she motioned to the man for more light.

"It seems he breathes still. Let us pray he may survive." Duncan's handsome face lay white and still on the straw, a pool of red blood oozing from his arm.

I'll fetch a bandage to bind up that wound. He may yet survive."

Duncan regained consciousness to find himself being stripped of his jacket, and then an elderly woman proceeded to bandage his arm. He was too weak to speak, but it seemed he was among friends. Later they carried him indoors and propped him up on a couch so that he could drink some hot broth.

"I thought you were ready for the grave, young man, but the good Lord has spared you."

"The prince's men lost the battle?" asked the man.

Duncan nodded, remembering the harrowing defeat. It was too painful to think about—all hope for the monarchy gone.

"'Tis a sad day for England," mourned the woman.

Duncan, sure now that he was among friends, introduced himself. "Duncan Talbot, son of Lord Talbot of Tadcaster," he said, proffering the hand of his good arm.

"Agatha and Matthew," said the old man. "You may stay with us until you are well enough to ride home."

Despite the fact that Duncan saw neither rosary nor crucifix, it was evident that Agatha and Matthew were Catholics from their prayers and their daily conversation. He did not have to ask. Their care of him undoubtedly flowed from hearts that respected human life and a belief that they ought to do unto others as they would that others should do unto them.

The wound on Duncan's arm had been inflicted by a Roundhead sword; however, it was a simple flesh wound, and under Agatha's care it was healing nicely. Her chicken broth and good bread restored his body, but his mind was taking longer to heal. The savagery of the battle had ravaged his heart, and the defeat of the king meant the loss of all hope for a brighter future. It irked him that Eleanor still did not know whether he was dead or alive or imprisoned, for news of the horrible defeat would have reached her by now. He was also concerned that in their mood of jubilation the Parliament and the army might take further action against those known to have opposed them.

The tranquility and kindness that surrounded him was balm to his soul after the clamor of fighting and the ignominy of defeat, but he was impatient to be on the road again. The little cottage hidden away from main roads was a sanctuary, but his horse stabled in the tiny barn was in danger of being discovered by passersby, and locals would know that his fine black mount belonged to a visitor. With the nation more thoroughly under Cromwell's control, he was nervous. Had he known that ships laden with prisoners were sailing for Barbados, he would have been even more nervous.

After a week he deemed himself well enough to undertake the trip back to Tadcaster. Agatha provided bread, cheese, and fresh apples for his journey, and he packed them into his saddlebags. He filled two water bottles from the well and tied them to his saddle. To be on the safe side, he had Agatha cut his hair. Short hair would make him look like a Puritan and avoid suspicion of being a Royalist soldier. With his sword arm still stiff and sore, he felt vulnerable. He would have to keep a sharp lookout for both highwaymen and those looking for Royalist soldiers. He could yet end up a prisoner awaiting execution or find himself transported to Barbados.

Chapter 36

The eagle owl spread its wings and glided silently through the forest. Without a warning sound the mouse was soon ambushed, and it was all over. The owl retired to its perch in the thick oak, gulped down its prey, and blinked. Perched in the oak tree, Prince Charles was silent witness to the demise of the mouse and determined all the more not to fall prey to those who hunted him. He would wait it out in the foliage of the oak until they abandoned their search, called off the dogs, and retired to the liquid comforts of the tavern.

The owl took off in search of another meal, and Charles remembered his own hunger. Darkness and lack of success was enough to discourage the hunters, and the barking of the dogs faded into stillness. From their perch in the oak tree at the edge of the coppice, Charles and Major William Careless had watched soldiers searching the woods. Night settled like a blanket, and Careless suggested they return to the lodge. Charles needed no persuasion. He was used to being in the saddle all day, hunting for pleasure, but tonight he was weary of body and soul. His hope of restoring the English crown was shattered, his spirit crushed.

Unlike the owl and Cromwell, his stealth had proved insufficient, and the New Model Army had routed his Royalist troops. Personal involvement in the battle had been a necessity, but it was his head they wanted just as they had wanted his father's head. Now flight was the only option. He envied the owl the ease and silence of its flight. Silence was what he most needed now, for should news of his whereabouts reach the ears of Cromwell, all hopes of the restoration of the English crown would probably die with him.

Over a chicken dinner they were told the latest news. The Penderel brothers had reconnoitered the area and found it unsafe. While Charles slept on a pallet in the secret hiding place, the brothers kept watch. Charles would rather have been a guest at the hunting lodge for more pleasurable reasons, but in the present necessity he was grateful for the protection it offered and the chance to plot an escape to the coast from where he could secure a boat back to France. Boscobel House, home of a Catholic family, was provided with a priest hole from where he could escape to the garden, but he had spent enough time in hiding. The sooner he could leave the shores of England, the sooner his head would feel secure on his shoulders.

The attempt to make good his escape over the Severn and into Wales and to the seaport of Swansea had proved fruitless since he and Richard Penderel had discovered the crossing places over the Severn guarded by Cromwell's men. After they walked the nine miles to Madeley, they'd had no option but to shelter in a sympathizer's barn until dark and then walk back to Boscobel. There they'd arrived footsore and weary at three o'clock in the morning. After several sleepless nights Prince Charles was glad of the comfort of the small pallet and the security of knowing that others were keeping watch.

Charles rose early and after his devotions spent some time watching the road from Tong to Brentwood from the gallery near the secret place. Their host was not known to buy meat, and to do so would have raised suspicion, so William Careless helped himself to a sheep from a neighbor's fold and killed it. Charles shared in the labor of cooking it, and after breakfast much of the day was spent in the arbor in the back garden. On a happier occasion he would have enjoyed this rural retreat, but the present crisis weighed heavily on him. It had been agreed that John Penderel be sent to enlist the help of Lord Wilmot at Moseley Old Hall a few miles east, and there was nothing he could do but wait. After four days on the run the strain was beginning to tell.

At Moseley Old Hall it was discovered that Lord Wilmot had gone to Bentley Hall five miles away with the intention of riding to Bristol with Colonel Lane's sister as a pillion passenger. It was decided that the Penderel brothers should bring Charles to Moseley Old Hall, where Wilmot would meet them, and that Charles should travel to Bristol disguised as the servant of Jane Lane.

In the early hours of Wednesday, September 10, Charles was pacing up and down the stable yard, striking his left hand with the one glove he had not lost. Other figures appeared, and then they all melted into the darkness.

"Pray God he will deliver them safely to Bristol!" whispered the groom.

"Aye! The hopes of three kingdoms depend on that!" agreed the maidservant. "We can do no more, sire. Come inside. We will need to wait patiently for news of his majesty now."

They did wait silently and anxiously, mindful of the proclamation that had gone out for the arrest of the prince and of any found harboring or helping him and the promised reward of one thousand pounds for anyone assisting in his capture. They had to wait a long six weeks before the welcome news of the prince's escape to France reached their ears.

Chapter 37

On a morning in September 1653 Simon surveyed Tall Chimneys as he returned from the church. Smoke curled up into the gray London sky, and yellow leaves hung limp on the plane trees. At a distance of fifty or so paces he paused, his black hat covering his short hair, thigh-length cape draped over his shoulders, and black britches tapering into black boots. He stood for a while, leaning on the cane he now used as an aid to his wounded leg, obviously in deep consideration over an issue, reluctant to arrive at home before his deliberations were successfully concluded. His eyes wandered over the house, drinking in the sight of it until he appeared to resolve an issue. Pressing his lips together more tightly and tossing the cane up a little way before catching it again, he resumed his journey.

Feathers fell at his feet as he lifted the latch of the front door because of the rapid departure of the resident swallow from her nest.

"Time for you to be going too," he said softly to the uncaring bird. It was early in September, migration time, when they would gather and fly south to Africa until the cold English winter was over. Migration was what Simon had on his mind too, but not to Africa. The swallows' high-pitched whistle as they gathered on the rooftops echoed the excitement within his own heart.

There had been several signs—circumstances really—that had persuaded him that the time was right to follow in the footsteps of Josiah and Martha to the New World. It was becoming more and more difficult to afford the upkeep of a home that was really unnecessarily large and the several servants needed to run it. His congregation, unsympathetic to his

Puritan doctrines, were refusing to pay their tithes and complaining to the bishop about his passionate preaching and lengthy sermons. Added to that, his mother and sister were still complaining about living in London, and Nell was finding it more and more difficult to tolerate Mary's high-minded ways, especially since the arrival of their second child, Verity. Simon recalled Nell's complaints at Mary's chiding when the children were just playing as children and how more than once she had scooped up both children in her arms and retreated to her own living room. It was time for change.

As he considered his options, some doors were closing, and the one that was opening the widest was the door to the New World. Earning a living, Simon decided, was going to be just as difficult in England as on the other side of the Atlantic. He could, he reckoned, farm or trade equally well in either land, and in the New World he would at least have the freedom to dwell with those of the same religious persuasions and avoid the continual hassle of trying to either fit in with or change the established church of which he had become a servant. He could no more stop the flow of the River Thames, he decided. It would continue after he had left much as it had for the last fifty years.

The previous week a letter had arrived, delivered by a messenger and dispatched by a friend of Josiah's who was revisiting his home shores. It contained both good news and bad. The lifestyle was hard and had been particularly difficult during the winter, but they had found true fellowship among their neighbors, had built a home from the local timber, and were making a good living from their small parcel of land. Josiah had been blessed to find a market for the silver utensils he was crafting. More than anything they were enjoying the freedom their independence had brought them and urged Simon and Nell to join them.

It was time to speak to his mother and sister about the need to sell Tall Chimneys and buy a smaller dwelling, perhaps in Worcestershire if they wished. He decided to do so over supper that night.

"Mother, I have been considering our present predicament. We can no longer afford to keep Tall Chimneys and so many servants. I have been considering selling this house and buying a smaller dwelling, one in Worcestershire if you like. I know you and Mary still miss Hartley. We could look for a suitable dwelling where you would be happy." Their response to this news was positive.

"Oh, yes, we should have done it long ago!" declared Mary.

"Why smaller?" asked his mother. "What about the servants?"

"Mother, we simply can't afford the upkeep of a large house and so many servants anymore. The money we had when father died has all gone. My congregation is refusing to pay their tithes and complaining to the bishop, so soon I shall be without a salary. Prices are escalating due to the poor harvests and—" he hesitated before he continued, "and Nell and I are being guided to sail to the New World."

Stunned silence was his answer as both his mother and sister gazed at him wide-eyed and open-mouthed. Finally Mary spoke.

"So you are leaving us, Simon? Two women on our own!"

"You are leaving us to fend for ourselves, taking the grandchildren away across the sea!" continued Margaret.

"Yes, mother, we are. But you will not be alone. Oliver and Thomas will be with you to care for the horses and the grounds and cut firewood."

"But how will we live, Simon? We will be without income!"

"No, mother, we will make a handsome profit from the sale of Tall Chimneys, and we will find a home in Worcestershire for a much more reasonable price than here in London and invest the surplus in such a way as to provide for you. We will make sure you and Mary are well provided for."

"Well, I can see you have it all worked out, Simon!" said his mother.

"It's a mercy, I suppose, that we shall have a roof over our heads!" said Mary.

A loud banging on the door precluded any response to Mary's sarcasm. Simon stood to answer it; however, the door flew open, and two uniformed men thrust Abigail, the maidservant through the door.

"It seems this is your maid, sir! She has just been found with a collection of bones in her petticoat pocket, and it seems she took them from here!" said the sergeant.

"We went to rescue her from the attack of a stray dog, and then we found out what the dog was after—the bones in her pocket! She's not the innocent little maid we thought," continued the other soldier. "Now tell me, miss. What might you be doing with bones in your pocket, eh?"

"I'm sorry, ma'am, sir," she began addressing Simon and Margaret. "I have taken in a little dog. He is so thin and starved, poor thing! I took the bones to feed him, ma'am. They were discarded, ma'am."

"I suggest she took them to lay them against someone's door! 'Twas witchcraft you had in mind, wench, not a dog!"

"No, sir! Please I did not, sir!" Abigail pleaded.

Margaret, who had been temporarily rendered speechless by the sudden intrusion, found her voice again.

"My servants are good Christian men and women, sir! I can assure you our Abigail would not be involving herself in witchcraft. Now take your leave if you please. We have no need of the army to keep our servants in order!"

The soldiers were in no hurry to obey her sharp command but stood where they were, one on either side of Abigail, wearing their new uniforms.

"We have orders from Cromwell, madam, to rid this nation of witches."

Margaret drew herself up to her full height and faced him defiantly.

"There are no witches in this house. We keep a strict observance here!"

The soldiers let go of Abigail's arms.

"Madam, we are watching this neighborhood for those engaged in witchcraft. Be warned! If anyone in this neighborhood suffers a sudden misfortune, she will be swum!"

Simon, observing the look of terror on Abigail's face, sprang to her defense.

"And what kind of justice would that be! To be swum means certain death! If she drowned, she would be pronounced innocent. If she lived, she would be supposed guilty and hanged as a witch. And you call that God's justice! 'Tis nothing more that the fruit of superstition itself! Murderers! Get out of my house!"

For a moment Simon feared his passionate outburst had sparked a physical combat, as his unwelcome visitors moved toward him, but his mother intervened between them.

"That will not be necessary, sergeant! We shall say our prayers for the good folks in this neighborhood, and I keep no witches under my roof! Good day to you!"

"Very well, ma'am. We shall be watching." The men stood to attention and then turned sharply and took their leave. As the large oak door closed behind them, Margaret turned to Abigail, who was still quaking from her ordeal.

"You may return to your duties, and might I suggest you refrain from taking victuals or anything else from this house!"

"Yes, ma'am." She sobbed and hurried away to the kitchen.

"Now she will pray very diligently no doubt, so as to avoid the ducking stool." Simon's mother sank down on to her dining chair.

"Lord, have mercy on me! My son is leaving the country, and the army accuses me of having witches in my house!"

Later that night Nell's' face was softly illuminated by the glow of the candle as she sat at her private desk and read from the family Bible. Her reading lessons with Simon had paid off, and she treasured these moments when she could pore over the scriptures that had been closed to her for so long. Literacy gave her not only the joy of reading for herself. It was also appropriate to her status as Simon's wife, and it restored her self-esteem. Tonight she was reading the book of Psalms, her favorite. She read aloud as she still found it easier to pronounce the words out loud.

"And he led them forth by the right way, so that they might go to a city of habitation."

The words from Psalm 107 suddenly had personal meaning for her. Surely the Lord, who led his ancient people across a desert, could lead her and Simon to a city in the New World. Ever since Martha and Josiah had left, Simon had been restless, inspired by their vision to create a godly community in a nation not controlled by the institutional church. Nell was of the same mind. In a sense she had less to lose than Simon. She would leave behind no blood relatives. Nell's only concern was for their own children, Adam and Verity, and for the hardships they might face on the perilous sea journey and settling in a strange land. The Lord's Word gave her comfort. He would settle them. Surely it was his will they should go.

The candle flickered as Simon entered through the heavy oak door of their living room.

"Simon, look! A promise for us!" She showed him the word on the delicate page.

"Aye, Nell, we shall go to our new city and join the other pilgrims." She looked up into his earnest face, and he gazed down at hers, their eyes meeting in a pact that was at once serious and exciting.

"Nell, you were ever ready for a new adventure," said Simon, appreciating more than ever Nell's indomitable spirit. It had been her courage that had attracted him to her at first during that time at Josiah and Martha's as he had watched her recover from the grief and shock of Robert's death. Plenty of people mourned the loss of loved ones at that time, himself included, but Nell had lost all—her only known living relative.

Nell closed the book and blew out the candle. Another chapter in their lives was about to begin.

Abigail was going about her normal duties one morning when Nell realized she was sniffing and wiping away tears.

"Why, Abigail, what's the cause of this distress?" inquired Nell.

"My little dog died, ma'am, and you're leaving us. And where shall I find employment with so kind a mistress?"

"Sit down, girl, and wipe your face," instructed Nell kindly but firmly, for Abigail had been prone to emotional outbursts since the king's execution and the episode with the bones.

"Now tell me where your family is."

"My brother died in the fighting, ma'am, and I have no one else." Nell's sympathy was immediate. She knew the grief of being bereaved and alone.

"Oh, I'm so sorry, Abigail. You must pray that the good Lord will provide another home for you." Abigail nodded.

"Yes, ma'am." She had no idea that Nell had in fact done that very thing and seen an amazing answer to her prayers.

"You may be surprised where the Almighty takes you, Abigail. He has good plans for those who obey him."

Nell was seized with an idea that she later shared with Simon.

"The girl would be a good help in the New World, Simon. She can cook and sew and mind the children."

"Yes, she has a good heart," agreed Simon. "We'll ask her if she would be willing to travel with us and work for us as we settle there."

"I think she is also secretly afraid that she may be swum after the incident with the bones. There is such a fever of persecution of suspects. People see the Devil in such ordinary things, and most of it is nothing but fear and superstition!"

"She may well be pleased to leave Camberwell," said Simon. "You may ask her tomorrow, but tell her she is not to speak of it. We cannot afford the passage of more than one extra person."

Abigail was thrilled to be invited to leave with them and honored the secret. When they learned of Simon and Nell's plans to emigrate, Edward and Elizabeth donated three acres of land on which a house could be built for Margaret and Mary and the servants that would move with them. Margaret and Mary looked forward to the relative peace of Retford and to being close to family. Simon was assured that with the welfare of his mother and sister so established, he and Nell could leave for the New World, and preparations began.

Barrels of salted beef were delivered to be stored in their cellars. It would be fine fare indeed on the long sea voyage and precious supplies in the New World until they established themselves there. Simon would buy land, and they would farm it to sustain themselves. Until then they could live off the supplies they took with them as well as deer from the forests and fish from the rivers. They would build a simple log home and buy flour and other foodstuffs from local merchants. It would not be an easy life; however, Simon's faith was high, and he was spurred on by his vision of a new life—a life free from political wrangling and religious control. Maybe in the New World the hope that had been crushed by violence and bloodshed would find expression again. Maybe there he would find space to live again, and maybe he would find his place—that unique place that was his by destiny.

Chapter 38

It was February 1652, and Edmund Whyte was in the woods watching the filtered light play on a small waterfall in a shallow brook that gurgled on its way to join the River Witham. Two dead rabbits from his traps hung from his hand, so at least he and his family would eat, no matter what was going on at the hall. He sat on a log, enjoying the peace and seclusion of the woods. At least that had not changed. With the reduction of the army the resident redcoats had marched off to join another barracks, and Edmund had not left with them. The great house was deserted. Old Jacob had died and been put to rest in the graveyard. Matilda and the other servants, finding themselves unable to manage without other staff to provide food and firewood, had found work elsewhere. Edmund was in a reflective mood. No one it seemed was interested in the future of the house now that it had served its purpose in the war.

Edmund took the rabbits home to his wife, took the only horse from the stables, and rode up to the crest of the hill from where he could look down on the house. It stood still grand amidst its gardens but neglected and sad, brambles overtaking the kitchen garden and unpruned roses crawling over the flower beds. He had expected orders to come from Cromwell to commandeer it for some other purpose, but none had come forth. It would not be long, he reasoned, before its walls, lacking warmth and care, would simply begin to weather and crumble, and the beautiful home that had housed so many would become a useless ruin.

It was not just the fact that the house and all of the toil that had preserved it for so long was going to waste, but Edmund was having a deeper crisis in his own heart, a crisis of conscience. He had fought for religious freedom, for toleration, but despite the fact that the villagers were no longer fined for nonattendance at church, the gloom that was hanging over the nation under Cromwell's rule was oppressive. Here in the woods he felt free, but how long could he stand by and watch Haresby Hall disintegrate and do nothing about it? He had to face facts. He had been mistaken to join the Roundheads. He should have kept out of the war and kept his peace. He had preached much about free will, but had it been right to drive the rightful owners of Haresby away at the barrel of a gun? He resolved to try to make things right with his former mistress.

"There's a man to see you, ma'am, the same man who came before from the south," announced Eleanor's maid. Eleanor frowned, trying to remember the identity of the gentleman in question, and then she frowned some more when she remembered.

"Very well. Show him into the parlor, and I will be there in a moment." She took a moment to steel herself to see Edmund Whyte again. After the last unpleasant visit, she was unsure whether she ought to invite him in, but then he had allowed Duncan to escape. She left the maid with instructions that she was not to be disturbed unless she rang.

Edmund stood at her entrance into the parlor and bowed slightly.

"Mistress Eleanor, good morning. I hope my visit does not inconvenience you, ma'am."

"Good morning. It does not. But I hope to find it a more pleasant experience than your last visit, sir."

"Indeed, ma'am. I have come to set some things to right, ma'am, if I may." He had Eleanor's interest, and she nodded to him to continue.

"I first of all desire to apologize, ma'am, for my behavior on the last visit. I was rather unpleasant and have regretted my rudeness. I do pray you will forgive me, ma'am." Eleanor was intrigued.

"Why, yes, Edmund. What brings this change of heart?"

"It seems, ma'am, that the Roundheads have shown no respect to their fellow men in their pursuit of religious freedom. It seems to me that what started as a godly cause has run away downhill like a cart out of control and landed as a pile of broken firewood at the bottom, doing much harm on the way down. It was not the vision I signed up for, ma'am." He paused, and there ensued a rather awkward silence as Eleanor waited for him to continue.

"In any case I must tell you that Haresby Hall now sits empty and derelict since the soldiers who occupied it have been commissioned elsewhere, and I know not what is to become of it. I have done my best, ma'am, to care for the estate, but with no staff and no money, it is sadly in need of repair. Now I, too, am about to leave it, for I intend to take my family to the New World."

Eleanor was silent for a moment, digesting the information.

"I thank you for the good service you have done me in bringing this news and indeed for your labor at Haresby. Is there no news of plans for its future?"

"None that I know of, ma'am. It seems that with the end of the civil war the army has no need of it."

"And what of the servants?"

"Old Jacob died, and the others left to find other employment."

"And you too, it seems."

"Yes, ma'am. The Lord has blessed us with more children, and we have outgrown the little cottage. Moreover, a new fire burns in our spirits to seek to settle in a land without tyranny from monarch or military dictator, and for that we are willing to sail to the New World."

"And how will you live there?"

"We will live there as we do here, ma'am. I shall build a log house and fish and grow crops, and maybe later we shall be blessed with some livestock."

"But how will you gain land?"

"I shall indenture myself for three years, ma'am, to a settler who needs a servant, following which labor I shall receive my freedom and a parcel of land of my own."

"Does that mean you must go alone and leave your wife and family here?"

"Aye, ma'am. Then I shall send for them to come—if you would be so kind as to allow them to remain in the cottage until then."

"That is very wearisome indeed! Shall they not be in want without a father?"

"My wife is a good woman, ma'am. She will have the older children to help with chores." Eleanor looked solemn and sat in silence for a full minute, considering her thoughts.

"Mr. Whyte, would you not rather stay and help me rebuild Haresby Hall. I could build a larger home for you, and you would not have the inconvenience of uprooting to another land and being separated from your wife and family."

"Thank you, Mistress Eleanor. That would be a fine offer indeed, were it not for the fact that should Cromwell think he needs my services again, I should be conscripted into the army and my family would in any case be deprived of me."

"Is that likely?"

"I know not, ma'am, but having once enlisted, it is possible that my name is still on their list."

Eleanor was pensive again for a moment and then turned the conversation to Haresby Hall. "Is Haresby Hall secured?"

"Yes, ma'am." He reached into his leather pouch, a rare smile pushing into his thin cheeks and a twinkle in his eyes. "And here is the key!" He held out the large key to the main door. "The other doors are bolted on the inside, ma'am."

"Are you not under orders to deliver the key to the army?" asked Eleanor, taking the key, a look of wonder and delight on her face.

"No, ma'am, I buried it the day you fled, ma'am! 'Twas considered lost!" Tears welled up in Eleanor's eyes.

"You have been a champion all along, Edmund Whyte!"

"Yes, ma'am, but I was confounded about whose cause I might champion."

Behind Eleanor a man appeared, his blonde hair falling over his shoulders, his figure framed in the doorway. Eleanor turned toward him.

"Duncan! Look! Mr. Whyte has brought us the key to Haresby Hall!"

Their return to Haresby was not really made possible by the return of the key, but the key was a sign to them, a symbol. Without it the damaged and boarded walls at the rear of the house would have offered little resistance to their entry, but having the key to the main door seemed to be a sign from heaven that things had come full circle and that it was time to repossess what was rightfully theirs.

Eleanor insisted on riding rather than using the carriage. That way, she argued, they could better reconnoiter without attracting too much attention. It was mid-afternoon by the time they cantered their mounts into the courtyard. The sun's rays were slanting across the stone walls and patches of dappled sunlight illuminated daffodil heads bravely pushing up through the dark earth into the spring air.

It was a bittersweet homecoming. The great key turned in the ancient lock, and the door swung open, its creaking echoing in the empty hall. They stood silent for a while, taking in the scene. Everywhere they saw the result of abuse and neglect. Furnishings, dirty and torn, were strewn around every room, the floor covered in filth, fine furniture ruined. It was a sorry sight, but most of the house seemed structurally sound. Edmund had spoken the truth when he had said he had restrained the rebels from destroying it. Eleanor turned into the drawing room on the left.

"Oh, look, Duncan, my father's portrait!"

"That is a mercy! To be sure, I would have thought the rebels would have destroyed it."

"Do you remember, Duncan, when you first came into this room that day after the battle at Winceby?"

"I do indeed! How I wished that day I had better news to deliver, my love."

"As did I, Duncan! But the messenger met with my approval!" They embraced in front of the fireplace. The fine fire that had blazed that day was replaced by an empty black hole, but their love had weathered the storm. Duncan held her at arm's length and looked into her brown eyes.

"We have one another, Eleanor. Shall we stay at The Grange or come here to restore Haresby Hall?"

"I don't know. My home is with you, wherever you are. Do you think we would be safer at Tadcaster?"

"In this world, Eleanor, we are not safe anywhere. And our possessions aren't guaranteed to be ours without contest, but we cannot therefore spend our lives in retreat. So let us return here and rebuild and trust the good Lord to deliver us from evil. We must not give way to fear. We shall hold loosely onto these things, Eleanor, but treasure one another and the children given to us."

"More children?"

"Yes, by God's grace, more children, and Haresby Hall will see happier days again."

Chapter 39

On a cool March morning in 1654 Eleanor stood on the quayside at Blackwall in her green silk dress, the southwest wind tugging at her bonnet. She looked out of place among the rough-looking, barefoot seamen busy loading and unloading goods of all kinds into and out of barges that would ferry them to the waiting ships.

The sun was still low in the sky as she strained after the progress of the *Ark* now swaying clumsily down the Thames toward the open sea. *It looks so vulnerable,* she thought. She could not imagine what it would be like to sail off into the unknown like that. What hardships would they have to face on the voyage in the crowded cabins? How would they cope with sharing living space with so much livestock? What challenges would they have to face on their arrival? Would the natives prove hostile or friendly? Would they have enough food and enough resources to build a home? Was it worth all the hardships just to be able to worship God the way you wanted to? Questions filled her mind as she watched the *Ark* disappear from sight with its precious cargo. She was glad that she and Duncan had at least been able to give the Whytes enough money to enable them to go together as free settlers.

A sudden gust threatened to send her bonnet into the mud, and she remembered that Duncan would be waiting for her in the carriage and that their hosts would be expecting them for a meal. As she turned, she was aware of another woman who was similarly dressed, wisps of auburn hair showing at the edges of a blue bonnet and blue eyes that were also focused on the ships anchored offshore. The latter turned to meet her gaze, and her face registered the shock of recognition.

"Mistress Eleanor!" The words escaped from her lips before she had time to check them. Her hand flew to her mouth as she questioned the wisdom of making herself known to her former mistress. Eleanor moved closer, her eyes wide with unbelief, but there was a smile on her lips.

"Are you really Nell Thornby?" Eleanor seemed to bear her no grudge, and Nell relaxed.

"Yes, I'm Nell," she answered.

"What brings you here, Nell? Are you also come to farewell friends?"

"No, I'm here with my husband to supervise the loading of our goods on the *Constance*."

Now Eleanor had more questions, but she was mindful of Duncan waiting in the carriage and reluctant to delay further.

"Might I see you again?" asked Eleanor.

"We sail tomorrow on the morning tide."

"Could we meet early … before you sail? I would so like to see you again."

"Yes, we could meet at seven o'clock if you wish."

The following day the *Constance* lay at anchor, gently rocking on the morning tide. Nell surveyed her three towering masts and bowsprit, pondering on the fact that soon they would trust themselves and all they now owned to this floating cradle. Simon was already on board with Abigail and the children. At seven o'clock, true to her word, Eleanor approached carrying a bundle. When she was near enough, Nell smelled fresh bread.

"Good morning, Nell. I wanted you to have something fresh for your journey. It will last for a few days. It was baked this morning."

"It's so very kind of you. Thank you! It's such a surprise to see you, my lady."

"I have often wondered what became of you, Nell.

"I left to find my brother, ma'am. I was afraid you wouldn't let me go. I wanted most desperately to find my brother and make a life for ourselves somewhere."

"Did you find him?"

"Yes, after much searching, but only to discover him mortally wounded at the battle on Marston Moor."

"He was a Roundhead, I suppose."

"No, ma'am, he gave his life for the king's cause." The memory pained her, and it irked her a little to have to talk about the past when she was about to leave it behind.

"Yet it seems that you have become a Puritan, Nell?" Eleanor's fashionable green brocades and parasol were catching slightly in the stiff breeze, and the venue did not seem suitable for an in-depth conversation. Neither did Nell feel inclined to pursue it; however, Eleanor was not one to give up easily, and she was intrigued by the change in Nell and her obvious change of circumstance. Nell nodded.

"I admit I am a little curious as to why people embrace that lifestyle," Eleanor continued. "My best workers have just left for the New World, and I fail to understand how that could be better than what they have here."

"It's the pursuit of freedom, ma'am. We desire to follow our own religion, and we desire to have the liberty to find our own way in it."

Eleanor considered her answer for a moment and then asked, "How about you, Nell? What prompted you to accept the Puritan religion?"

"I found work in a Puritan household and there came to learn of their ways. When I heard the scriptures read daily in English, it caused me to consider what the Savior did for me, and it caused me to consider why the Anglicans do things the way they do when none of those rituals are found in the New Testament."

"I see. Are you happy now?"

"I'm satisfied, ma'am."

Eleanor smiled. Despite her haughtiness, Nell could see kindness in the brown eyes.

"Well, I'm glad for you, Nell, that you have at least found something you were looking for. I pray you will prosper in your new life and that it will go well with you. It seems that your circumstances have changed considerably already."

"Indeed they have. The good Lord has seen fit to bless me with a fine husband."

"I am glad, Nell. I, too, have a wonderful man whose generous heart is a great comfort to me. God has blessed me too." Nell smiled.

"I am glad to hear that Haresby Hall has a new master, ma'am."

"Haresby Hall has suffered much at the hands of the Roundheads, Nell. It is a blessing that I have a man who can share the task of restoring it."

"I pray that it may go well with you now," said Nell. She was genuinely solicitous; however, so much information was hard to digest, and Nell was loath to ask for more details. Eleanor's loss at the hands of Cromwell's men was scarcely an issue she wanted to dwell on when her thoughts were on joining Simon to sail far away from England and Haresby Hall and everything she had known in her life hitherto. Eleanor noticed her gaze had shifted to the vessel.

"I have a small present for you. I would like to give you these. I hear it gets pretty cold on the other side of the Atlantic." Nell looked at the gift Eleanor held out to her. It was a pair of gloves made of buckskin. She had never owned a pair of gloves before.

"Oh, thank you, ma'am!" said Nell a little awkwardly. Suddenly she was back in Tadcaster, picking up Eleanor's glove from the snowy road. She had felt so different then with the soft doeskin between her work-worn fingers, and the halfpenny reward had seemed such a fortune.

"Did you know it was me, ma'am?" she ventured to ask.

Eleanor's puzzled expression told Nell she had no idea of her find.

"I found your glove in the snow, ma'am. That day you left Tadcaster on the stage coach. I took it to Lord Talbot. I trust he returned it to you. I knew it was special to you."

"Why, Nell, I had no idea! Yes, it was one my father had had fashioned for me from a doe I'd brought down while we were hunting together. I little thought I had you to thank for its return!" Eleanor laughed at the coincidence. "Take care you don't lose yours!"

"I will. They're beautiful. I shall treasure them always. I shall need these in the harsh New World winter. I'm most grateful."

Eleanor's countenance returned to seriousness, but it had lost some of its aloofness.

"There is something I wanted to say to you, Nell." Eleanor seemed to summon up courage to bring it forth, and Nell waited, awkward and a little anxious, searching Eleanor's face for clues about the nature of what was about to come forth from her prim features.

"I owe you an apology, Nell," she finally began. A fresh sea breeze had them both attending to their bonnets and blinking away the dust from their eyes.

"You do, ma'am?" Nell was a little embarrassed, but Eleanor obviously had a mind to put something right between them.

"My family could have cared for you better, Nell. When you were a child and your mother came to work at Haresby ... we could have sheltered you. I realize that now. Your poor mother was so heartbroken too. I can see it differently now, Nell. I have often wished we'd done more for you. Perhaps you might have stayed on." Eleanor's tone was somehow formal, as if the emotions attached to her sentiment had been locked away in a far corner of her soul, but her voice was tinged with regret. Again Nell was forced to reach back into the past when she'd have preferred to leave it all behind.

Nell looked at Eleanor and saw behind the self-control a heart that wanted to make things right between them. She reached down into her own heart, seeking a genuine response. Neither could turn back the clock to those days of want. Silently she reached out to the One who had forgiven her, seeing again the nails and the welcoming arms. Grace came as she reached out to Eleanor—across the divide of their previous social status, past the pain and heartache—to a place where two hearts met in mutual recognition that it was past.

"It's all right, ma'am. I needed to discover many things just as I now need to begin this new journey."

They both looked in the direction of the *Constance*.

"I'm grateful to you, ma'am, for coming to see me. Rest assured I harbor no grudge."

"Nor I. I shall remember you always."

"And I you, Nell."

"I must be going."

"Godspeed, Nell."

"And you, ma'am." Nell bobbed a curtsey from habit rather than necessity. As they went their separate ways, both women brushed away tears, and both felt the weight of burdens lifted. Nell could now sail away leaving some unwanted baggage behind.

Chapter 40

Ahead of Nell a rough-looking man was boarding the *Constance*. He had a pair of dead pigeons slung around his neck, hanging from his huge frame—supplies for the trip, no doubt—probably to eke out the provisions that would be his as an indentured passenger, From his unkempt appearance, Nell surmised that he was not one of those who was leaving with religious aspirations but an adventurer seeking his fortune in the New World. He appeared to possess little apart from the pigeons.

Nell was thankful that she and Simon had the means to be free settlers. At a time when the price of the passage was equivalent to five years wages for unskilled labor, she knew that many would have indentured themselves to the ship's captain. The captain would provide for them on the voyage, and on arrival he would advertise them as indentured servants. The responsibility for their provision would then pass to the new owners. After they served up to seven years, they would be given suits and their freedom and begin their own farms or use their newfound skills to earn a living. Nell was reminded of her own servitude and was so grateful to be a free woman.

Simon had supervised the loading of their goods—a dresser and a chest of clothes, crates of implements, Simon's tools for building their new home, plates, pots, pans, vegetables, fruit, salted beef, dried beans, two casks of water, a supply of flour that hopefully would last until they could buy more, and seeds to plant. They were precious provisions that would be needed in their new homeland as well as on the journey. Josiah and Martha had written with news of the challenges they themselves had faced. A lack of implements had been one of them, so Simon was bringing carpentry tools for building a home and as many farm implements as they could take. These they would be able to share with Martha and Josiah, while the latter sheltered them initially in the house they had already built. They had shared living space with Martha and Josiah before.

Here on the ship they would have to share living space with many others in cramped conditions. When they had settled below decks, they gathered on the top deck to wave farewell to their homeland. Relatives had been farewelled earlier when they had left Margaret and Mary in the care of Edward and Elizabeth, but as Nell surveyed the faces on the quayside, she saw Eleanor frantically waving a handkerchief, her face framed by her green bonnet. She had not expected such a royal send-off. Grabbing Simon's large white handkerchief, she frantically waved back. It was a meeting of hearts that had been separated by social distance and would now be separated by the Atlantic. She hoped Eleanor might find peace the way she herself had. Soon Eleanor's face blurred into the sea of faces, and the ship made its way down the Thames. They had said good-bye to life the way they had known it. Before them lay unknown adventures. Nell was thankful for the supernatural peace in her heart that overrode the turmoil of mixed emotions threatening to engulf her. Simon squeezed her hand.

"He will guide us, Nell," said Simon, sensing her feelings.

"I know," she answered. She turned her eyes to the horizon, where a pale sun was climbing up into the sky and sending streaks of pale gold across the river. She looked at the children. Her silent prayer rose heavenward for their future in a land where Christians could worship in freedom, uncluttered by ritual and tradition.

First though they had to survive the Atlantic crossing. Among the Puritans there was a fellowship, a camaraderie born of common beliefs and common goals. The other passengers consisted of men and women with a variety of motives, and Nell was at pains to keep the children away from such company.

With little else to do on the long voyage, Simon took upon himself the job of educating his own children, and Adam and Verity were joined by half a dozen others whose parents were glad of the opportunity to keep them occupied. There was little play space on board. To the children, the seven-week crossing was going to seem like a long time. Simon did well, though reading materials were scarce. Bible stories formed a large part of the daily tuition. In the New World there were many things they would need to do for themselves, and one of the most important would be to educate their children. Seven year-old Adam was learning to read. At all events their daily lessons kept them away from the unsavory company that met in a corner of the deck, kept them from hearing words unfit for younger ears. Nell was happy to tuck them into their cots every night, knowing that they were one day closer to their Promised Land.

Two weeks later the square rigger was gliding through the Atlantic toward its destination. Several passengers stood around on the main deck, enjoying the spring sunshine. A fresh breeze blew fluffy white clouds across the sky, and the voyage was almost pleasurable. Lessons had finished for the day, and Adam was enjoying some activity on the deck with the other children. The fresh air was a welcome relief from the stuffy and unsavory quarters below. Nell and other women were chatting toward the stern, and the children were playing on the deck. Simon and their men-folk were engaged in discussion below decks.

Most of the deck was enclosed by the high sides of the ship, making a relatively safe playground for Adam and his playmates. Toward the center the solid sides gave way to a gap across which was fixed several vertical rails and a horizontal rope. It was the only place where a child could actually see the sea apart from on the poop deck, which was closed to all except crew. Adam had once been found peering through the rails, watching the gray water glide by.

"Play down this end of the ship!" Nell called out.

Bart and his drinking companions were gathered farther along the deck, playing cards on the top of a barrel. They drank as they played and made noisy wagers. The women ignored them, finding their behavior unsavory. Their attention was on two-year-old Verity, cute in her little white bonnet and blue shift, clinging onto Nell's skirts; however, the gaze of so many faces intimidated Verity, and she cried to be picked up. Nell was stooping to lift her when a commotion broke out behind her—men's voices loud in argument and then shouting and the noise of a barrel rolling across the wooden deck. A child's scream was followed by the sound of a splash.

"Adam!" Nell screamed as she realized the shocking truth that her son had been sent overboard by the barrel. Thrusting Verity into Abigail's arms, she rushed to the side of the ship. Adam himself was screaming, but all too soon his screams faded to silence. There was no way of stopping the square-rigger to rescue him. The women rushed to the deck rail, crying out helplessly as the square-rigger abandoned the child to the cold Atlantic. Adam's fair hair bobbed above the surface for a few short moments. Then they watched helplessly as the ocean swallowed him up, and he disappeared from sight.

"Man overboard!" The cry rang out, but to no avail. At best the ship could have made a wide circle, but it was already too late for that.

Simon responded quickly to the shouts of those on deck, but by the time he had reached the ship's side, his son's blond head was disappearing below the waves, his little life claimed by the cold sea. His anguish was too great for words. He paced the deck, head in hands, seeking to understand how his son had so suddenly come to be in a watery grave when a few moments before he had been happily playing on the deck.

Bart stood ashen-faced and sheepish as his two drinking companions hurled accusations at him.

"You drunken fool!"

"You pushed the barrel!"

"'Twas your fault!" he yelled back.

"The child was swinging on the rope! I rolled it at you, not him!"

"You should have kept your temper!"

"'Twouldn't have happened if you kept sober!"

The captain appeared, his face grim. On being acquainted with the details, he shrank back in unbelief and then exploded in anger.

"If you scoundrels were crew, I'd put you in irons!" he bellowed. "As it is, if the child's parents want to press charges, I will hand you over to the custody of the magistrate on arrival." Turning to Nell and Simon weeping in one another's arms, he gently and flatly said, "My utmost apologies. It seems the disorderly behavior of your fellow passengers has resulted in the loss of your son. I offer my sincere condolences. I fear we are powerless to rescue him. It seems he was standing by the rails at the time the barrel was pushed and it rolled over and propelled him over the side." To the rest of the passengers now crowded on the deck he barked, "See to it that your children are kept away from the side of the ship!"

The offending barrel lay on its side at the edge of the deck where it had come to rest. Simon kicked it, feeling angry and powerless. Then they stood together for a long time, gazing into the gray waters that had claimed the life of their only son. Nell licked her lips where the sea and her tears had deposited bitter salt.

"My boy! My poor boy!" she cried.

The brawlers had scattered like scalded cats and disappeared below decks. The Puritans gathered around Nell and Simon with Bibles and committed the boy to his heavenly Father. The loss was too shocking for Simon and Nell to register. The hopes and dreams of so bright a future evaporated in a moment.

Nell blamed herself for not watching over him more carefully.

"I told them to keep away from the side of the ship, Simon. I little thought he would disobey me." Simon shook his head.

"Caught up in boyish fun, Nell. We are all prone to be disobedient," he said. Others added comments, some helpful, some hurtful.

"Poor wee lad meant no harm."

"It happened so suddenly!"

"No one could have prevented it."

"It was the fruit of ungodliness—drinking and gambling and such! The wages of sin is death, is it not?"

"They must be brought to justice!"

"Nothing will bring Adam back now," said Simon. "He will be in the arms of our Lord."

Simon and Nell decided that pressing charges against Bart would only hinder them in their settlement in the new land.

"Better to forgive and leave him to God's justice, Nell. Bart's prosecution and trial would necessitate staying behind until the trial was over. Bart's guilt will be punishment enough."

"Yes, after all, it was an accident, not a deliberate murder."

Those who shared their faith joined them in a simple prayer to commit Adam to the Lord.

"The Lord gives, and the Lord takes away," said one.

"No," said Nell quietly but firmly. "The Lord gave us Adam, and the Devil has taken him away. We will find comfort in the Lord and in knowing we shall see our son one day in heaven. We must just give him to the Lord now."

There was a somber mood on board that night. Nell sat with her head in her lap and Simon with his right arm around her. Footsteps sounded on the narrow stepladder that descended from the hatch, and Simon caught sight of the haggard face of Bart peering down into the gloom.

"I'm most sorry, sir, ma'am, for this tragedy. I never meant the lad any harm. It was just those braggarts cheating me." He reached down his hand to Simon proffering a sovereign.

"Money cannot bring back our son!" said Simon, angry at Bart for thinking their loss could be recompensed so cheaply.

"No, but it's all I can do, sir," replied Bart earnestly.

"What's done cannot be undone," said Simon.

Nell, understanding that for Bart money was the price of freedom, appreciated more the sacrifice that he was offering.

"Money is precious to you, but no amount of money can make up for the loss of our son," she said. "You may keep your sovereign." Bart put the sovereign in his pocket.

"We shall not be pressing charges, but I pray you give up your drunken ways and lead a sober life. We shall speak no more of this tragedy." Bart looked heavy with the guilt he bore, his eyes crazed and moist. Money had been the source of the problem. If he could have won it by a wager, he could have paid off his indenture and entered the new country as a free man. It was the threat of being cheated of it that had led to the outburst that resulted in Adam's death. To give it away might ease his conscience, but they had no wish to take it. In the face of such pain, money was superfluous.

"I'm asking your pardon, sir. I am not a godly man, but I would never have harmed the little one deliberately."

"Children are apt to wander. You have my pardon. You must ask the good Lord for his."

"Aye, sir. Thank you, sir." He turned and disappeared through the hatch.

Simon turned back to Nell.

"He's a tormented soul, Nell. Pray God he will leave his wicked ways and turn to God."

It was a difficult night. The loss of Adam, his little life so easily snuffed out, had created an even greater sense of insecurity among those who had just left all that had given them earthly security. Parents, apprehensive against a similar loss, snapped tense instructions to their children who reacted by becoming rebellious. The little ones were fretful, and Verity, feeling her brother's loss, whimpered pitifully by Adam's empty cot. The sighing of the wind and the creaking of the huge timbers at the movement of the vessel did nothing to create an atmosphere of comfort. They were very much aware that they were at the mercy of the elements. Many prayers were sent heavenward, especially from Nell and Simon.

The next day dawned gray and overcast. Nell was on deck by herself when something white caught her attention fluttering in the periphery of her vision. She looked up and was astonished to see a white dove perched on the rail close to her. They were much too far out at sea for it to have flown from land. Nell knew doves were not migratory. Surely this dove had come from heaven, a sign from God sent to comfort her and to reassure her of his presence. Why she should have been favored in that way she did not know, but if the Lord wished to manifest his love to one of his children in need, she qualified! It answered her prayer for reassurance that they were in his will, for Adam's death had caused her to doubt that they were. The dove flew off unseen by any other passengers, but Nell knew it was a visitation for her benefit. Later she would share it with Simon, but for now she kept it in her heart like hidden treasure. Both the loss of Adam and the comfort of the dove were at that moment too deep for words.

Chapter 41

Water was sliding by, clear, green water, cold water, so much water. Nell watched it, lost in her own thoughts. Water divides and separates, but it also unites. It just depends which way you look at it, she decided, but there was an awful lot of water—a vast expanse between the shores of Massachusetts and England. The sunlight shone through the wave created by the bows of the *Constance* as she slid through the water, slowly now, surfless, revealing dark depths below, depths that were becoming shallower as they sailed at last into Massachusetts Bay.

As they neared land, the wavy lines of the coast manifested trees and places where buildings crowded together, clustered for comfort in the vast wilderness. Nell's eyes searched the shore as orders rang out on deck and the great sails flapped noisily in the wind. The plaintive cries of seagulls wheeling over the masts filled the air with a sound they had not heard for seven weeks.

Nell, Abigail, and Simon, holding Verity in his arms, stood on deck, eagerly searching for Josiah and Martha among the clusters of people gathered on the shore. Hope was burning in the heart of each one. Had Josiah and Martha been able to make the journey to the coast? It would make things so much easier to find their friends waiting for them. Apart from Josiah and Martha, they knew not another soul. Josiah and Martha would be such a help in their relocation to this foreign land with the many challenges they would face. Even as Nell considered the daunting task of unloading their provisions, she knew what a blessing it would be for Simon to have Josiah at his side. If they had brought a wagon, it would save Simon the task of finding one before they could load their possessions and transport them to wherever they would settle. In any case it would be so good to see their friends again.

Simon and Nell hardly recognized their old friends, but it had to be them, waving frantically and with two boys at their side. It was a welcome sight—friendly faces in the midst of a sea of strangers. It had been eight years since their farewell at Poppleton; however, the bonds forged through that traumatic time endured still, and they would have much to share.

Abigail watched as warm hugs were exchanged. These people were the only family she had, and she was learning that the bonds of Christian fellowship could endure as well as any.

"Did you not have a son?" asked Martha suddenly.

"Our Adam fell overboard and lies in a watery grave," answered Nell, her tears rising to spill over again. Simon moved quickly to put a comforting arm around her.

"It has been a cruel grief to us to lose him so suddenly. We scarce thought we should have to build our new lives without him."

Martha and Josiah regarded them with open mouths and wide-eyed horror.

"Oh! I am so sorry!" exclaimed Martha, her own tears more eloquent than words.

"This is bad news indeed! A most grievous trial!" added Josiah.

Martha turned to her own two sons, Joseph and Jonathan.

"I'm afraid your little playmate will not be joining us. Adam was lost at sea—a great loss to us all. We shall not meet him in this life after all!" The boys received the news in silence and then retreated to sit dejectedly in the wagon.

"They were so looking forward to showing him how to catch fish in the river," Martha said sadly.

More conversation was difficult in the midst of the quayside activity, and Josiah suggested he help Simon unload their goods onto the waiting wagon, while the women waited with the children and assisted as they could to load their precious cargo ready for its journey to their final destination.

"What a blessing to have you here for us, Josiah!" said Simon, truly grateful for his support. They moved off in the direction of the *Constance*, and the women took the children to wait in the wagon.

Simon was ascending the gangplank of the ship again as Bart came down accompanied by the ship's captain. His shoulders were stooped, and he looked up from under a brow that was creased with anxiety and pain.

"I'm much obliged to ye for not pressing charges mister," he said sheepishly.

"'Tis more than you deserved!" growled the captain. Simon observed the guilt-racked man as he was led toward the building where he would need to wait until whoever had hired him came to sign the indenture papers. His heart was suddenly touched for the man, whose slavery to sin was more apparent in that moment than the servitude of his coming indenture.

"Bart!" he called out after him. The big man turned and looked at Simon like a dog unsure whether it were about to be kicked or offered a bone.

"We have forgiven you, but you will never be free of guilt until you ask the Lord to pardon you. You must confess your sins to him, the maker of heaven and earth and the Father of our Lord, Jesus Christ!"

"Move along!" said the captain angrily. "This is no time for religion! There's no place in heaven for the likes of him!" he added, scowling at Simon.

"There is room for all who repent!" declared Simon, seeing the desperation on Bart's face.

"Thank you, sir," said Bart quietly. Then he nodded and allowed himself to be marched away to await his indenture.

Josiah, who had been watching the scene nonplussed, looked at Simon questioningly.

"He has need of the Savior," said Simon. "Maybe he will find him. Come, let's find my barrels. I'll tell you about Bart later."

The wagon lurched uncomfortably along the rough road, but it was good to be on dry land again. Simon sat with Josiah on the driver's seat, and the others crowded on the wagon, as comfortably as they could between barrels and sacks. It was several hours before they reached their homestead on the edge of town. It was a simple home, the furniture Spartan, but their welcome was as warm as the fire that was soon blazing in the great stone hearth.

"Welcome!" Josiah flung down the last bag on the wooden floor and stood with his arms in open invitation. "You won't regret the journey, though I am saddened to hear of little Adam's loss."

"It was such a shock not to see him with you!" joined in Martha.

"Such a terrible shock when he fell into those cruel waters." Nell brushed away a tear. "We'll take comfort that he is in the arms of the Father. We must look to the future now … and to establishing a home here for Verity and her brother or sister," said Nell with a sad smile.

Martha looked at Nell, and a smile brightened her serious face.

"You are carrying another child, Nell?" she exclaimed. All eyes were on Nell.

"I believe so," she said.

"So! We populate the New World with true believers!" laughed Simon.

Chapter 42

Nell longed for the day when Simon could start to build their home. Rustic as it would be, it would be the first time she had had a home of her own since childhood. For that she would gladly put up with the hardships and deprivations of pioneer life. It would not be easy, but the promise of a future with her husband and family, a future with purpose and destiny burned bright in her soul. Here at last she would be the mistress in her own home. Here at last she could settle. The restlessness she had known in England was over. The good Lord had surely led them here to give them hope and a future.

For now they were guests of Josiah and Martha, and again she was grateful for their hospitality. It would give them the chance to regain their strength after the long sea voyage and to find a few acres of land and plan their future home.

The two women were happy to be together again, to share their lives, their burdens, and their thoughts.

"It's a new life, Nell. Our only battle has been against the elements. Our first winter was the worst, as our crops were sparse at first, but there was always plenty of firewood and fresh fish from the river, so we were neither cold nor starved."

"Do you miss the old country, Martha?"

"Aye, Nell, sometimes. The country I knew as a girl, when all the village children would gather on the green and play games and the mothers would gossip as they watched and cuddled the young ones and the men would play tipcat. When I met Josiah, we would walk for miles over the moors and watch the wind send waves through the long grass and the skylarks ascend into the blue summer sky and trill away for all they were worth. It seemed that the fair land of England was like heaven itself. Yes, I miss that sometimes, Nell. But those times are gone. When our parents refused to see us because we would not follow the old traditions, we had to make a choice."

"You chose to follow a new path, didn't you?"

"Yes, we chose to follow the Lord wherever he would lead us."

"And he led you here."

"Aye, he led us here, and he leads us still."

"Have you been happy here, Martha?"

"I have never regretted the journey, hard though it was. There were times when we had to pray for God to strengthen us, to sustain or heal us, and he has shown us his mighty hand in this land."

"Is it a fair land like England?"

"Wait until you see it from the top of the ridge! There you can see the land spread out before your eyes—emerald forests under an azure sky in the summer or glorious with color in the autumn."

"I shall be glad to see it," said Nell. "Simon has been up there already."

This is a good land, Nell."

"I am happy to hear it. Simon was telling me about the bear tracks he found in the forest. We weren't used to living with such danger in the woods back in England. He had forgotten about the bears when he was enjoying being up there on the ridge. He was so relieved when he found that the paw prints were leading away from his path. He so enjoys being up there in the fresh air!"

"He carries his rifle, does he not? We have had no trouble with bears, but it is as well to be aware of their presence if they are around. You can usually see their prints and the broken undergrowth."

"I am sure Simon is enjoying the challenge of his new surroundings, Martha. I think this life suits him, Martha. He won't mind the hard work of building and plowing. Here he is happy to expend his energy to build us a new future."

Chapter 43

A week later as he was returning from his newly acquired land near Josiah and Martha's cultivated acres, Simon was almost at their hosts' home when he heard the familiar sound of Josiah's wagon approaching from behind. On turning he saw Josiah at the reins and beside him the larger figure of another man—a figure that was at the same time familiar and yet unknown. As they drew near, Simon recognized the man. He stood rooted to the spot, gripped by a sense of unreality and unable to respond to Josiah's wave of greeting. Suddenly he was back on the *Constance* with Nell's screams echoing inside his head and the sight of the cold, gray sea covering Adam's little head.

The wagon drew up, and Josiah jumped down and tethered the horse to the gatepost.

"Simon! I've brought us some help for our labor!" called Josiah. Simon gazed at the newcomer in the wagon, unable to answer. The man himself also sat in stunned silence.

"I was in town collecting mail and buying supplies when I happened to see this fellow advertised for hire as an indentured servant. It seemed good to contract him to work for three years, after which we shall be better established and he shall that way gain his freedom and a living of his own. What think ye, Simon?"

Simon thrust the spade he was carrying into the dark soil and leaned heavily against it, his gaze now on the ground, while he searched for the strength to look again on the face of Bart. Grace had prevailed enough to enable him to release words of forgiveness toward Bart, but to have him here sharing his life on a daily basis, being in close proximity to those he held most dear, being part of his new life here was unthinkable.

"He is a good strong fellow, Simon. He will serve us well," added Josiah, noticing Simon's reticence. Then coming closer, he said, "Simon, whatever ails you?"

"Josiah," explained Simon, hesitating before he went on, "this is the man who caused Adam's death." The words came out quietly, matter-of-factly as he tried to communicate the truth unencumbered with emotion. It was Josiah's turn to be at a loss for words. Finally he recovered his equilibrium enough to say, "Simon, I'm sorry. He seemed like a decent fellow to me." He shook his head, baffled. "I was so sure it was the good Lord that led me to him today, Simon. I am so sorry. I must have been mistaken."

By now Bart had climbed slowly down from the cart. He walked haltingly over to Simon and stopped a few feet away.

"I am as surprised as you are, sir, to see you again." He stood awkwardly, shifting the weight of his huge frame from one foot to another and trying to summon the courage to look directly at Simon. Finally he lifted his creased brows on a level with Simon's and their eyes met.

"Permit me, sir, to tell you that I did as you said," he said, his voice thick with emotion. "I asked God to forgive me, and indeed I do feel a weight of guilt has lifted off me and I am left in a sober but more hopeful state of mind. I want to thank you, sir, for your former goodwill toward me. However, should your friend not wish to honor our contract, I do understand. I would implore you though to return me to the town from where I might have opportunity to be indentured."

The three men regarded each other for several moments, considering all that had passed between them before anyone spoke. Finally it was Simon who spoke first.

"Josiah, maybe it was indeed divine providence that you found Bart today. I have an inkling that the Lord kept him for us so that we should have opportunity to practice what we preach and to show charity to one who might have been more likely to receive our wrath."

"That may be so, my friend," replied Josiah, "but it is hardly a kindness to Nell to bring home the man who has caused her so much anguish."

"I think my Nell is more resilient than you know," returned Simon, "but who can know the depths of the pain she has suffered?"

Bart, not wishing to intrude in their private discussion, turned and walked back to the wagon, calling over his shoulder,

"I shall wait in the wagon, sir, for my return to the town. I have no wish to be a cause of more pain to you or to your family, sir."

The attention of all three men was arrested as the front door of Martha and Josiah's home burst open, and Simon saw Nell come through it backward, followed by Martha, who was sharing the load of a laundry basket.

"We'll soon have this on the line!" declared Nell.

"Indeed we will! And this beautiful day the wind will soon dry it! Then we shall eat some of your delicious chowder and corn bread!" The two women were in high spirits as they maneuvered the bulky basket through the doorway. Then Martha hesitated, her eyes taking in the scene and sensing all was not well. Simon watched as Nell put down her end of the basket in tandem with Martha and turned to see for herself who had claimed Martha's attention. On seeing Bart sitting in the wagon, she shrank back, her hands over her mouth.

Before either of them could step away from the laundry basket, Simon and Josiah rushed to Nell's side.

"Nell, I brought this man to work for us here, little knowing what Simon has just told me of his unfortunate past."

"Rest assured, my dear Nell, that Bart has himself offered to return to the town to seek employment elsewhere."

Nell looked straight past both of them and kept her gaze on Bart, studying him from the doorway, her blue eyes penetrating and her expression pensive.

"He looks different somehow," she said, "sort of softer."

"He says he has repented of his sins, so maybe that is the reason for the change of countenance you discern, my dear. The poor man is exceedingly embarrassed by our staring. Let us dispatch him to town at once and release him from this unfortunate engagement."

"You mean he has indentured himself to us?" asked Nell incredulously.

"Yes, it was my fault," said Josiah.

"Why is that such a bad thing?" inquired Martha. "We could use some help to get you established, and he could build himself a small cabin on our land. What has he done that is so contrary?"

"He was instrumental in the accident that caused our Adam to be propelled over the side of the ship and drowned, Martha," said Nell calmly.

"Oh, Nell, I am so sorry. He must go at once!"

Martha encircled Nell with her arms and drew her toward herself, turning her away from the sight of Bart in the wagon, but Nell resisted her comfort and drew herself upright.

"Wait!" she exclaimed with sudden resolve. "I will speak with him myself."

So saying, she marched down to where the wagon still waited by the gateway with the horse still tethered to the post and Bart shifting uncomfortably on the wooden seat. At her approach he climbed down once again and stood by the side of the wagon with his head bowed.

"Ma'am," he said, nodding, "I am most sorry for this unfortunate meeting. I am waiting to be taken back to the town and have no wish to give you further cause for grief."

"We meet again, Bart. I scarce thought I would see you again."

"Nor I, ma'am. It was not my purpose that our paths would cross again."

"No, but it may have been the Almighty's. His ways are higher than our ways, Bart, and he works curiously, so I have found." Nell paused before she continued, "Maybe it is right that you should work for us, Bart." She hesitated again, searching for a way forward, measuring her words carefully, seeking for wisdom from somewhere outside of her tangled emotions. "Simon tells me that you have asked the good Lord to forgive you?" It was a question, not a statement.

Bart answered, "Yes, ma'am, indeed I have, and it has given me a measure of peace unknown to me before. A miracle indeed, ma'am."

"Then if you are a man of peace, you may stay and make a new life with us. We will be dependent on his divine grace to preserve us all."

"You are very gracious, ma'am, but I should not wish to trouble you further."

A flurry of white wings drew Nell's attention to the dove cote that Josiah and Martha had built, and Nell was once more on the deck of the *Constance* with the white dove perched on the rail in the morning air. Peace flooded her heart, and she smiled a welcome.

"God will keep us all in his peace, Bart. You must learn of his ways now, and you can learn from us."

Before Bart could answer, Nell nodded, turned, and walked back to where the other three were watching speechless in the doorway.

"I have settled it," she said. "He is staying."

"Are you sure?"

"Yes, I'm most certain. He was sent to us."

"Are we all agreed then?" asked Josiah.

"If Nell is sure, then I am willing too," said Simon.

"Then we will ask him to stay for one month and see if both he and our families can get along together. After that if all is well, he will work for us for three years, and then we will provide him with the means to buy his own land and some tools of his own. Are we all agreed then?" asked Josiah again.

"Aye!" they chorused.

"Then so be it," said Josiah, "I shall put it to the man that he may stay."

Nell and Martha stooped to pick up the laundry basket just as Martha's boys came running at full tilt around the corner of the house and demanded to know who the visitor was.

"He's our new friend, boys, come to help us here. You may call him Uncle Bart."

Chapter 44

The days slipped by, and Bart passed the test and stayed. He was indeed much subdued, and his inclusion in a caring community was doing much to soften the roughness of his former life and character. Both households traveled to town for the weekly religious meetings, and Bart went with them. The time came when Martha and Josiah were willing to trust Bart to accompany the boys to fish in the river.

"Uncle Bart can catch two fish at once!" declared Joseph in tones of admiration.

"That's good because he eats them twice as fast as you do!" joked Martha.

There was no shortage of fish in the river, and the boys enjoyed the sport of catching them, competing to see whose catch was the largest. They relished the thrill of pulling in the struggling fish and landing it successfully on the riverbank. Joseph was becoming adept at casting his line into the fast-flowing waters of the river and had concentration enough to yank it toward him when he felt the tug of a bite. His younger brother was apt to become frustrated at his lack of skill, but usually Bart and Joseph were quick to help him to get his hook into a likely spot for a bite.

It was spring, and the river was full with meltwater from faraway mountains. Bart and Joseph were both occupied with their own lines. Jonathan drew back his rod to cast it as the others had done, but the line flipped back behind him and tangled itself around a bush on the riverbank.

"Aw, I've got my line stuck in the bush!" he complained.

"There's no fish in there, lad!" Bart said and chuckled. "I'll help you in a moment." The boy was tugging at it for all he was worth when it suddenly released and he toppled backward into the swirling water. It was Bart's worst nightmare. He could not lose another boy! Without hesitation he threw himself in after the boy and managed to grab him by the cuff of his sleeve. Bart was not a great swimmer; however, his bulk made him buoyant, and keeping afloat, he held onto Jonathan's wrist as they were both pulled downriver in the current. Joseph shouted helplessly from the shore.

"Go! Bring your father!" Bart managed to shout. Joseph raced off in obedience. *At least,* thought Bart, *if the boy and I perish, Joseph will be safe.*

Jonathan had stopped struggling, which caused Bart some concern, but it made it easier to hold him.

"I've got you, son! Hold still! I'll get you back to the bank."

How he was going to do that Bart had no idea. He was fast becoming exhausted with the struggle of keeping them both afloat in the current. With relief he noticed that they were coming to a bend in the river and the current was carrying him in the direction of the bank. With all his strength he pulled against the water, forcing himself out of the main current and into the quieter waters by the bank where he could grab hold of a low hanging branch. As his feet sank in the quieter water, he also found he could stand. Thankfully he dragged Jonathan on to the bank, and after he laid him on the slope, he drained the water from his lungs.

"We're safe, lad. We're safe now!" he gasped.

Jonathan lay like a landed fish, spluttering and coughing; however, he was breathing normally again, and his eyes were open. Bart sank down beside him, recovering his own breath and anxiously watching the boy. Finally Jonathan spoke, "I'm cold, Uncle Bart. Can we go home?"

Despite the difficulty of answering that question, Bart smiled at the boy's trust.

"Yes, we'll go home as soon as I'm able to carry you," said Bart, wondering how he was going to find the shortest route home. He was shivering himself and had no idea how long it might take to carry the boy home. If he traveled through the uncleared land along the riverbank, his journey would be arduous and long since the river had curved around several bends. To find a more direct route would be difficult since his attention had been entirely taken up by his efforts to survive in the cold, swirling water and he had lost his sense of direction.

Bart was unprepared for what happened next, for he had neither seen nor heard the shooter of the arrow that suddenly landed at his feet. He started to his feet and in the gloom of the forest detected the figures of three native men. Clad mostly in leather, they were swarthy and brown and stood watching and waiting from the shelter of the trees. Finally the tallest one moved forward, still keeping an arrow at the ready in his bow. Bart raised his hands, demonstrating that he was without weapons, and the native relaxed his bow and called the other two to join him. They regarded him with brown eyes staring from curious faces, taking in his waterlogged state and the poor condition of the boy.

Jonathan recoiled in fear and moved closer to Bart.

"Must be Algonquian. I think they mean no harm." By waving his arms at the river and trying other sign language, Bart made an effort to communicate the fact that he had just pulled Jonathan from the river and needed to know which direction he needed to travel home. It appeared that his signs were understood, for the three talked among themselves, pointing this way and that until finally they seemed to agree and all pointed in the same direction. Then they moved in that direction and beckoned him to follow.

"Better jump on my back," said Bart. Jonathan did not argue, and the two followed behind their native guides. At times it was necessary to clear a path, which one of the natives did with a tomahawk, while the other two pulled away the undergrowth to make a space for them to pass. At no time did they hesitate, seeming sure of the way. Bart hoped they were headed to the settlement where Josiah and Martha had their home.

Although the undergrowth was thick and the going difficult, the knowledge that they were both alive cheered him. He was less at ease though about the kind of reception he was going to get on their arrival. Dread began to rise within him. He was blaming himself for not untangling the boy's line sooner, and surely the boy's parents would blame him for not taking greater care of the boy. Shame flooded his spirit. He had caused the drowning of one boy, and now he had almost done it again. He reproached himself, and surely Josiah and Martha would too. Joseph would have told them how it happened, and it would look as though he had been negligent. The boy was heavy, but not as heavy as his heart.

The forest became less dark as they approached the track that was revealed along the edge of it. The three natives indicated for Bart to follow the track. Bart acknowledged his thanks with a bow, smiled, waved, and turned to continue his journey. Jonathan insisted on walking by himself for a while; however, soon he was ready to be carried again, and Bart simply scooped him up in his arms and carried him that way.

The track was little more than a space from which the larger trees had been cleared and where the vegetation had been flattened by the passage of carts; however, it was easier walking than the forest, and there was a sense that sooner or later he was going to arrive somewhere, which without their native help was more than he would have had in the forest.

The sound of cartwheels jerked Bart out of his brooding thoughts, and when he looked up, he saw Josiah and Simon approaching from the opposite direction.

"Bart! Jonathan!"

"Father! Father!" The cart slowed to a halt alongside them.

"Jonathan! Bart! We thought you were lost!"

"Even when we saw you, we were unsure whether you were carrying the boy or his corpse!" explained Simon.

"We were relieved to hear your voice, son," agreed Josiah.

"I'm well, father! Bart jumped in and saved me!"

"Bart is a brave man, Jonathan."

"I am indebted to you for my son's life, Bart."

"I am sorry. He fell into the river."

"I am sure it was not your fault. You have shown true courage, it seems. I am most thankful to you."

Josiah took hold of his son.

"We'll soon have you warmed up, son! We have blankets in the wagon."

"We will soon be home, and the others will be glad to see you unharmed."

Bart kept reliving the awful moment when Jonathan had hit the water with a splash, when the dread of another drowning seemed like an imminent reality. Memories of Adam's splash in the Atlantic haunted his mind still and tormented his soul with regret and shame. Joseph and Jonathan were full of admiration for Bart's heroism.

"It seems you risked your own life to save Jonathan," said Josiah. "You are truly a hero!"

At Josiah's words the brooding cloud over Bart's spirit evaporated. What had seemed like a conspiracy of evil had indeed been turned around for good, and how thankful he was to have had the opportunity to redeem himself and to live in their memories as a hero rather than a scoundrel. He had known their forgiveness, but it was even sweeter to know their respect.

Chapter 45

In the local church meeting the somber chanting of psalms was followed by much preaching. Nell could see that the preaching was spiritual food for them all, but the joylessness of the worship left her feeling empty. When she was out working on the land alone, she sang from her heart to her Redeemer, the melodies springing from within her inmost being as she released them to the skies, her arms raised to heaven. This was her secret refuge whenever the physical hardships of their pioneering life became too much for her. In that secret place she was refreshed. It was a private place where she met alone with her Creator, and she needed no hymn or prayer book, no one else's approval for her worship, no order of service or any rituals.

Sometimes it seemed to Nell that the Puritans were as intolerant of the views of others as the church they had left behind, and her free spirit shunned such control. She was, however, content in her new life. There was security in knowing that her neighbors were God-fearing folk and a degree of protection in living in a community in a land where the native people and animals were not always friendly. She kept her opinions to herself, and no one asked for them. She knew Simon to be a fair-minded man of genuine faith, and she trusted him with her future.

Six months later Nell crooned a gentle lullaby as she rocked the tiny form of the new arrival backward and forward. Benjamin's tiny form was hope for the future—a blessing from God. The gift of his life helped fill the space left by Adam's loss. Here was new life. Here, she believed, was a child who would grow up in a land full of promise, unhindered by the traditions of previous centuries. She looked forward to watching him grow and to seeing whatever gifts this child possessed being used to build a new life in a new land.

Chapter 46

Simon was outside creating a trellis over the gateway to their newly completed log house. He reflected on Nell's enjoyment of their rustic home. In their new land timber was plentiful, and Simon, aided now and then by Josiah and Bart, had built a home of logs. It was so devoid of the luxuries they had been used to, but Nell seemed to be taking it all in her stride, counting every day as a day full of opportunities. He valued the fact that she had not enjoyed a life of luxury in England long enough to be softened by it, and she knew how to endure discomfort. He appreciated how she leaned on the Almighty for strength when she lacked it, and she had the courage to persist in adverse circumstances when others would have given up.

When the trellis was complete, Simon appeared at his neighbors' doorway, carrying a spade in one hand and a bush ready for planting in the other.

"Nell, Martha, come and join us to plant this—the first of our flowers!"

"Flowers!" exclaimed Martha. "That's a luxury!"

"Just a little reminder of our homeland. We will plant it by the gateway, and soon it will form a fragrant arch over our pathway."

"What is it?" inquired Martha.

"It's a red rose—the one we had at Tall Chimneys. I brought it wrapped in a cloth with soil around the roots and have kept it planted in a barrel until now."

Soon Nell, the children, Martha, Josiah, and their boys made a little group gathered around the hole Simon had dug. There he placed the soil and the rose from England in its new home.

"We'll plant it in memory of our Adam," said Simon.

They were silent for a while, remembering the loss of their son.

"We will call this rose Adam Brierley after him," added Simon.

"I pray it will transplant to the land of America as well as your family has done," said Nell, looking at Josiah and Martha and their boys.

"May we all grow and blossom here and live in peace!" answered Martha.

"Amen!" the others chorused.

Lightning Source UK Ltd.
Milton Keynes UK
UKOW03f0532100914

238314UK00003B/3/P

9 781490 820651